Going Buck Wild

By Nina Foxx

GOING BUCK WILD
GET SOME LOVE

Going Buck Wild

Nina Foxx

AVON
TRADE

An Imprint of HarperCollinsPublishers

HarperCollins books may be purchased for education, business, or sales promotional use. For information please write: Special Markets Department, HarperCollins Publishers Inc., 10 East 53rd Street, New York, NY 10022.

FIRST EDITION

Designed by Elizabeth M. Glover

Library of Congress Cataloging-in-Publication Data

Foxx, Nina.
   Going buck wild / by Nina Foxx.—1st ed.
      p. cm.
   ISBN 0-06-056449-0 (alk. paper)
   1. Single women—Fiction. 2. Mate selection—Fiction. 3. Unmarried couples—Fiction.
   I. Title.

PS3556.O98G65 2004
813'.6—dc22   2003062948

04 05 06 07 08 JTC/JRRD 10 9 8 7 6 5 4 3 2

Acknowledgments

Nothing or no one exists in a vacuum. Fortunately for me, my world is full of great spirits and people who guide and encourage me daily. Thanks and praise to the spirits of my ancestors, most recently, my friend and Soror Joan Jackson, my child's godmother. It was a blessing to have known you, and to the spirits of my parents, Brison Hamilton and Elvie Jackson. Thank you for your gifts and guidance.

My family and friends that encourage and guide me daily: my husband and daughters, the Hortons, the Scotts, the Hamiltons, the Greers, the Harolds, the Alis, the Varners, the Robinsons, the Millers, and the Davidsons. Thanks to the myriad of writers that have become my community, for your words of support, encouragement and advice: Marissa, Lolita, Victoria, Eric, Victor, Earl, Trisha, and Chet.

Thanks to Pam Walker Williams and the Good Book Club, L. Peggy Hicks; the bookstore owners; and the readers, for supporting all of my books; and to Alpha Kappa Alpha Sorority incorporated, as well as Jack & Jill of Austin.

I would also like to thank Elaine Koster, Carrie Feron, and Selina McLemore, for the encouragement and patience.

Chapter 1

There was nothing like smell to make an experience whole. Claudia grabbed a cart as she headed into Central Market and inhaled. The smell of ripe fruit greeted her nose. She immediately felt warm; there was something about the market on Saturday morning that made her feel good, something about the way the various exotic fruits blended together that made her feel calm and relaxed.

Central Market had become her oasis in the midst of a hectic week.

Central Market was Austin's semi-upscale, semi-trendy supermarket. Its aisles were stocked with the hard-to-find and exotic. Nothing ordinary here. If you were looking for organic food and top-notch catering, this was the place to go.

There was no rest for the weary in Claudia's household, especially when the weary was the wannabe superwoman type. Even though she had left him at home over twenty minutes ago, Claudia knew exactly what her fiancé was doing right now—nothing. He needed to "decompress" from his stressful week at the office. She frowned and stopped at the coffee counter. Must be nice. Claudia had no time for decompression, though her week had been as stressful as most—she'd closed two major deals that the office had been working on for over a year, filled in as the "snack mother" for her best friend's kid's class, and taken her cat to the veterinarian three times. For Claudia, it was important that everything get done, and get done well. Nothing could slip through the cracks. She liked feeling efficient, but efficiency had its price: exhaustion.

"Decaf latte please, soy milk." She scrounged in her bag for some cash. Claudia never had time to make it to the ATM, but shopping wasn't complete without her coffee. Maybe a cooking class was going on too. Central Market was famous for those, and although she'd never had the time to formally sign up, Claudia had eavesdropped on quite a few.

"Okay, you know they are much more fun when they are fully loaded. Decaf and skim—what would the point be? I will take one fully loaded, with a double shot, please."

Claudia turned around and looked up into a face that was vaguely familiar, surrounded by curly, dark brown hair. His long eyelashes framed his almond-shaped eyes perfectly. She tried to place his face but couldn't. Was he wearing mascara?

"Excuse me? But caffeine is bad for you. The way you asked for it will give me wrinkles, and I don't make enough to afford a plastic surgeon." She sipped at her cup and grimaced.

"I sincerely doubt that you have to worry about that. You take care of yourself. You are not about to wrinkle, and there are so many plastic surgeons in Austin we might as well be in L.A. I'm sure you can find one within your budget." He took the cup the person behind the counter handed him. "And you should try your latte with whipped cream on top. It will make your day." He sipped and dabbed at his mouth with a napkin. "I'm Cody, I work downstairs from you, in IT—"

"I knew you looked familiar." Claudia placed her coffee cup on the counter and extended her hand. They must have ridden in the elevator together once or twice. "I'm—"

"Claudia Barrett." Claudia was immediately overcome as his massive fingers wrapped around hers in the strongest handshake she had ever felt.

"I know who you are. Everyone does now. That was a major coup you pulled off with Boeing. They were about to drop us. The whole office is talking about it. Good job."

Claudia worked for Pittsford Electronics, and Boeing was their largest customer, one usually handled with kid gloves. Their last account executive had said something to set them off, and they'd repeatedly threatened to take their business elsewhere until Claudia had stepped in and signed them to a ten-year exclusive agreement. She'd ended her stress-filled week as the star of the office.

Claudia blushed. "Thanks. They had to come around sooner or later. We do have the best product." Cody stopped shaking her hand, but he didn't let go. She shook her hand free and fidgeted. The tightness of his grip had been uncomfortable. She still could not seem to recall the exact place she'd seen Cody before. "You have a good shopping trip. You may be the only man in here."

"You might be right about that, but I love to cook so I am here all the time. I'm used to it."

"Really? Your wife must love that. My fiancé doesn't even know how to *get* to the kitchen." Claudia thought about the last time Jackson had tried to cook anything. He'd scorched one of her best pots so badly that it had set off the smoke alarm.

"No wife. No girlfriend." He shook his head. "That's too bad about that fiancé. I find cooking therapeutic. It calms me after a long day at the office. He should try it sometime." Gingerly, he balanced his cup in his shopping cart. "Take care." He paused, not trying to hide the fact that he was checking her out. "And I like those shoes. I know you didn't buy those here in Austin."

"No, no I didn't." She glanced down at her new sandals, half frowning. "You know shoes? These are Taryn Rose. I got them in Houston." Claudia opened her eyes wide in recognition as her "gay-dar" perked up. Not many men would dare make a shoe comment to a woman they didn't know. Or any woman, for that matter.

"I wouldn't say I know them. I just appreciate women who take care of their feet."

"Oh, okay, I am surprised you noticed. Men usually don't. It was nice talking with you."

Claudia picked up her coffee and headed into the market. Central Market was set up so that the traffic flowed through smoothly. This was a good thing; they were known to have crowds and crowds of people in the store at any given time. She was used to thinking while she shopped and didn't really want to talk, although Cody wasn't too bad to look at. He smelled good too, like Egyptian Musk. Claudia raised her hand to her nose and sniffed. The smell was unmistakable. It used to be her favorite scent.

Gay or not, the attention from Cody was flattering. How many men would notice anything on a woman below the ankles? Woman's shoes? Jackson certainly didn't. He hadn't noticed her feet or anything else in a long time.

Claudia had stayed up late last night, after answering all of the e-mail she hadn't gotten to in the office, just to give herself a pedicure. Her new alligator sandals needed to be highlighted properly. Claudia wiggled her toes, feeling the leather against her feet. The new shoes had cost her a grip, the only things in her wardrobe she regularly spent any kind of money on. It made Claudia feel good even if Jackson didn't care.

Claudia squeezed a cantaloupe, looking for just the right one. Jackson was a good man. She knew that. But sometimes he was plain old boring. He could be a little overbearing too, the way he was always trying to protect her, as if she were a damsel in distress or something. Her mother's words echoed in her ears: Gotta take the good with the bad, she would say. But Jackson had become predictable. Marrying him would be worth it, even if it wasn't exciting. She would have security and knew that he would help provide for their family beyond her wildest dreams. He would make her family happy too, and they would stop worrying about her becoming an old maid. All that would rate real high with her mother.

"You have to smell your melons. Like this." Cody was back again. He held a melon to his nose and inhaled, long and slow. His eyes were closed, and it looked to Claudia like he was kissing the melon. She stifled the urge to laugh. "And *then* you squeeze it, like this."

She watched as he squeezed the melon with his massive hand. A chuckle escaped her lips.

"Is *that* how you do it?"

"Yes." He was suddenly curt. His eyes narrowed slightly, although a smile still played around his mouth. "No part of this is funny. Don't blame me when you get home and your melon isn't the best. I was just trying to help."

"No doubt. But I am not doing that. Do I look like I would do that?"

"Lady, I just want you to get the best melon possible. But I guess you can't be as beautiful as you are and know how to pick your produce. No one person can have everything."

Claudia picked up a melon and then stopped in midair. If she didn't know better, she would think he was flirting with her. Uh-uh. He had to be gay. No man was this serious about shopping for groceries. She shook her head. Didn't he see the two-and-a-half-carat ring that adorned her finger? And what did he know? As far as she was concerned, she did have everything. Vice President before thirty-five, a staff of fourteen, and a budget to match.

"You should know better than to flirt with an almost married woman in a supermarket. It's not a good thing."

"That's a mamey sapote." He pointed to a brown fruit on their left. "From Central America. Tastes like apricot." He picked one up too and turned it over in his hand with a flicking motion. He handed it to Claudia. "What might happen if I did? Harmless conversation? And who said I was flirting?"

"I know what it is. I can read." She returned it to the display and wiped her hands. "I can spot a flirt when I see one. You *are* flirting. You just keep your melon advice to yourself, okay?" Claudia moved over to the grapes but smirked to herself.

"If it offends you, no problem. You just let me know if you need anything else. I know a lot of stuff about produce. About the supermarket. You would be surprised what growing up in a house full of women will teach you if you pay attention." He winked at her and pushed ahead.

Claudia stood in the middle of the aisle with a bunch of grapes poised above the scale. What had just happened? That boy had to be ten years younger than she was, and

Claudia knew that had been a come-on. These young boys were bold these days. She dropped the grapes onto the scale and entered the code into the computer. Claudia smiled. She was even admitting to herself that she was getting old. She grabbed the ticket the scale spit out and stuck it onto the plastic bag. Her biological clock was ticking even if she didn't want to talk about it. But what if her mother was right about wasting her childbearing years? Women had children well into their forties now, right?

She wondered if that Cody fellow thought she was helpless? Claudia dropped the grapes into her cart, shaking her head. Probably not. She could not possibly be giving off the "helpless" vibe. She was a strong woman. She puffed out her chest a little as she pushed her cart. Everybody thought so. There was no doubt about it, he'd been flirting. And he was still wet behind the ears.

Claudia sighed and moved forward through the aisles, heading toward dairy. She had to admit that the extra attention felt good to her. She peered through an opening in the dairy cases, trying to catch a glimpse of Cody, but he was nowhere to be found. She picked up a carton of yogurt and stared at the expiration date, not really seeing it. She had not seen him on the elevator. No way. She would have remembered those dimples. If nothing else, she would have definitely remembered his smell. That selfsame smell is what had first attracted her to Jackson. Not being able to place him nagged at her; she prided herself on being good at remembering things, faces. She shrugged. It would come to her eventually. She hummed and continued her grocery shopping. That young man had made her day, engaged or not.

Chapter 2

Letting go was hard. Cody tried to settle in for the night, but he couldn't get comfortable. His heartache had transformed itself into physical symptoms; he hurt everywhere. He wanted to watch the final episode of *Survivor*, but he could not concentrate. His apartment was small, and the walls were as thin as a cheap motel's. His neighbors were active tonight; the constant thumping on the wall reminded him that he was alone again. They were in lust in a big way. By now, he knew their pattern. Sometimes they went at it at least twice a night.

He scratched his head and headed toward his office to find a book instead. He needed to get himself together. He banged on the wall as he left the living room, and he laughed. He had become his father. His father had gotten crazier and crazier after his mother had died, and Cody had to live with it. He'd dropped out of college to help pay his father's medical costs and moved back home for awhile. He shuddered. Sometimes it had been really ugly between them, and he'd finally had to put him in a home. He remembered his father thumping on the ceiling in their apartment when the upstairs neighbors had been too loud. They were always having parties, and people had come and gone way too often for normal folk. The thumping had changed to terrible confrontations as his father had slowly descended into senility.

He wanted to get to bed early; it was back to work as usual tomorrow. Just as he reached his office door, the doorbell buzzed, and Cody glanced at his watch. It was after nine. He still didn't know too many people in Austin, so he knew without even looking through the peephole who it was. He flung open the door and walked away without even looking.

Ever since they were kids, Barry had been just plain loud. Even his house was loud. His had been one of those too busy apartments in their building. Cody's father used to say that Barry had to be loud to survive. He had so many kids in his family that he had to speak up to be noticed. Cody didn't even cringe as his friend barreled into the room.

"Hey, man. You ain't sleeping already, are you? Are you watching the *Survivor* finale? Can you believe the sister-girl won? That is history in the making right there. Man, I think we can do that. I know I can." He paused and picked up the picture from Cody's coffee table as he dropped a stack of mail onto it.

"What are you trying to say? And put that back." Cody snatched the small picture frame from his friend's hand and dusted it off. "If I was about to sleep, I ain't now. Don't you ever talk quietly?" He frowned.

"Nope. I brought you your mail. I thought you were over that girl. She did you wrong, man. Didn't you come here to get away from her and her drama? You should put that away somewhere. As pretty as you are, you think you would have the ladies wrapped around your little pinky finger."

Cody felt a twinge of guilt. He never had told Barry the whole story. Marina didn't want him, all right. As a matter of fact, she'd let her new husband pay him to walk away. Over the past year, he'd had to admit to himself that he had been bought. All his bills were paid, and he had been relocated free of charge—if he agreed to never talk to Marina again. Overall, it had been the best decision for all involved, but he'd never told anyone how he'd come to just walk away. "I *am* over her. I just haven't gotten rid of this yet. You wish you were as good-looking as I am." He held his hand up in the air, looking at his pinky. "And don't be talking about my pinky ring. You gotta be real sure of your manhood to wear a ring like this."

"You got that right." Barry twisted his mouth to the side and chuckled. "Always thought that you had a lot of nerve. I can't believe that you would boldly display a picture of another man's wife anyway."

"And if I had known you were going to be giving me grief every day, I would have moved somewhere where I really didn't know anyone. She was my girlfriend before she was his wife. I was first, remember that. Just because she got married does not mean she stopped being special to me."

"Yeah, whatever." Barry rolled his eyes. "You know I'm family. And whatever you want to do is your business, but you got about six or seven other pictures of Marina in this place. We need to do some spring-cleaning and get rid of them. She is gone, man. It's been well over a year. She left you and chose to be with him, remember? Just like I told you she would. Can't say I blame her, though. Most people would choose security over happiness." He flopped down on the dilapidated brown couch. "I thought you was making the big bucks? You need to buy you some furniture." He patted the cushion next to where he was sitting, and a cloud of dust rose into the air. He coughed. "I think one of the springs in this couch just gave me an enema."

Cody leaned against the wall. "Very funny. You know how I am. I can live with that couch until I find exactly what I want. That came with the apartment. So why did you come here if not to pick on me? Don't you sleep? Normal folks have to work in the morning." He put two fingers over his eye and rubbed; his head ached.

Barry looked around the disheveled room. Cody used to be the neat one between the two of them. He seemed to have lost it when he lost Marina. Everything was a mess.

"I ain't never been normal a day in my life. You know that. You need to go over to the doctor and get you some Claritin, man. I swear by the stuff. Austin must be the allergy capital of the world. I thought I was going to die when I first got here. I have a few clients in the morning, over in Barton Creek. No more long hours like before. I work when I want to work. Benefits of being retired at an early age."

"I wish I was a dot-com dropout like you. Must be nice. And you ain't retired, man. That little bit of change you got won't last you too long. With my luck, I will be one of those they let go in the next round, even if they did pay a whole lot to transfer me here."

"Don't you worry about me now. I got a plan. Are we working out in the morning?"

Cody and Barry usually met first thing in the morning to work out together. Barry insisted on it. It was his own special brand of therapy. He believed that a healthy body led to a healthy mind.

"Nah, man. I got another plan. I think I'm going to go run down at Town Lake."

Barry narrowed his eyes. "Again? Running is too hard on my knees." He rubbed both his knees with the palms of his hands. "I can't believe you're all into that. A few weeks ago I could hardly get you into a gym. You gonna run a race next?"

"Maybe. I like it. And running by the water is nice. It relaxes me."

"If I didn't know better I would think you were ditching me for a woman. But you ain't like that, right, man?" He narrowed his eyes. It wouldn't be the first time. Back before Marina, they used to hang out all the time. "Running is new for you, isn't it? Back in New York, the only running you did was when you were being chased."

Cody chuckled. "This ain't New York. I'm trying to get in shape, change up my routine. I just might run one of those races, maybe do a triathlon. I can be the next Lance Armstrong. Lots of people train at the lake before work."

"The next whom? You're kidding me, right? You ain't even *got* a bike. I know you better be careful down there. Women ain't the only ones who can disappear, you know. It happens all the time here. People disappear off that jogging track, but they pull dead men out of the lake every other day." He put his feet on the table, crossing his legs.

Cody half-laughed. "You can't be serious. I am from New York. You Austinites don't know from crime. A man is running around parking lots feeling women's behinds here and that makes the news. They even named the dude The Northwest Stalker, like it was a big deal. You know, back home that wouldn't be happening. A sister-girl would grab

that man by the wrist and he would draw back a stump."
Barry relaxed as they both laughed.

Cody gently eased his friend's feet off the table. "Watch
that. I know you weren't raised in a barn. That's an expen-
sive finish on that table. I did it myself."

They'd grown up in Lefrak City in New York, an area
that had once been nice but over the years had become
more run-down as the high-rise apartments that were sup-
posed to have been the wave of the future for the working
class had become overcrowded and crime-ridden.

"And ain't nobody throwing me in no lake. You talking
crazy now, you got to go. That wife of yours will be looking
for you soon." Cody pointed toward the door, jokingly
shooing his friend out. He really did need his sleep if he
was going to run at six-thirty in the morning.

Barry stood up and rubbed his hands on his tan-colored
pants. "A'right man. Hope you have fun, but I can't run.
You just be careful. What you know about New York don't
apply here. You are in Texas now. We do things differently."

They walked toward the door. "What is this 'we' shit?
You ain't no more Texan than I am."

"Yes, I am. I am a naturalized Texan. I have been here for
going on ten years now. I know what I am saying."

Barry stopped and searched his friend's face. His move
to Austin was supposed to have taken his mind off Marina
and all the mess he had gotten himself into back home, but
Cody didn't look any more rested or less worried than he
had two months ago, and he had been in Austin almost a
year now. Barry couldn't help but wonder if Cody was
holding onto the memory of Marina until something better
came along, the same way he was holding onto that old

sofa. He shook his head. There was a thin line between ded-
ication and obsession, and Cody seemed to have a leg on
both sides of it.

Although Barry was going to miss working out with him
in the morning, he wished his friend *were* meeting a woman.
Cody needed some feminine companionship. Cody always
seemed right on the edge, but Barry couldn't tell just what
he was on the edge of; he kept to himself most of the time,
almost as if he was hiding some deep, dark secret.

Cody closed the door behind Barry. He glanced out his
window as he passed. He could see stars from his balcony,
something he had not been able to do back home in New
York. The light pollution and the tall buildings had made it
virtually impossible to see the sky clearly, something he'd
never understood before. If nothing else positive came of
the move to Austin, at least he would be able to live at a
slightly slower pace.

Cody picked up the stack of mail that Barry had thrown
on the coffee table and walked into his office. The room was
cramped, filled to the brim by just his oversized desk and a
bookcase. He bumped his toe on his telescope as he passed,
swearing under his breath as he made his way over to the
desk. The telescope was the first thing he'd bought when
he'd realized that the stars he'd read about could actually
be seen and recognized here, but it made the already small
room more cluttered. Seeing the runners in the park was
just an unexpected bonus.

Cody left the lights low. He discovered that it relaxed
him and let him use his telescope in private. Absentmind-
edly, he flipped through the mail, immediately sticking bills
and other things he deemed important into his accordion
file by anticipated due date. He liked his office to remain as

organized as possible. A letter in an official-looking enve-lope caught his eye, and he stopped, reached for the letter opener, and sliced open the envelope. Cody unfolded the letter and swept his eyes over the document in his hand. His headache intensified immediately. It was what he'd been waiting for, but not the news he'd hoped for.

It was official. His children were adopted and the records were sealed. He knew they would be. Although he'd never been allowed to see them, he knew that they were beautiful and perfect. He felt an empty space in his heart and missed both them and their mother. But it was the best thing. His heart had hardened.

Although he shouldn't have, Cody had tried several times to find his children. He could believe that Marina's husband wasn't happy when he found out about the two of them and their affair, but why had Marina pushed him away so hard? She had not even called him to say good-bye. She could have gotten an annulment. She'd found out she was pregnant two days after their wedding day, but in-stead, she'd chosen to stay with her new husband. Now the kids had been adopted away, heaven knew where, and Cody had no legal rights in the matter. Marina and Wesley were married, so Cody's name was not even on the original birth certificate: Wesley's was, even though it would even-tually be obvious that the children were not his. He was just as white as she was, and eventually, the kids would darken up, they always did. Cody imagined them with his hair and eyes as he fingered the letter.

Barry was right, he needed to get rid of her photos and move on. He felt like he could now, even if he could not find his children yet. He smiled. Maybe a good romance could take his mind off a lot of things. It was time for him to direct his energies elsewhere, move on from Marina and what she had done to him. She had made her choice, it was time for him to make some of his own. He needed someone else to help him soothe his pain. And Claudia was the best candidate.

Chapter 3

Record heat blanketed New York for six days in a row, leaving Wesley and Marina taking refuge, day after day, in the only air-conditioned room in their house. Their small home in Forest Hills was upscale, Queens style, but it was still over seventy years old and lacked central air-conditioning. The sole air conditioner jutted out from the side of their storybook-looking manor, spoiling the perfect lines of the house that Marina loved, but it was the only thing that made the house and their bedroom livable during the hot summer.

The bathroom-bedroom was decorated in black, gray, and gold, with lots of frills everywhere. It made Marina feel as if she were going to sleep in one of the dollhouses her father made for her when she was a girl. Normally, she would feel immediately at ease as soon as she entered, but the heat and humidity were taking their toll on her, as well as everyone else in the city. Rather than relaxed, she just felt annoyed.

Wesley dressed behind her as she sat at her vanity. She leaned her head in her hands, her elbows propped on the table beside the myriad bottles she kept there—close to one hundred bottles to make her smell good, perk up, or look more gorgeous, but she knew that nothing on the vanity would help her tonight. She just did not want to go to another one of these boring functions. But that was her job.

"You better get a move on. We don't want to be late. Do you think you could help with these cuff links?" Wesley looked over her shoulder into the mirror as he tugged on the sleeve of his tuxedo shirt.

She rubbed her fingertips together, although she knew they were clean. She scowled. God forbid she should get any makeup on his shirt. She would never hear the end of it even though he had six others in the closet ready and waiting. She had seen to it. *That* was her job too.

She turned around to face her husband but felt no emotion. She smiled anyway.

"Why are you moving so slow? I told you about this days ago. This is important, my first event as president of the division."

"I know. I'm trying to hurry," she lied. "Maybe my period is coming or something."

"This must be the third one this month. Can't you take something for that? It will be fun, honey." He rubbed her shoulders. "You usually like to talk to the other wives, right? Don't you guys always get a little too toasted together?"

"No, I get toasted so I can forget that I am there. I have nothing in common with those women. They are just nice to me because my father owns the company." She sighed. "They are always talking about their kids. I have a hard time relating to that." Marina was used to people sucking up to her because they thought it would get them things. It had been that way all her life.

A shadow darkened Wesley's face, and his grip on his wife's shoulders became a little too hard.

"You are hurting me," Marina whined and tried to pull away.

Wesley's chest began to heave with anger. They had been over the issue of children time and time again, and he could not believe Marina would try and take a shot at him like this.

"You know how I feel. We are not going to discuss children again. I don't want anyone messing around with my parts. I do not want to conceive a child by any of those godforsaken 'new technologies' as you call them, and I refuse to adopt a child. If we can't do it naturally, we shouldn't do it. End of discussion. Get dressed now." His voice became firm. "And wear that blue dress I bought you. I like it." He pushed Marina backward onto the vanity and stormed out.

There was no use arguing. Marina ran her hands over her face and then rubbed the spot on her shoulder where he had held her. It hurt and she could see a bruise coming already. Over the past year or so, she had become an expert at using concealer. She could cover this bruise up easily. It could be worse. It could be on her face, like last time.

She opened the plastic shower curtain surrounding their old-fashioned tub and turned on the water full blast. Perhaps a good shower would make her feel better. Wesley got really upset when she wasn't nice at these things, and she didn't feel like fighting with him more than she already had. It was bad enough he wanted her to wear that blue dress. She hated it. But he probably knew that too.

The water was a little too warm, just the way Marina liked it. She stepped inside the shower and paused a minute to get used to the heat. It cascaded over her body and she ground her teeth; the heat was just short of punishing. Her skin prickled and she shivered as she let the water envelop her fully from head to toe.

Although they never talked about it, she was grieving for her children. Not a day passed that she didn't think of them. When Wesley had suggested they put the twins up for adoption, she'd thought it would be the best thing to do. Cody had never tried to call her or anything. He must have known something was wrong. Wesley had tried to find him, but he couldn't, so Cody obviously did not care anything about her or his children. He had lied to her about loving her all those years. She pursed her lips, remembering him saying that their love was bigger than anything.

Marina had had no idea that it would hurt so bad and continue to hurt the way it did. But she was the one who had chosen to marry someone else. She spent most of her days numb now, just going through the motions, doing various things to keep her mind off them. She couldn't help but wonder when her children's first steps were, or if they looked like her at all.

She'd done what her father had wanted when she'd married Wesley. At the time, she thought she was doing the right thing. She'd been convinced that he would be a better provider, just like her father said. But she knew that Cody would never have treated her like Wesley did. She shook her head. Who would have thought that she would ever be a trophy wife? Why couldn't her father see that this had not made her happy?

For most of the time, Cody had been so caring and open to her feelings. Except for the fact that her father would never accept him, they'd had a great relationship. She couldn't believe it when he disappeared after she got married. It just didn't fit.

The phone rang and Marina could faintly hear it over the hiss of the shower. She rinsed the soap from her body. Wesley would get it. He got so upset with her lately if she answered the phone. That was understandable; she was the one who had obviously slept with someone else right before they'd gotten married. It had been a mistake, she knew that now, but she had been so vulnerable and Cody had felt so safe at the time.

Wesley was guarding her. The counselor said he would be insecure for a while; Marina knew she'd violated his trust in the biggest way possible. She just hadn't known it would take this long to win it back. Had she let true love just slip through her fingers? At the time, it had all seemed logical and right, but now it felt as if she'd traded happiness for a weekly dose of bruises that she could no longer cover up.

The shower curtain tore open and Wesley stuck his head in. "Get out. Shower time is up." His face was dark. Water splattered on the floor as Marina rushed to get the last bits of soap off her. What was he so upset about? His mood swings were getting to be too much for her to handle.

Wesley went into the closet and grabbed the blue dress. He couldn't believe the nerve of that Cody. The whole thing was supposed to be water under the bridge, something that he wanted to just put behind him. It was getting harder and harder for him to keep things under wraps. He jumped out of his skin every time the phone rang now. Cody must not have believed him when he'd said that they would come to collect if he did not hold up his end of the bargain. He was supposed to have taken the money and disappeared into oblivion. People like him never did what they were told.

Wesley watched as Marina dried herself off. He hung the

dress over her vanity chair. This was the best thing for Marina, he still believed that. Cody was good for nothing. He could never provide the lifestyle that Wesley did for her. And she could never live with the stares she would surely have gotten as part of an interracial couple. She should thank him for saving her.

"Are you going to stand here and watch me get dressed, or what? Don't you have something else to do? I promise to hurry."

Marina's voice was sounding just as edgy as he felt.

"Sorry." She was right. He didn't want to piss her off any more than he already had. He wanted to have a nice, peaceful night. This was the second phone call he'd gotten about Cody. He was snooping around. His friends down at the Queens County courthouse called to let him know. Wesley had lots of friends in strategic places. Thanks to their help, there was no way Cody could ever hope to trace the whereabouts of those children. The files had been lost "accidentally on purpose."

"We need to leave in about twenty minutes, honey." He kissed Marina on the cheek. "I'm sorry I was so short with you. I guess I am just a little on edge. I think I will go and have a small cocktail to relax while you finish, okay?"

Marina didn't answer. Wesley didn't expect her to. It was time for Wesley to make some phone calls of his own, call in a favor or two. He knew just whom to call, too. One thing about growing up in south Queens, you made all kinds of friends, in all kinds of businesses. Wesley had one particular friend in mind that he had not talked to in a while. One that specialized in collections.

Chapter 4

It was the middle of summer, but Austin mornings remained cool. Claudia looked at her watch. It was six-fifteen in the morning and she was grateful for the breeze that came off the lake. She tapped her foot, eager to get started before the central Texas heat came on full force.

A new pedestrian bridge stretched over Town Lake and marked an entrance to the well-used running path. Claudia's natural light brown hair was drawn into a ponytail held down by a baseball cap that matched her running clothes. She would definitely be seen while she was running; the size twelve, hot pink ensemble screamed out as it clung to her full-figured body. Claudia was not thin, but she was generally fit. She did not appear obese, but she knew she wasn't Twiggy either. Like most women, she was never satisfied with her body, but she covered it like an expert with what she thought were decent clothes and good, conservative makeup.

Several bicyclists passed by, a little too close for comfort. The wind from their passing startled Claudia; they whizzed by so close that you would never think that the bridge was as wide as a four-lane highway.

The sun was barely up in the sky, and the trail was already getting crowded with all sorts of runners, walkers, and bikers.

Claudia paced impatiently and began to stretch. She always had to wait for Pam. She swung her arms back and forth to warm them up. It was not within Pam's power to be on time, but that didn't stop Claudia from being annoyed.

As if on cue, Pam appeared, running between the heavy traffic to reach her friend. Claudia frowned. She wished she had at least taken the time to coordinate her outfit. She couldn't understand it. Usually, Pam lived for clothes. For all the beautiful body she had under it, Pam's clothing was oversized and unmatched: a wrinkled black T-shirt with blue running shorts. Still, Claudia could feel the confidence that flowed from Pam, as if she were clad in the most expensive, high-tech running gear. Pam was that way.

"I'm sorry, girl, you know how it is. The kids wouldn't act right, my husband needed this thing and that thing. I don't know what he would do without me."

"Unfortunately, I don't know how it is." Claudia pursed her lips. She could not help herself, but she really wasn't a morning person, and Pam appeared too unconcerned for someone who was late. "You ready? I have to get to the office. I have back-to-back meetings today. I don't know why you don't get yourself a nanny, girl. Let's go."

"Please. We ain't rolling in dough like you and Mr. Baxter, you know that. Not all of us have the luxury of being able to throw our money around the way you do. Do I have time to stretch?"

"You used up your stretching time getting here. Let's just go. I won't go too fast, okay? We'll just take two loops around the short path."

The jogging path rimmed Town Lake, really part of the

Colorado River, in the shadow of downtown Austin. In most places, the gravel-covered path was just below the street, giving the illusion of tranquility in the midst of Austin's tallest buildings and waterfront historic hotels. The path was popular and often crowded.

The two friends crossed the pedestrian bridge and started running, Pam immediately huffing as she tried her best to keep up with the pace that Claudia set. They ran in near silence for about ten minutes as Pam tried to catch her breath.

"How ya doing?" Claudia looked over at Pam. Her T-shirt was now thoroughly wet and clung to her skin.

"I'm okay. You gotta remember that we all ain't as in shape as you. Could you slow down the pace just a bit?"

"It's your own fault. All that stuff you eat isn't good for you. And if you got in shape the old-fashioned way instead of visiting your plastic surgery friend—"

"Don't go there. I see no need to kill myself. Life is too short. Everybody has their temptations. Ice cream just happens to be mine." Pam wiped at her forehead with the back of her hand. Her bleached blond hair was plastered to her face, and she tried to push it back. "Besides, exercise is just too hard. You need to get with it and *buy* you some new body parts. You guys can afford it."

"Why are you always telling me what I can afford? *You* can afford a nanny so you can meet me on time." Claudia's voice was sharp as she flashed a sarcastic smile at her friend. Pam had no right to talk about her body. Sure, her stomach was a little round, but it was all natural. It looked good. "And I told you before, please stop referring to Jackson and I as if we are an old married couple. He has his money and I have mine. We are not married just yet."

"Okay, sweetie. I don't know what it is with you. Makes absolutely no sense to me. You kill yourself working out for mediocre results. You kill yourself on your job and your fiancé is a big fancy lawyer, making enough money for all of us. You need to go ahead and marry that man and call it a day. I don't get it. You plan on setting a date anytime soon?"

Claudia rolled her eyes. "Whatever. Are you in cahoots with my mother? You two seem in such a big hurry to get me married off." She didn't understand what the big rush was all about. 'Til death do us part was serious business and sometimes a woman had to do it for herself first. "And they don't do liposuction on butts, so forget it. We all know that is where I need the work. I am just going to have to learn to work it and start eating right. I don't want to die early, and that is something that liposuction can't change." She paused. "I like having my own money, anyway. I can't see myself sitting around depending on some man, even Jackson. You and I have different lifestyles, that's all."

"That's true. But I also have a family and a good life insurance policy. You can tell me you don't want those things."

Claudia laughed. Pam always managed to break through her icy morning temperament. "Yes, I can. Having my own stuff, that I got without anyone else's help, makes up for a lot."

"Yeah, sure it does. But it can't keep you warm at night, now, can it? You will understand it one day. Mark my words. Once you two are married, you will understand a lot of things you didn't before." She wiped at the sweat on her brow with the end of her T-shirt, using up the only dry space. "Did you and Jackson decide what you are doing for your anniversary? Setting a date, maybe? You two have been engaged for so long, you just ought to go on down to city hall and get it over with."

"Back to the date thing again? We will get married when it is time. I don't get it. Back when we announced our engagement, everyone said, 'Oh, there is no rush. Take your time. Have a long engagement.'"

"Yeah, but we didn't expect you to take it so *literally*. We were worried about you. You did get engaged kinda fast."

Claudia did not want to rehash the past with her friend once again. Every other day Pam seemed to be inquiring about her wedding date, and Claudia could not understand it. She didn't bring up the fact that Pam had been four months' pregnant when she'd gotten married, now did she? "To answer your other question, anniversaries are no big deal between Jackson and I. We don't get all excited and sentimental about those things. Every day is like an anniversary," Claudia said. "I promise that when we finally tie the knot, you will be the first to know, okay?"

"Don't get excited? What does that mean? He lets you buy whatever you want? You better wake up and smell the coffee, girlfriend. You are lucky, and you two need to celebrate it. Not everybody makes it to five years, married or otherwise. He is a good man and he might not wait around forever, you know. Men might not act like it, but they want the picket fence and kids too. If you aren't acting like you want to give it to him, he might just go somewhere else and find it."

Claudia paused. Five years with Jackson had flown by like five weeks. Pam and her husband had already been separated twice in the four they were married. They had been in and out of counseling several times. "He just isn't into all that. If I don't plan it, nothing will happen."

"Well then, make it happen. You be in the house cooking in lingerie when he comes over or something."

"Maybe that happens in your world, but not mine. First of all, you know I don't cook. You know as well as I do that I could be in the kitchen cooking butt naked and I would probably just burn myself or something with hot grease. Jackson would walk right past me and go get on the computer when he came in or turn on the TV. He just isn't the romantic type."

Pam grabbed Claudia's side, forcing them to slow down. "And that is okay with you? Didn't he used to be? Maybe he isn't romantic because you don't act like you want it or you won't let him be. It's okay to let someone be in control a little. Didn't anyone ever tell you that when you are dating, men are the best they will ever be? And don't tell me that is how you want it to be, because I know the real deal. You try to act all hard on the outside, but to quote my mother, sometimes even steel has water on the inside."

When they first started dating, Jackson would send Claudia flowers at the drop of a hat. "Well, I used to be mad at him a lot. But it's okay. You can't change people. In general, I like him the way he is. That is what marriage is about, right?"

"How would you know what marriage is about, you won't try it. All I know is that I want to get buck wild occasionally. And my man knows that he better be coming with me or I am going alone."

Claudia stopped running. They had run almost a mile and a half and stood in front of a fountain. She walked in circles while Pam wiped the sweat from her forehead with the end of her Keep Austin Weird T-shirt.

"You should stretch. It will make it better."

"Ain't nothing going to make this better." Pam stopped pacing momentarily and bent over at the waist. "You just don't worry about me."

A light breeze rippled the water as they stood in the shadow near the bridge on Congress Avenue, a major thoroughfare and crossing place for auto traffic. Not too far from where they stood, a group of runners was preparing for the day's run. They watched as the group went through a series of stretches, most holding onto jogging strollers the whole time. A few, double strollers.

"Claudia, maybe we ought to join them and bring my little ones out here to run."

Claudia stopped in her tracks. "Pam, what do you notice about those women? How many Black people do you see over there?" Her face was peppered with disbelief.

"What's color got to do with it? It's a great way for the kids to get some air, and you could get some practice for when you have a family of your own. Aren't you the one worried about getting rid of your onion-butt? Think what pushing a jogging stroller will do for your gluteus maximus."

"No, sweetie, the only way my kiddos are going to get out here is when they can run themselves. Why should I push yours? And which one of us would get the baby? You can try if you want to, you might fit in, but you can't even run by yourself. What makes you think it is going to be any easier pushing a thirty-plus-pound kid in a stroller? I don't think so. Let's get back to reality." Claudia wiped the sweat from her brow with the end of her shirt. Her biological clock was ticking. If she didn't do something soon, she might not ever have any kids to push around at all. It was not a subject she wanted to talk about with Perfect Pam anyway. "Okay, so, were you saying that you would cheat on your husband?"

Pam looked at Claudia knowingly. "Not necessarily. But I might give him the illusion of cheating to help him put things in perspective. But do you think if I did I would ever tell?" She grinned and winked. "Didn't your momma teach you anything?"

Claudia narrowed her eyes as they started walking back toward the bridge where they'd started their run. Pam would never tell, she knew that, and she probably knew her better than anyone else. They'd been best friends since high school.

Claudia thought about her mother. She could not imagine her ever doing anything to displease her father—at least not so anyone else could see. Her mother was a perfect June Cleaver whose husband had ruled their house with an iron fist for forty years.

"She used to joke with my aunts all the time about getting a houseboy when she turned thirty-five. But that was a *joke.*" Claudia laughed. "She and Daddy always seemed happy. You know that stuff only happens on *Sex and the City.*"

"Uh-huh. You better ask somebody, girl. Our mothers knew how to keep their men happy. It made them happy. We should take a lesson from them. When was the last time you did something romantic for Jackson? You don't have to cook naked, but you need to make him feel like a man."

Claudia stopped in her tracks. She looked at Pam, and couldn't believe that she was talking with a straight face. What made her the expert? "You losing it or what? If you say I need to stay at home, be barefoot and pregnant, I am going to throw you in the lake." She started walking again. "Let's pick the pace up again. If you can't run, we can walk fast."

Claudia laughed, swinging her arms as she attempted to

power-walk. Pam was making her a little angry and she needed some punishment, and Claudia knew she hated the way she looked when she was power-walking. Girlfriend just couldn't get the stride right and just ended up looking like an out-of-breath one-legged duck.

"I'm not saying all that. You are sure breaking your mother's heart, you know that? She has been planning your wedding for five years. The only thing missing is the date." Pam knew that Claudia had picked up the pace out of sheer meanness, but she refused to let her see that she knew that too. She thrust her arms back and forth to try and concentrate on something other than the pain she was feeling. "Home works for me, but I see you going a little nuts if you were to try it. Everyone in your house would mutiny. But you could dress a little nice for him and smell good. Be feminine. You know what I mean."

"Just what are you saying? I do dress nice. All the time."

Pam didn't answer. She concentrated on pushing with the backs of her legs and watched the gravel pass under her feet. Claudia dressed *nice,* but that wasn't what Pam meant. Pam knew she equated nice with expensive, and the two were not necessarily the same, at least not the way Claudia put them together.

"Oh, so you are going to get into the workout now, huh?" Claudia tripped but quickly regained her footing. "Silence is not good from you."

Pam pursed her lips and wiped sweat from her brow. She knew Claudia would not like what she was about to say.

"Yes, you buy nice clothes. But I am talking about the way you put them together. Sometimes you gotta be a little raunchy. Stop trying to look like Lilith from *Cheers* and be more . . . you know what I am trying to say."

"I do not look like Lilith. That's horrible, how could you say something like that?" Claudia hated Bebe Neuwirth in that role, like the show's writers were trying to make a negative statement about intelligent and successful women or something. "That woman was all pasty and stiff. My clothing is . . . professional."

"Look, I am just calling it like I see it. Professional is nice in the office, but you have to be a little 'Frederick's of Hollywood' at home. For a smart woman, you sure are dense. When was the last time you had sex? I bet you two just get together and watch TV all the time."

"I'm not answering that. Who made you an expert, anyway?"

They slowed their walk. They had almost made a complete circle.

"You don't have to answer. Just ask yourself truthfully. I bet you sleep in an old T-shirt? Am I right?"

Claudia tried to keep a poker face but could not help rolling her eyes. She hated that Pam was right. She couldn't remember the last time she'd had sex. "And you sleep in nice lingerie every night? C'mon now."

"Girl, some nights I don't get a chance to get it on. What do you think is the real reason I am late. I even wear exercise thongs." She winked.

"Okay, that is too much information. And that's not realistic. If Jackson and I spent all our time doing the nasty—"

"You would have a healthy sex life and be married already. He wouldn't be able to live without you instead of stringing you along the way he has been for so long. Just give me a chance. I can teach you a thing or two that will make this anniversary the best one yet."

Back where they started, Pam and Claudia began their

cool down. Claudia stretched and Pam followed suit, humming a tune under her breath. Claudia was pensive as she eyed her friend. She knew that Pam and her husband had a healthy sex life—Pam always talked about it—but she'd had no idea that her best buddy was a secret Xavier Hollander.

"Who said he was stringing me along? Maybe I am the one doing the stringing along. Maybe I am the one hesitant to set a date."

"You see, now the truth really comes out. Like I said before, he ain't going to wait forever. I don't see why he is wasting his time with you. You never let him be a man. That's okay sometimes. It doesn't mean you are a weakling. I know you would hate for anyone to think that." She rolled her eyes. "What is he getting out of the deal?"

Pam was right, Claudia knew she could use a little improvement in that area. What did she have to lose? A spiced-up sex life might give her the excitement she was looking for.

"Okay, I'm game."

Pam was bent over at the waist, stretching the backs of her legs. She stopped midstretch and smiled devilishly.

"Really? I knew your momma didn't raise no fool." She stood up. "You need some work, so we have to take it slow."

Claudia nodded but could not help but feel a little apprehension. There could be no harm in humoring Pam just a little. At the worst, a few makeup tips would be a Martha Stewart good thing. She had been wearing the same face for years and might learn something she didn't know. Maybe. Or Pam just might turn her into the freak of the week. She shuddered, waved good-bye to Pam, and headed back to her car.

Chapter 5

The sunrise crept up on the small balcony outside Cody's apartment, and he was there to watch the way the sun glinted off the soft ripples of Town Lake. Sweat beads popped onto his forehead as he struggled to drag his telescope outside with him. He grunted from the exertion, rubbing his hip after he bumped it on the narrow doorway. There would be a bruise tomorrow. Pains shot through the hip, but that did not deter him from his plan.

Pointing the telescope toward the area known as Auditorium Shores, he adjusted it just as daylight broke over the Austin sky. This was his favorite part of the Austin day. Austin itself wasn't too bad, considering the fact that he'd been practically forced to move there. The people almost had a certain "Woodstock" quality to them, and that seemed to agree with Cody. There was even a fair share of all-night restaurants and other displaced New Yorkers if one knew where to look.

The telescope was the most powerful one the store had. Cody swung it around, searching the area over by the new pedestrian bridge on Lamar. He saw various people milling around. None of the walkers, runners, or bikers looked like the woman he was looking for. He could not pick Claudia from among any of the people he could see. Cody glanced at his watch. It was 5:45 A.M. It was still too early to see much. From his calculations, she usually arrived at Auditorium Shores about 6:30, if her friend arrived on time. He wanted to wait until he saw her pass, and then leave his apartment. The lake was less than five minutes away if he hustled.

His stomach grumbled, and Cody rubbed it. He had time for coffee. He stepped back into his office, his eyes immediately coming to rest on last night's stack of mail. A momentary feeling of remorse swept over him and then flitted away. He'd told Barry that he was going to run, which was not exactly true. He really was not interested in the fitness part at all. Instead he was going to just exercise his eyes and *watch* the runners. He felt bad for lying to his friend, but sometimes Barry was just a little too nosey and a little too righteous. What did he know about it? He hadn't married love, he'd married comfort. That seemed to suit Barry just fine. He appeared happy, but Cody wanted more. He wanted to love the woman he married from the start, so he could stay that way until death did them part, as the vows said.

He paused in the living room briefly. He snatched up the three remaining pictures of Marina and scowled. He would always have fond memories of her, but he hated how they'd ended. It was his own fault anyway. He should have broken it off with her, like any sane person would have done, when she'd started dating someone else. Instead he'd held on like an idiot, as if she were going to change her mind about it. He should have known that Marina would do whatever her father wanted.

Cody strode to the kitchen, where his automatic cof-

feemaker was waiting for him. The coffee smell was what
had started his stomach growling in the first place as it had
softly wafted through the apartment. He reached up, open-
ing his white cabinets to grab a cup and stepping on the
foot pedal of his stainless steel garbage pail at the same
time. He removed a cup with his right hand and simulta-
neously dropped the pictures he held into the trash with his
left. It was time to move on. She was the past. The pictures
hit the bottom of the empty can with a thud; Cody swallowed
and released his foot. Marina was crazy not to want him. He
knew he was a good man, even if her family couldn't see it.
Cody grabbed the coffeepot, hurriedly filling his cup. Some of
the hot coffee splashed on his hand. An omen. Marina had
burned him before. He sucked his finger to cool the burn and
hurried back to the balcony. Good riddance. Too bad it had
taken him over a year to arrive at this point.

Six-fifteen. He put his eye up to the telescope. No signs
of who he was looking for. He knew that if he left just when
she passed Auditorium Shores, he could get to his spot in
the park before she did. She and her friend usually stopped
running by then. They would be walking. He could be sit-
ting on a rock across from that funky statue on the edge of
the water and it would look like he had been there all morn-
ing. He could get a close look at her and she would only
know if he let her. And he would, when the time was right.

The running mother group began to arrive at the clear-
ing. He watched so often now that he was beginning to rec-
ognize them too. They ran three times a week. He knew
who would be early, who would come running up at the
last moment. He even knew who would not finish the run.
It was a shame that people were so predictable. That's why
life got boring for them, he thought. They let things get too

run-of-the-mill—their lives lacked excitement. It was a good thing he wasn't a criminal or anything, he thought. Most of those folks would probably welcome a little intrigue and spice in their lives. He hoped Claudia would.

It was time to go. He grabbed his keys and left his apartment. He sprinted the few blocks to the Town Lake track, getting there within a few minutes. He sat facing the water, the statue across from him. No matter what time he came, that statue would always have fresh flowers in its outstretched hand. Someone got up pretty early in the morning to take care of that. Cody opened the book he'd brought with him and waited, not reading a word on the page, instead peering over the top of the book. He smiled to himself.

This was the fifth time he'd sat on the rock, with the exact same book. Claudia had never noticed him. Couldn't she feel the special electricity that happened every time they were near each other? It was almost as if they'd known each other in a different life or something. The only other person that had happened with was Marina. And they'd had several good years, even if he'd had to share her with someone else.

Claudia and her friend were keeping up a pretty stiff pace, even if they were only walking. They strode past Cody, and he held his breath for a minute. As usual, she was perfectly coordinated and eerily attractive. He had been watching her for almost two months, and time still seemed to slow down just a bit when he saw her. She and her friend were talking up a storm, and neither one of them bothered to look sideways at all. They obviously had never lived in New York and were used to the security that a town the size of Austin and its low crime rate offered.

His stomach quivered. He was not ready yet, but one day

he would tell her how he was beginning to feel. He lowered his chin just in case she decided to look over, so he could avert his eyes and appear to be reading, if necessary. He shifted his body on the rock as she walked by. There was something about her that was so beautiful. Her skin was the deepest chocolate brown he had ever seen, and what he could see of her wavy hair he loved. He would love to run his hands through that hair. The end of her ponytail stuck out of her baseball cap. He knew that underneath it would be smoothed down into the waves she always wore at work. She seemed so comfortable with herself, even as she tripped on a small rock in her path. Tripping did not even make her miss a beat in her conversation. His stomach got warm. Claudia just had it together. She was smart, stable, and knew where she wanted to go. Exactly what he needed in a woman now.

After they were a safe distance away, he stood up and slowly followed behind them. The water rippled and the air felt freshly wet, but Cody didn't notice. The only thing on his mind were the two figures in the distance. He day-dreamed, keeping Claudia's hot pink jogging outfit in sight. He imagined peeling it from her sweaty body and helping her shower. Cody watched as long as he dared, then ambled back to his apartment.

Cody straightened his tie and calculated his next move. He smiled into his small bathroom mirror. He wanted to make Claudia feel as if she were the most beautiful woman in the world. He wasn't a bad-looking guy and was positive that he could make her like him, even just a little bit. Thoughts of her propelled him through his morning dressing routine faster than usual. That woman sure looked good, even when she was covered with sweat from running.

His thoughts were interrupted by the phone. He glanced over at his caller ID box, which read Unknown Number, Unknown Name, and he opted not to answer. Cody wasn't ready to talk with anyone just yet. He wanted to spend a few more minutes basking in the high he got from watching other people work out.

He made it out of his apartment in less than thirty-five minutes, rather than his standard hour and fifteen. Capitol of Texas Highway stretched out across Austin in a south-to-north concrete ribbon, divided in the middle by a grassy median that was often covered with wildflowers in the early spring. It climbed up and down Austin's hills, meandering through the bottom of the Texas Hill Country. The flanks of the road were rimmed at points by remnants of hills blasted through to lay the roadway. Various home and office developments were hidden along the side, and cars often darted out to cross over.

The stoplights along the highway were not synchronized and never had been. Barry was really into the local government and city planning, and he ran his mouth nonstop about what road improvement was planned for Austin and when. Thanks to him, Cody knew that if he traveled at just the right speed, he could miss virtually every traffic light on the way to his office. He drove the road without thinking, bopping his head in time to the music that played on his radio, intermittently fishing in his briefcase.

His cell phone chimed, and Cody snapped to as he flipped it open.

"This is Cody," he said.

"How was your run?" Barry's voice boomed at him so loudly that Cody had to remove the phone from his ear.

"Good morning to you."

"Are we still going to meet later? Or are you standing me up for that too? You know how obsessive you can be."

Cody squinted. "Excuse me?" He slowed his car as the light turned red in front of him. Barry might have messed up his pace, but he would not let him mess up his day, too. This wasn't the first time his friend had teased him about the way he went about doing things.

"You get all into running and things, and I know you might not want to hang with me anymore. We're supposed to get together after work. To go and get *professional* haircuts. Remember?"

Cody didn't remember. But he did need a haircut. The last time he'd let Barry cut his hair he'd ended up a with mess. He ran his hand across the side of his head. His "fade" still didn't fade at all. His hair just stopped abruptly, as if someone had sat a bowl on top of his head and shaved around it.

Austin was so divided that he had to go to the other side of town, the east side, just to get a decent haircut. He hadn't believed it when he'd first arrived, but all the services for "People of Color" were on the other side by Interstate 35.

"Yeah, I'm game. But what do I have to be obsessive about? Haven't you ever heard the adage that anything worth doing is worth doing well? Half-stepping isn't as acceptable for everyone else as it is for you."

Barry guffawed into the phone. "I meant you no harm, but you know how it is. I thought you may have been running again now that you decided you are a runner. Every time you decide that you are going to try something new, you go all the way, man. Tell me I am lying."

"That doesn't make me obsessive, that just makes me a perfectionist. Like I said, I just don't believe in half-stepping, in anything. You only live once." He paused. "Shoot me an e-mail and give the details of where we are going to meet. Is this a nice place? You know that I don't want to sit on any folding chairs." The last time he'd let Barry talk him into going to a barbershop, the place had been a dump. Cody shivered as he remembered the hard, cold, metal chairs and holes in the wall. That place had been right next door to a greasy spoon, and he'd come out feeling as if his cholesterol level had gone up just by inhaling the fumes. Some things just shouldn't have to be, he thought.

"How about I just pick you up? We need to be there as soon as possible after work if we don't want to stay all night."

"Whatever. Anything will be better than you cutting my hair again. I have to run a few errands too. You can help with that. See you then." He hung up the phone and turned his thoughts back to Claudia.

Chapter 6

Marina stood up from her vanity, checking herself one last time in the mirror. She pursed her lips and shook her head. She was perfect, she thought to herself—at least for Wesley. He had even chosen her makeup colors. She grabbed a lipstick for her bag and headed toward the living room, where she knew Wesley was waiting impatiently. He was probably pacing up and down the room by now. One more minute, and he would have dragged her out to the car by her hair, caveman style. Marina grimaced at the thought.

She walked down the short carpeted hallway balanced on her toes. She grabbed the banister as soon as she reached it. Marina wanted to conserve her feet; they could only stand so many hours in these shoes. She caught a glimpse of herself in the full-length mirror at the top of the stairs and decided that she looked every bit the femme fatale. No one would ever guess the misery that lurked inside her. Her father always said she should have been an actress. She could win an Academy Award for this part. Unfortunately, she did not feel as if she had an Academy Award life; it was more like she lived a bad daytime soap opera than an award-winning motion picture.

At the bottom of the stairs, she turned the corner into the

living room. Wesley was standing by the phone table, his back to the stairs.

"I'm ready." Marina's voice was flat as she announced her presence. "Is the car here yet?"

Wesley jumped, returning the phone to the cradle. He spun around, wiping his hands on his suit pants.

"What?" He looked dazed for a minute. "Uh, they should be pulling up any minute." His face softened. "I'm sorry if I got a little angry earlier. You know that is a sensitive area for me."

Marina didn't answer. His anger was nothing new. Who had he been talking to? He looked at her like a kid that had been caught doing something he was not supposed to. She knew that he was just apologizing because he was so afraid that she might embarrass him at his little function. Did he think she was a fool?

Wesley rested his hands on her slender waist, holding her at arm's length. "You look wonderful."

"Do I?"

"You will probably be the best-looking and best-dressed wife there."

Marina raised her eyebrows at his comment. "Of course I will. I will stand out because of the lack of a flowered caftan. Isn't that what all the other 'corporate wives' will be wearing?" She made quote marks in the air with her fingers.

Wesley removed his hands. She flinched. Her shoulder still smarted from earlier. If he so much as raised his hand to her she was going to fall down and scream. Not that anyone would run to her rescue. The neighbors were used to them by now. She could see his eyes darken a little, but he did not attempt to push her or hit her again. Instead he moved away from her and looked out one of the front windows, then glanced at his watch. They did not speak again, and Marina found herself wondering what he was up to. He was so secretive sometimes.

The car arrived, and they left the house in silence. Wesley held the door open on the long, black car before the driver even had a chance to. They were outside now, and he would want to appear to be a perfect gentleman. The company had always paid for its executives to be driven to work by car service. Formerly it had been the only way to make sure that they did not have to ride the subway into work, but now it was a necessity. Like many other companies that had once been headquartered in the Wall Street District, they'd moved the executive offices across the river to New Jersey after September eleventh. They were being taken to some nondescript and overdone catering hall in New Jersey, near the office, and getting through downtown Manhattan could be difficult. She and Wesley would have just been more agitated with each other if they'd had to drive themselves through that tangle of traffic. Besides, the car was air-conditioned, and she could get a break from the heat.

Marina found herself wondering why Wesley had hung up the phone so quickly. It seemed to have happened too often over the past few months, and Marina was beginning to feel as if there was a big part of Wesley that she knew nothing about.

She glanced up at the driver. He seemed to be in his own world, listening to the earplug that was stuck in his ear.

"Isn't there a baseball game tonight?" she asked. The driver made eye contact with her in the rearview mirror and nodded. Claudia knew there was a "silent ride" policy in effect, just like the yellow cabbies had now, but she did not want him to listen to the conversation. He took the hint and reached for the radio. He turned it on and tuned to the station broadcasting the Yankees game. Marina met his eyes in the rearview mirror again and smiled, reassuring him that it was okay. He nodded, silently guiding the car onto the Long Island Expressway.

Claudia looked at Wesley's profile. He was still as handsome as he had been when they married. He'd just never had the ability to make her heart do that little flip-flop thing that Cody had made it do. She loved Cody, but she did not have the guts to stand up to her father. She wanted him to be proud of her, but now it was clear that the only way she could make him happy was if she turned into a son instead of a daughter.

Although she had become fond of Wesley, she didn't love him. Her mother had told her that the kind of love she and Cody had would not last. She'd said that she would grow to love Wesley. He was from the right kind of family and would take care of her. What she'd really meant is that her father could get him to do anything he wanted him to, and he was white. Sure, Wesley provided for her, but he seemed to keep a part of him locked away, even though he had been there when Cody had left the way he had. Wesley had become increasingly secretive, and there could only be one explanation.

"Wesley, are you seeing someone else?"

"What now?" His voice dripped with annoyance. "When would I have time to see anyone else? I work fourteen hours a day, Marina."

"I don't know. You hung up the phone so abruptly when I walked in the room."

Wesley removed her arm from his. "I should be the one having problems trusting you, not the other way around. You are the one who—"

It was just like Wesley to turn things around and make her feel as if it were her fault. She held up her hand.

"Let's not talk about that. It's in the past." Every time Wesley brought the twins up, it was as if he were throwing salt on an open wound. "You remember what the therapist said. You are the one who wanted to stay together. You are the one who said you could forgive me. You wanted this." She wiped at the tears that were forcing their way to her eyes. "I just asked a question, you didn't have to bite my head off. What else have I done wrong?"

Wesley hated it when Marina cried. He didn't want her to cry, especially now. They would have to arrive at the banquet with her face streaked with tears and her makeup ruined. That would not be good. Her father would look at him as if he had done something wrong. In her father's eyes, Wesley's biggest job was keeping his daughter happy, but he was supposed to "keep her in line" too. He cupped her face in his hands. "You haven't done anything. I did forgive you, I swear. It was business, Marina. The call? It was business. I just didn't want you to worry. Problems at the office. Nothing for you to concern yourself over. That's all." Wesley shook his head. He had forgiven her, just not Cody. Cody had known that Wesley and Marina were going to get married, but he couldn't do the right thing and just bow out. And now, here he was digging around and stirring things up again. But soon he would be reminded that he needed to stay away and not dredge up the past.

Marina looked into her husband's solemn eyes, searching for some clue that told her that they had done the right thing or that he was telling her the truth. She found nothing but the emptiness that lived inside her.

Chapter 7

It did not take long for Claudia to make it back to her neighborhood. She lived on Austin's West side, just inside the city limits. The pretty neighborhood was a cornucopia of race and ethnicity, one of the reasons that Claudia chose to live there. There were a few other African American families, two Asian, and a smattering of families from various other places around the globe. Very few native Austinites like herself.

She was the only single person living in the development, but Jackson stayed over so much that her neighbors treated her as if they were already a couple.

The little strip of town houses was sandwiched in between the other homes, all "bigger than small" but not quite mansions, all crowned with meticulously manicured lawns.

She swore under her breath as she pulled into her driveway. The garage door had been left open once again. *What was so hard about closing it?* Claudia wondered. Jackson was a smart man, but he didn't seem to be quite housebroken. He never seemed to forget to put his own garage door down, not that he stayed at his place much during the week. When he did, he rarely invited Claudia anymore. At first he'd said his apartment lacked the creature comforts and feminine touch that Claudia's had. But she was beginning to think he liked staying at her place just because it was closer to where he worked.

Small social graces seemed to slip by him. Claudia didn't have time to worry about that now. She had to hurry to get herself together.

She hit the automatic garage door opener and watched the door as it came down, just a few inches shy of the rear end of her small car. The space barely qualified as a garage at all—it was more like a closet with an automatic door. She was barely out of the car, but she could hear the alarm clock she'd bought for Jackson chiming away all the way inside the bedroom. She shook her head. That meant he was still asleep in her bed with his head under the covers. Her nose flared thinking about it. He needed to be up working out for her as hard as she worked out for him.

Just as she thought, Jackson was a lump under the covers. Claudia peeled off her running clothes on the way past him, shaking him on the way. He groaned and turned over. She always teased him about sleeping the way he did. He must have gone right back to sleep after he'd put the garbage out. The first time he stayed at her place, he'd wanted to sleep with all the lights on to be sure he would get up. That didn't work for Claudia. She slept so lightly that a car passing on the street might wake her up. It had taken her all of their five years to get Jackson to just trust an alarm clock. Even so, he still hit the snooze button multiple times and never remembered doing it. The first thing he would do when he finally did get up was blame her for his oversleeping, as if he weren't a grown man.

She reached for a fresh towel, wanting to have it ready

when she was done. Just as she opened the shower door, her phone rang. Claudia pursed her lips, immediately annoyed. Why was it that although everyone who knew her claimed they understood that she didn't like to talk in the morning, they still called her? She knew without looking that it was her mother, and she contemplated not answering it for half a minute but then picked it up anyway.

"Hey, Ma." Claudia's voice was flat. She immediately regretted having answered. Her mother had a flair for the melodramatic, and there was no telling what the drama in her life would be this morning.

"Well, don't be so excited. I was just calling to fill you in on my tests. You know how I hate doctors."

Her mother was in one of her talkative moods. "Yes, Ma, I do know. Are you okay? I can't talk long. I have to get to the office."

"Oh, don't you care about me and my health? I am only calling to tell you if I am going to live or die. You work too much anyway. You need to be concentrating on setting a date with that wonderful man instead of giving away all your milk for free. How is he, anyway?"

"Fine." Claudia did not want to get into it with her mother. It would be too easy for her to ruin a day that had started out good. "The tests—? I really do have to run, Ma. I am running the shower, wasting water." Claudia knew that the idea of any kind of waste would make her mother cringe.

"Oh, it's fine. Turn the shower off, then. You need to conserve water for those grandbabies you are going to make me."

Just as Claudia thought. She folded her arms.

Her mother continued. "At the rate you are going I won't be around to see them. You know I been having that bad gas. Remember after I eat I have to make that big old burp that embarrassed you so much?"

Claudia closed her eyes and pressed her fingers into the space between. There was no winning with her mother. If she was not going to chatter on endlessly about the virtues of marriage and motherhood, Claudia would have to hear about the more unpleasant bodily functions. She did not know what was worse, the belching problem her mother was referring to or having to hear an essay about it. If she was nicer, maybe her mother wouldn't talk so long.

"What do you mean, Ma? It is not embarrassing. I understand. You told me you couldn't help it." Claudia crossed her fingers and hoped that lightning would not strike her for lying. She tilted her head to the side, closing her eyes, just as Jackson stumbled into the bathroom. Claudia motioned to him that it was her mother. He shook his head adamantly, obviously wanting to talk with her even less than Claudia did.

Claudia sighed and stepped aside, letting Jackson get into her shower. He grumbled something at her that she did not quite catch, but she knew that it was his customary "Why didn't you wake me up?" or a variation of it. Hopefully he would not use up all the hot water with his love of long showers. She might as well let him go first; this conversation between her and her mother had become a weekly one, and she knew there was no way she could get off the phone without hearing her mother's whole story, short of hanging up. And there was no way that was happening. If she did, she would have to hear about how disrespectful she was for the next ten years.

Claudia stood outside the shower stall, half listening to her mother, plucking her eyebrows at the same time. It had been so long since she'd had them professionally done that they were officially approaching "uni-brow." She interjected an occasional "Okay," where appropriate, to at least make her mother feel as if she had one hundred percent of her attention.

"I am not going to keep you, Claudia. Like I said, I just wanted to let you know that all is okay and the colonoscopy was negative. I think that old doctor was just trying to milk my insurance anyway. You know me and your father have good insurance, right? His benefits are still good, even though he retired. We are some of the lucky ones. At least he got something out of slaving for the man all those years." She paused. "What are you going to have? You better make a life for yourself, you hear?"

Claudia wanted her mother to be finished with her diatribe. It had taken longer than Claudia expected for her mother to get around to talking about her favorite subject: everything she felt Claudia was not doing but should be. Claudia was no more in the mood now than she had been when the phone had first rung.

"Thank you for understanding, Ma. I will see you soon, okay?" Sometimes the best strategy was to just ignore her comments until she went away.

"You think we would get together more. We see each other so infrequently now that we have moved down to Houston. But I have a surprise for you."

Claudia felt her chest tighten. Surprises from her mother were not necessarily a good thing. "A surprise?" She could not imagine what it might be, and she was still recovering from the last "surprise." Her mother had set up unwanted and unasked for premarital counseling with a priest who was an old family friend. Claudia's face turned red just remembering how embarrassed she'd been, sitting there, along with Jackson, half-nodding and smiling as Jackson squeezed her hand in a "I-am-going-to-kill-you-when-this-is-over" fashion.

Jackson opened the shower door and stepped out, totally missing the shower mat. He walked, naked and dripping, across the carpet to get a towel. Claudia rolled her eyes. She hated stepping on the carpet when he did that.

"Your father is going on a trip with his friends to play golf, and rather than stay here all by myself, I am going to come and stay with you for a few days. I thought it would be good for us to visit and catch up. Talk about things like we used to."

With her mother, a few days could quickly turn into an eternity. And "catching up" meant nitpicking to death until Claudia wanted to pull her hair out.

"Do you think that is a good idea, Ma? What would you do here? You and Dad are not used to being apart. All of your friends have moved away from here, and I have to work. You know I can't—"

"Nonsense, girl. You have to come home at night. I don't have too many good days left, and I just want to be near you. Help you plan for the wedding. You two are setting a date soon, right? We might as well get started on the preparations. A wedding takes so much. I want so much to be a part of it all. Your brother cheated me out of it when he eloped with that girl."

Claudia felt her head begin to pound. Henrietta was laying on the guilt extra heavy. Still, this was not the most opportune time for her to visit. Her mother was talking as if a date had already been set, and here she was contemplating whether she did indeed want to marry Jackson or not. She definitely did not need her mother around; she had a way of just jumping right in the middle of things, especially Claudia's things. That would just make matters more confusing. "Ma, that was ten years ago. They didn't elope, they just went to a justice of the peace. And she gave you grandchildren already. It turned out good."

"Hmmph. If you say so. I never see those kids. She made him move all the way to Washington State. And there is nothing like your daughter's kids. It's different with a son, you know."

Jackson walked out of the bedroom, clutching the towel to his front. Claudia watched him go, bare-assed. Boring or not, he did have a nice behind. She glanced at her watch and jumped, startled at how long she had been on the phone being tortured. If she argued, it would only get worse. The best thing to do was to head her off at her own game, talk her off the phone without giving her much of a chance to protest.

She took a deep breath. "Ma, I really, really, really have to get to work. I will give you a call this afternoon to talk about this, okay? I promise." Claudia did not give her mother a chance to answer. Instead, she cringed and pressed the Talk button on the phone, hoping it did not sound too much like she had hung up the phone on purpose. That would be worse than listening to her mother talk her ear off. Claudia would have to sit through her mother's crying about how she was an ungrateful daughter. Worse yet, she would have to hear about how her aunts were so close with their perfect daughters, like her mother felt she should be.

Claudia peeled off the rest of her still sweaty clothes in front of the mirror, casting her eyes downwards. She didn't have time to look at herself; she knew all she would see were flaws. If she couldn't love what she saw, she might as well just not look.

The water enveloped Claudia's body fully as she stepped into the large double shower. She inhaled and savored the feeling of the water cascading over her. She relaxed, letting the water run over her shoulders and down across the rest of her body without a thought. After her run and shower, she would have enough energy to face the long day in corporate America.

Pam popped into her head. Claudia smiled as she thought about her friend and the ups and downs in their relationship. As long as they had known each other, Pam had both loved and fought hard, but overall she seemed happy. There was no lack of excitement in her relationship, that was for sure. She and her husband fought like they were still newlyweds. Claudia shrugged. At least they were feeling. That was good. They had not let the tedium of everyday routine take the excitement away from them. That girl probably still swung from the ceiling every other night. Claudia and Jackson were not even married yet, and they treated each other like old blue jeans worn thin.

It was as much her fault as it was his; she had been caught up in her career too. The problem was that you never knew when old jeans just might rip.

Pam could say that she'd cheated on her husband, but Claudia wondered how far she had actually gone. Was Pam telling her that she kept a little sugar daddy on the side for when her husband wasn't acting right? Was it something she'd just thought of doing? And just how did you find one of those? It was not as if you could take out an ad that said "Sugar Daddy Wanted." Surely, she didn't mean that she cheated on her husband for real, right? Pam was probably just talking some of that crap that she was famous for.

Claudia turned the brass handle on the shower, stopping the water. Pam *was* kinda crazy. There was no telling what she had or had not done. Back in the day, she'd been the one who'd always been getting rescued from some dilemma, usually of her own creation. Before she was married, several men had gone stone crazy over her. Claudia still had vivid memories of one poor guy standing outside Pam's dorm door for hours. He'd vowed that he would camp out there until Pam went out with him again. He'd thought he was in love. Apparently, he had been the only one who had been; and he'd stayed so long that the campus police had had to remove him.

Claudia grabbed one of the white towels she had stacked next to the shower and began to dry off. She frowned. One of the towels in the middle of the pile was just a little yellowed. She removed it and threw it into the trash bin under her vanity, making a mental note to go through the laundry process just one more time with her housekeeper. She wrapped her towel around her and picked up the Saks catalog that sat on the edge of her sink. She opened it and flipped through the pages. What did Pam think was wrong with her wardrobe? Her clothes were okay enough for her. She liked classic things and generally stayed away from fads. Her clothes were good clothes, and they camouflaged what she needed hidden and accentuated what she didn't. Trendy might be okay for Pam, but it wouldn't work for Claudia. It did not make sense to spend good money on clothing that she would only be able to wear for one season.

"Hey." Jackson, now fully awake and dressed, stormed back into the bathroom.

Claudia jumped, frowning, and dropped her towel and the catalog. "I thought you left. You scared me." Although she was annoyed, she had to admit he looked good. He was wearing a dark brown double-breasted suit, with wingtip shoes. His haircut, perfect as it always was, was immaculately brushed into place, and he moved so smoothly that he was almost graceful. Jackson exuded confidence. He always had; that was one of the things that had attracted Claudia in the first place.

"I did," Jackson said. "I had to come back. I forgot my phone." He picked up her catalog, handing it back to her. The smell of his Pleasures for Men cologne caressed her nose. The musky, powdery scent was pleasant, but Claudia did not like it as much as the plain old musk oil Jackson used to wear back before he'd graduated from law school, and she sure wished he would "pleasure" her much more often. There was no hope for that. She knew that once he got his clothes on there was not much she could do to coax him back into bed. It was just as well that she didn't have time either.

Jackson kept his cellular phone right next to the sink. When he stayed over, he usually plugged it in to charge up overnight. Claudia watched as he reached for it.

"Have you seen my pen?" he asked. "The gold one?" Claudia's heart sank. She shook her head no as she fought back the tears. Jackson was socially handicapped. He didn't even kiss her hello, good morning, or good-bye. He had not even asked her how she was or how her run had turned out. This was not new to her, but it still hurt. It was all about him, as usual. They weren't even married yet and she was already keeping track of everything for him. She shook her head. He would be asking for his socks next, even though he only kept a pair or two at the house.

She headed for her closet to choose her clothes. Jackson followed.

"Do you think we can get together for dinner?" he asked. "I have some things I would like to discuss with you."

She rolled her eyes. Everything always sounded so businesslike with him, like they were part of a corporate merger instead of a long-term relationship. She looked around her closet, her back to him. It was lined with rows and rows of suits, mostly brown and black, all very conservative. At least it all matched. "I was actually planning on working a little late, and then I was supposed to meet Pam. Can it wait until the weekend?"

Jackson looked at the floor. "Well, actually it can't." He put his hands on her shoulders. "I thought we were going to set a date. This is important to me."

"It's important to me too." Claudia breathed deeply and turned to look at Jackson. Her stomach was suddenly in knots. Who was she kidding? The uncertainty was gnawing at her, and she felt as if they were just killing time until something better came along. It wasn't all his fault. She knew that Pam was right. Either she would have to move on or put some serious thought into getting some spice back into their relationship. At the rate they were going, they would never make it to the altar, much less to "death do them part."

Jackson removed his hands from her shoulders and stepped back. He folded his arms against his chest. Claudia walked back into the bathroom, clutching the black, double-breasted suit she had chosen. She watched him in the mirror as he leaned against the bathroom wall.

He licked his lips, and Claudia could tell that he was about to say something that was hard for him. She had seen him make that same gesture a thousand times, but it was usually when he was trying to be diplomatic as he delivered bad news to other people. Her stomach tightened, and she slipped her skirt on over her hips.

"You know, when we first met, I thought we were soul mates. I couldn't imagine ever being with anyone else. I knew we would be together forever, and I was so happy when you accepted my engagement ring." He spoke almost mechanically, as if he had rehearsed what he wanted to say several times.

Claudia turned around to face him and opened her mouth to speak. Before she could say anything, Jackson held up his hand, motioning for her to be quiet.

"Let me finish. I never thought we would be here, Claudia, and I don't understand what has happened between us. I know I still love you, but I don't think that you feel the same."

Claudia shook her head. "That is not true, Jackson. You know it isn't. I just don't think that we should rush into marriage. It is a big decision, and I only want to do it once."

"That may be, but actions speak louder than words. At least that is what you always tell me. And your actions are saying that you don't want me around anymore. You keep putting me off as to when we are going to get married, and I am just not going to have that any longer. We are not getting any younger, and I am ready to move to that next phase in my life. I understand if you aren't, but you need to tell me that and stop stringing me along." He lifted his eyebrows and stood up off the wall. From the way he tilted his head to the side, Claudia could tell that he was expecting her to say something. He was putting the ball in her court.

"I am not stringing you along. That is ridiculous." Her voice quivered. Claudia inhaled, and her nostrils flinched. Her eyes began to sting as she fought back tears that wanted to come through. She was slightly angry with herself. Why did she always feel the need to cry at the most inopportune times? She wiped at her eyes with the back of her hand. "I thought we both agreed that we would spend some time concentrating on our careers—"

"Yes. Some time, but not an eternity. I am ready to move on, and you are not. In my mind, that means we are no longer compatible. I want a family before I am too old to enjoy them, Claudia. Don't you want that too?" he paused. "I think it is best we move on."

"Move on? Have you met someone else? I can't believe you. I thought we wanted the same things. Am I not good enough anymore? I may not be a beauty queen, but I have a lot going for me." She stood up and reached for her blouse, fumbling with the buttons.

"I never doubted that. This is not about anyone else. It is about me and what I want, and, I thought, about what you wanted too. We are like a sailboat on a day with no breeze. This whole thing has become just boring. I know you are bored too, don't say you are not. I don't know what to do to pull us out of here." Jackson stopped and ran his hand over his curly hair. Frustration was written all over his face. "We should break our engagement. You can keep the ring."

Claudia's mouth dropped open. He was bored? How dare he! She was suddenly angry. "But—"

"No," Jackson said, "it's best. Really, before one of us gets hurt. I have already removed most of my things."

Claudia glanced around the bathroom. It was true. His toothbrush was gone from its usual place. The small travel bottles he kept in his little corner, those were gone too. What the hell did he think this was, anyway? She was not some one-night stand floozy he just met yesterday. She willed herself not to cry. *Son of a bitch.* Claudia struggled to look composed and semidignified. She sat back down and turned back toward the mirror. She played at beginning to apply her makeup.

Jackson paused, looking at Claudia as if he expected something. He knew that she would put him off once again, and he had prepared. He still loved her and probably always would. He just wasn't sure that he gave her what she needed anymore.

"If you want to talk, you call me, okay?"

"And the point of that would be what? Prolonging my getting dumped?" Claudia said. She slammed her compact down on the counter. Jackson had some nerve. What would make him think that she had anything else to say to him? Hadn't he said it all?

Jackson shook his head. He knew he was doing the right thing. He loved Claudia, but she obviously did not feel the same. She was hopeless. "You had better hurry. Wouldn't want you to be late for work."

Claudia waved good-bye over her shoulder as she sped up her dressing routine. He would be back. He needed her. She avoided looking in the mirror and did not want to turn around. If she made eye contact with him, she knew that the tears would start flowing. When she finally did look up, Jackson was gone.

Claudia took off her engagement ring and placed it on the jewelry tray on her counter. Men were such assholes, she thought. He hadn't even asked her anything about how she felt, not really. As usual, he'd just told her how it was going to be. She looked at the ring as it sparkled on the tray. Maybe she could sell it on eBay. Either that or find a pawnshop. Damn.

Chapter 8

The parking lot was still deserted. Cody pulled his car into a space at the back of the gray building and looked around. He could only see two other cars, and one looked as if it might have been there overnight. This building was one of the three that made up the Austin office of Pittsford Electronics, the only one that was in this small office park in north Austin. Claudia worked in this building, and Cody had visited it several times for meetings. Twice, he'd virtually walked straight past her desk.

Cody knew from past experience that his car was just outside the view of the security camera. When they'd installed it, they'd left a blind spot. Cody was not sure if the security company did not know or didn't care. The woman who sat in the lobby, overcome with Cody's flattery, had wasted no time in describing the things she could see on her monitors. Cody had smiled with her and filed it all away. She had all but asked him out on a date. He picked up his small package, sealing it as he remembered her. She wasn't bad looking, just not for him.

His palms were sweating. Cody wiped them on his jeans. Why was he so nervous, he wondered? It wasn't that he was committing a crime, not really. He just had no business reason for being inside this particular building at this moment. Still, he felt like a parasite, waiting to piggyback onto someone else entering the building. There was no sense in him taking chances. Cody didn't want to use his magnetic badge to open the door, although he did have clearance to do so. Most people were careless, and although the employees were warned time and time again to be careful of people coming in behind them, most didn't. He never would have thought of doing this before they'd given him the idea. Cody smiled and made a mental note to thank someone for the inspiration.

In the security office, there was a machine keeping track of who used what badge where. Cody had seen it when he'd first gotten the job and had had to go to the security office to get his picture taken. He'd asked questions about the system, innocently at the time, not realizing how the information would serve him in the future. Cody smiled. Maybe he was being overcautious, but he was not ready to be discovered yet. The mystery added to the romance.

A small, gray car pulled into a space a few feet away from where he was parked. Cody watched the man in the car reach over to his passenger seat. No one would park there unless they intended on using the door that Cody wanted opened. He glanced at his watch. He only had about five or ten minutes before this parking lot would be overrun with cars. He egged the man on under his breath and crossed his fingers. He willed him to hurry.

Cody waited just long enough for the man in the car to get a few steps ahead of him, and then he opened the door and jumped out. He carried a stack of papers, big enough to look awkward while hiding his small package at the same time. Cody kept his eyes focused on the man ahead of him.

He wore the standard yuppie uniform—khaki pants with a slightly darker, lightweight jacket. He was obviously in no hurry; he even stopped to check out something on the bottom of his shoe.

Cody could feel his anxiety level rising, and he inhaled deeply to calm himself a little. Claudia might be driving up at any minute. Just as his host reached the door, Cody juggled his papers the way he'd rehearsed. It was essential that he look as if he was having a hard time. Hopefully this one would not be one of those information security nuts, someone who would stop him and make him use his badge to get into the building anyway.

"Hey, man, can you hold the door for me, please?" Just for effect, he dropped one piece of the computer printout. Sure enough, it worked like a charm.

"No problem." The man held the door with one foot as he reached down to retrieve Cody's lost paper. He handed it to him.

"Thanks." Just as Cody thought would happen, he was let in, no questions asked. He paused a minute to let his eyes adjust to the slightly dimmer artificial light inside the building. This area was a maze of cubicles, too high to see over. Anyone already here probably would not bother moving their chair to look and see who was walking by. They would be too dedicated, having arrived at work extra early to start their day. At least that was what Cody was planning on. The walkway was lined with off-red industrial carpet. Cody stared down at it as he walked with alacrity toward Claudia's cubicle, making two lefts and then a right. He looked around one last time, then gingerly placed his small package on Claudia's chair without stopping. He ran his hand over his head, dropped all of his papers in a waste-basket marked for shredding, and continued down the hall-way to a door on the other side of the building. He glanced at his watch. That had not even taken five minutes. It was time to get to work.

Chapter 9

Capitol of Texas Highway was known for traffic jams and accidents during rush hour, especially when Claudia was late. Her back was already hurting, and she was more tense than usual as she maneuvered her way through traffic. Talk about having a bad day. It wasn't even nine A.M. and Claudia felt like she was already nearing a ten on her stress scale. Her jaw began to ache from clenching her teeth.

Jackson had some nerve. How dare he just throw her away like that? What did he think this was? She was the person who was supposed to do the breaking up, not him. In between swearing at him, she silently prayed that there would be no major holdups on the road. Being late for her own staff meeting would really be the icing on her cake.

Claudia made it to the office a few minutes shy of eight o'clock and pulled into the parking lot. She scowled as she pulled into her self-designated parking spot. Everything else in Texas was big, but someone had drawn the line at parking. Gingerly, she maneuvered her way into the space between two sport utilities. Everyone except her seemed to drive one of those monstrous things. Not in the mood to be cautious, she opened her door, thumping the car next to hers. Claudia pursed her lips and shrugged her shoulders. Door dings happened. If they shared some paint, she would just have to take care of it later.

Claudia hurried into the building with the hordes of other people that were arriving at the same time. Everyone stared straight ahead as they rushed through the hallways, eager to start their day. It was like that most days; people rushed in, then all but a select few rushed out too. The people without lives stayed behind. That had always included her. Now she really had no life. A sinking feeling hit her stomach as she realized she now had less of a reason not to work late.

A few people called hello and Claudia reciprocated, forcing a smile she really did not feel like giving.

Just as she was about to step into her cube, she was stopped by Mary, the administrative secretary she shared with three other people.

"Good morning, Claudia," she said. "I have that paperwork you asked for on Friday. Do you want to go over it this morning at the staff meeting?"

Mary was a good woman, but it had taken a lot of work to get her to this point. Mary and Claudia came from two different worlds; Mary had been raised on a farm out in West Texas, and working in an office was a new experience for her. She spoke with a heavy Texas drawl, the kind you usually found outside Austin, in the rest of Texas. Claudia could tell from her reaction during their first meeting that Mary was not used to seeing a whole lot of Black people either.

Claudia ran her eyes over Mary. As usual, she looked as if she dressed straight from Wal-Mart. Mary's wardrobe seemed to consist of only five flowered dresses with bows in the back, which she rotated throughout the week. If not, then everything in her closet looked virtually the same. Claudia could tell which day of the week it was by which dress Mary was wearing. She frowned; according to Pam, her own wardrobe suffered from the same ailment, only in shades of brown, navy blue, and black instead of knockoff Laura Ashley prints. Maybe they weren't that different after all.

Mary's hair was stereotypically big, frozen in place by what seemed like whole cans of old-fashioned hair spray. She usually used so much that her perfume was overpowered. Claudia remembered that when they'd first met, Mary had seemed surprised that Claudia was the boss and a college graduate, whereas the furthest she had ever gotten was to beauty school.

Claudia stopped and smiled, smoothing her simple black skirt as she did. She realized Mary's worth, even if she did lack fashion sense. What did Pam know? Claudia knew she had fashion savvy, at least compared to Mary, and Mary might not know clothes, but she sure did know what was going on in the company before Claudia ever did. Mary could be a gossip if she wanted to, but she lacked the mean spirit that would have made her that way. She was just well-informed, and if she liked you, you would be too.

"How are you today, Mary?" Claudia stopped and smiled at her. Mary was always in a good mood and had a way of brightening everyone else up. It didn't hurt to be nice to her. "That will be fine. Just bring them to the staff meeting."

Mary nodded and looked past Claudia. Claudia moved over to let her look. It was better to let her satisfy her curiosity than have her guessing about what she imagined was in the Black woman's cube. It was the same as everyone else's, except she had the "executive" chair. Mary blushed when she realized she'd been caught.

"Can I help you with something else?" Claudia stepped inside her cubicle and laughed. Mary's embarrassment was all over her face.

"Looks like someone has sent you a package." Mary leaned up against the cubicle wall. It swayed a little under her weight.

Claudia swung her chair around and looked at the small box on her seat. It was long and flat, not much thicker than an envelope, and wrapped with raffia tied into a neat bow. Where had that come from? She had hurried in so quickly that she must have walked right past it.

"Looks that way. You wouldn't happen to know who put it here?" she asked.

"No, it was here when I came in," Mary said.

Claudia raised her eyebrows. Did that mean that Mary snooped around the cubicles before people arrived? That would not be surprising. There had been a couple of times when Claudia had suspected as much.

"I mean, I think it wasn't. At least I didn't notice it when I walked by. I wasn't as early as I normally am this morning." Mary generally liked to arrive before anyone else did.

Claudia shrugged her shoulders. "It's probably an invitation to one of those human resources shindigs or something." Someone in the corporate communications department knew how to spend company money on being overcreative, and Claudia was always getting interestingly packaged invitations to "rah-rah" meetings. Did they really believe these things boosted employee morale? Whatever it was, Claudia didn't want her business broadcast across the office by Mary's loose lips.

"No one else got one."

"Oh? I am not going to worry about it. I don't have time to look at it now." Claudia turned around in her cube and grabbed her mouse, moving it. Her computer screen flickered to life. Claudia could feel Mary still lurking behind her. She looked up. "That's it, then. Can you get a vacation schedule together for me before the staff meeting? We should go over that." Claudia removed the small package from her chair and put it on the corner of her desk.

Mary looked from the package to Claudia, craning her neck a little to get a glimpse of it again. There was an awkward silence for a minute, then Mary mumbled, "Oh, okay," when she got the message, backing out of Claudia's cube, giving her an awkward smile. It was obvious that she was disappointed, but Claudia did not want to give her the satisfaction of seeing what was in the less-than-corporate-looking package. If whoever sent it had meant for everyone to see it, they would not have wrapped it up. She flashed Mary a phony smile. *Don't hurt yourself now,* she thought. Mary needed to know just how far she could pry. No use in letting her get too familiar.

"I'll see you in the staff meeting. We can start off by you reading over the tasks we assigned last time." Mary's footsteps reached the end of the row of cubicles and reapproached on the other side. Her desk was almost directly opposite Claudia's.

Claudia threw her light sweater across the back of her chair. Pam would probably not approve of that either. It was classic and not exciting, but it was the kind of thing that would never go out of style, would fit nicely, and be almost inconspicuous under her suit jacket. She sat at her desk and opened her inbox. She had 144 messages since she checked her e-mail last night. Didn't people call anymore? She could barely get any real work done for the e-mails she got daily. The package caught her eye again and she reached for it just as her phone began ringing. Her caller ID said it was her boss. The day was beginning. Another hectic week. Claudia picked up the phone.

"This is Claudia," she said. The mysterious package would have to wait, at least until after the meeting.

Claudia punched at the elevator button impatiently. There was no reason on earth why a simple staff meeting had to take so long. Her shoulders hurt. She had been sitting in that uncomfortable chair for over two hours. Claudia stretched as she reached up and rubbed her right shoulder. It would be lunchtime soon for most people, but she had come out of the meeting with more action items than she had delegated. Once again she would eat at her desk.

The elevator doors swung open. It was crowded, and everyone looked at the floor. For a split second, Claudia considered walking down the few flights of stairs to her desk, then quickly reconsidered. She just did not have the energy. She pushed her way in and stood in the very front of the car, inhaling as the door just missed her nose. The remnants of everyone's perfume and cologne mixed together, making Claudia aware of her stomach. Conversations resumed.

"They think if they outsource that call center then—"

Claudia's ears perked up at the mention of a call center. She was responsible for one of the company's two. Hers had the most volume, and it was also the one with the least complaints. She fought the urge to turn around and see who was doing the talking.

"Outsource? But that is a lot of people that work there. What about their jobs?"

"Either they find jobs inside the company or they go elsewhere. But you are missing the point. The point is that we can drive cost through the floor. They could be managed from here, but the new hot spot is India, or so they say."

"Who says? How do you know?"

"Look, I'm just telling you what I heard."

"I'm not sure that works too well. Has anyone done any studies on what the customer thinks about this?"

"Who do you think is driving this? Our customers want lower costs. Taking out heads is one way to get it."

The elevator was silent as the doors opened. Claudia's heart raced. What those people were talking about would affect her directly. She stepped out of the elevator and waited for it to empty. She paused, watching as the other people got out too. She recognized the voice as belonging to Jason Marlboro. She didn't know him well, but they had been in a few meetings together. Claudia let him go ahead, and then walked a little behind him.

"Hey, Jason, how are you? I couldn't help overhear your conversation. You know anything else?"

He smiled thinly, letting his eyes run over her clothing. He shrugged and shook his head. "Not really. What's it to you?"

Claudia licked her lips. "Nothing really." She didn't want to appear too flustered. "But if there is any shred of truth to what you are saying, that could directly impact me."

"Oh, right. You still have the call center, huh?" He glanced at his watch. "From what I understand, it won't affect you directly. Just the people that work for you. They would all be *Indian*." He patted her on the shoulder and walked off.

Claudia's mouth dropped open as she watched him walk away. This was shaping up to be one hell of a day.

Chapter 10

Forest Hills was tucked away in the center of Queens, its own private enclave. Most of the time, it felt quiet and safe, lurking silently on the other side of hectic Queens Boulevard. Marina loved it; she could walk almost anywhere she wanted to, and most of the time, she would much rather walk than be driven. She and Wesley had settled not too far from where Marina had grown up, and that was fine with her. Until recently, she couldn't have imagined moving. She frowned as she looked at the houses she passed. She walked the same way at least three times a week, and she used to find something new almost every time, a new bush, a new flower, maybe notice some home improvement one of her neighbors made. Not anymore. Wesley was acting weirder than ever, and everything she used to appreciate appeared more and more drab. They didn't excite her anymore. She needed a change. The two of them were more different than she'd thought they would be. She'd thought that the house and the picket fence were what she wanted and that if she did what her father wanted, she would never have to worry about anything. Instead, she spent most of her time bored, unsatisfied with her choices, and afraid of her husband.

Usually, Marina liked to walk, but it occurred to her that

she wasn't sure if she liked to walk so much because it was good exercise, or because Wesley didn't want her to. He thought that walking was beneath her, for commoners. She pursed her lips. What did he know? He was from a plebeian background himself. His mother had been a supermarket checker when she'd met him. If it were not for her father feeling he owed Wesley's father a debt, where would Wesley be?

Her cell phone chimed just as she rounded the corner to enter the boulevard. She removed her bag from her shoulder and opened it quickly, swearing under her breath. She couldn't even take a walk in peace without someone calling her for one thing or the other. Thank goodness for caller ID. She was on the way to her morning yoga class, and then on to run errands. She did not want to be forced into the daily "rushing" routine early. The yoga class would usually relax her before she had to start running around like a chicken with her head cut off.

Wesley's cell phone number flashed on the screen. She put the phone back in her bag without answering. He probably didn't want anything anyway. He would be calling her to remind her to do one thing or the other, as if she needed reminding. And he would want to nag her. Just once, couldn't he get his own shirts from the cleaners? Who needed that? She would just have to call him back later. She refused to let her level of annoyance rise this early.

The boulevard was bustling with activity. Old-fashioned neighborhood shops lined the street, some that had been there for years, many owned by the same families that had owned them when Marina was a child. She knew many of the shop owners by name, and many of them knew her and her family too. She waved and smiled as she walked briskly to the recently added yoga studio, savoring the various smells that greeted her as she passed by. She glanced into the windows of her favorite store. The Italian bakery always brought a smile to her lips. The smell of warm fresh bread caressed her nose, and the treats displayed there looked wonderfully fattening. Marina licked her lips. She would have to visit after her class. Pastry would be her well-deserved reward.

Yoga was slow and uneventful, but it did serve to relax her. It was just enough exercise for Marina, but not enough to make her sweat heavily. After class, she stopped into the bathroom to reapply her makeup even though it had not smeared, and make sure she had no visible sweat stains anywhere.

Cody used to tease her about putting on makeup to exercise. He didn't understand the point, since she would sweat it all away anyway. And he would always tell her she was so beautiful she didn't need it. Marina blinked, trying to put thoughts of Cody and what she had done wrong out of her mind. She had done well not thinking about him for a good period of time, but lately he was creeping back into her thoughts again. He always had been what Wesley was not. In the beginning she'd had high hopes for her marriage. At the time, it had been the right thing to do, but her husband had turned out to be narrow-minded and uncaring, focused on only one thing—his career. Lately, she was starting to feel as if she had made the wrong decision in staying with him. She shrugged at the thought. What did it matter now? Everyone had made it so hard for her and Cody to be together, almost as if they had been the only interracial couple in New York. Even her mother, who was normally understanding, had urged her to give it up and move on.

Marina jumped as the bathroom door opened. She was joined by two women. Although she had known them since childhood, Marina felt she had nothing in common with them. Their exercise clothes were just as stylish as hers, but they seemed to just enjoy being "housewives" just a little too much. Marina hated the thought of even being called that. She was no more married to her house than the next person. Her nose flared. There had to be more to a relationship than this. It was not supposed to be about material things. What had happened to the love?

"Hey, Marina. You sure were looking strong in there." Justine talked first, chewing a big wad of gum as she spoke. She and Marina had actually almost been friends at one point back in high school.

"Thanks." Marina could tell she was waiting for her to say something similar back to her, but she didn't feel like small talk. She used to be at least cordial to Justine and her friend, but she didn't feel the need for that anymore. Since having the twins, she had become distant from any of her remaining friends. She did not want to encourage them or be close to anyone. If she did, she might feel the need to share, and Wesley would die if she did that. He'd made good and sure that she'd stayed out of the country while she was pregnant, just so no one would know. Marina knew she had nearly driven the nuns down in Puerto Rico crazy, with her incessant crying every day. When it was over she'd pulled herself together, just as she'd been expected to.

Marina halfway smiled at Justine, who was standing, waiting with a curious look on her face. She applied her lipstick, blotted it, and then put it back in her bag. She nodded. Marina could feel Justine's eyes boring into the side of her face. She sighed. *What is her problem?* She still had to pee, so there was no use in being too rude.

Justine and her friend looked at each other and raised their eyebrows. They did not even try to hide their looks of disapproval from Marina. "Everything going okay with you? How is that fine husband of yours?"

At the mention of Wesley, Marina froze. "He's fine. How about yours?" They really did not want to know. They were just being nosey.

"Oh, honey, he is fine. Still working it like he should." Justine flashed a phony smile, rolling her eyes upward and gyrating at the same time. "You ever hear from that guy you used to date. That *Black* guy?" She spit out the word *Black* as if it were some kind of crime.

Marina felt her breath stop in her throat. She cringed at Justine's nerve and vulgarity and shook her head. Cody would be the one to stick out in their heads, as if she were the only one who'd ever dated someone who was not white. There was no way she was going to discuss Cody with them. She couldn't. She stepped past them and into a bathroom stall and slammed the door bolt. Marina rested her head against the door, trying to catch her breath. Had they been sent here to torment her? Was this God's way of making her pay for her sins?

Outside the stall, Justine and her friend laughed together. They tried to whisper but didn't do a very good job. Everything echoed in the otherwise quiet bathroom—even whispers. Marina hoped they would not stay long. She did not want to look at them again, so she tried to stay in the stall to wait them out. Lipstick clattered on the sink. Justine swore under her breath. The bathroom was so quiet that Marina could even hear Justine smacking her lips as she chewed the wad of gum that was perpetually in her mouth. Marina wiped her eyes with the back of her hand, clenching her teeth. Her makeup would be smeared now. She let their whispers blend together until she thought she heard her name. They were talking about her. She was sure it wasn't the first time, but her ears immediately perked up as she strained to hear.

"As I was saying, he was handsome enough, but we used to joke about her having little brown babies. She made a smart choice, 'cause I don't know how people do it. Relationships are hard enough in this city, you know what I mean? On the other hand, though, I don't know how Wesley stays married to her. She is okay looking, but *he* could have done better."

Marina flushed the toilet to remind them that she was still there. *Done better than what? They have no idea what they are talking about.* She was the one putting up with him. She did not want to listen to them berate her, and she definitely was not up to facing them. She felt a sinking feeling in her stomach, as if the flush was taking away what little feelings she had left inside.

Justine immediately stopped talking. The bathroom became even quieter as the two women paused. One of them cleared her throat. Marina heard the water being turned on, then off. The door opened and closed. She exhaled, realizing that she had been holding her breath. Marina had been hiding from everyone for a whole year, and she was tired of it. She did not like the situation Wesley had forced her into. She opened the stall door and headed toward the door, glancing once again at her face. It wasn't as bad as she'd thought. Marina removed a tissue from her bag and gently dabbed at her eyes to remove the tears that had gathered there. She sniffled. *Whatever. Who are they and what do they know about my life?* They didn't matter in the scheme of things.

Justine and her friend had not made Marina feel any worse than she had already been feeling. They'd just made it easier for her to head toward the bakery. Actually, she thought to herself, their little snide comments had been just what she'd needed to justify the guilt she might have felt for indulging herself the way she'd planned. Now the calories would be a reward.

Marina left the yoga studio and headed back the way she'd come, toward the bakery. She opened the door, and the warmth that was always inside the place hit her in the face. She had fond memories of getting treats in this same store with her father when she was a kid. She'd never imagined that she would not be able to share this type of thing with her own children here.

The door jingled. The woman behind the counter, the granddaughter of the original owner, looked up as Marina entered, and she waved at her. She wiped her hands on her ample-sized apron.

There were several people ahead of her in the old-fashioned store. It was small, just enough room for a few people, with a large, white counter in the back. Anyone standing in the waiting area could see back to the kitchen through a hole that had been cut in the wall.

Marina loved the fact that things did not change much in her neighborhood. All over the city, many of the mom-and-pop shops were going out of business or selling out because of the chain stores. That seemed so far away from the place she was now. Every time she came inside one of these stores, she felt as if she had stepped back in time. She felt herself relax again. She was so tense from listening to those women in the bathroom that it was almost as if she had not been to yoga at all. The smell of bread made her feel better.

The door jingled again. Marina felt someone else come in and stand beside her. People had to stand so close in the small store that it made her uncomfortable. Her daydream was over. She focused on the treats displayed ahead of her instead of the body too close behind her.

"I'll be right with you, Dominic." The clerk did not look up as she signaled to the customer now right behind Marina in the line. She apparently knew this person too. This was not unusual here, even in a big city like New York.

Marina tensed. She could almost feel the man's hot breath on her neck as he stood behind her. His breathing sounded labored and heavy, and Marina could tell that it belonged to a person of substantial size.

"I heard you won that baseball pool." The clerk smiled at the customers as she continued to direct her attention to her work.

"Yeah, I did. I went in with Wesley."

Marina jumped at the sound of her husband's name. There were probably fifty trillion other people with the same name, but what were the chances?

"You lucky dog. I wish I had won that money. It's not every day you fall into five thousand like that."

Marina could not resist. She turned around and mustered up a smile. She looked straight into the eyes of a very rotund person that she did not recognize. He was about her height, with black hair that was greasy, speckled with telltale flecks of dandruff. A Head & Shoulders commercial ran through Marina's mind. His hair was combed over the top of his head in an attempt to cover a growing bald spot, and he smelled like tobacco. He wore a vest left open to reveal a well-worn white shirt.

"Hi, I'm sorry to interrupt you. Would you be talking about Wesley Piscato?" She increased the intensity of her smile.

The stranger placed his large hand on his chest, pausing a moment. His nails appeared freshly manicured.

"Yes," he said, raising his eyebrows. "And you might be?"

"Oh, I'm sorry. I am Marina Piscato. Wesley's wife." She extended her hand.

"Dominic." He smiled, taking it. "The famous wife. I sometimes do work with your husband. He might have mentioned me. So nice to meet you." He kept shaking her hand. "Your pictures do you no justice."

Marina blushed slightly. He was missing one of his incisor teeth on the right side. She smiled again and shook her head. *What did he mean by "famous"?* "No, he hasn't, and he sure didn't mention winning any money, either."

The man guffawed, and the clerk chimed in.

"Uh-oh. You got him in trouble, now."

It was Marina's turn at the counter, and she stepped up. She pointed at three different kinds of éclair.

"I didn't mean to. We just found out—"

"He's in no trouble." She tried to make her voice sound as sugarcoated as possible as she shook her head. "I assure you, Wesley is his own man."

"That may be the case, but I know more than one fella that got into trouble over sports pools, at least with their wives. He is a good guy, he was probably going to send you on a surprise shopping spree or something." His childish grin exposed more gaps in his mouth where teeth had once been.

The clerk laughed again. "He is now."

"You think so?" Marina tilted her head to the side. This guy obviously did not know her husband. This wouldn't be the first secret he'd kept from her. The clerk handed her the bag of éclairs over the counter. "It's really okay. You take care. I will tell Wesley I bumped into you." She turned and headed toward the door.

"Wait. Can you let him know something?"

Marina turned as Dominic addressed her. He hurriedly paid and joined her at the door. She stepped outside, and he followed. She raised her eyebrows. "Yes?"

"I was supposed to call him, but I haven't been able to get through. See, I was supposed to deliver a message for him, to some guy in Austin. Can you let him know that it's been all taken care of now. He shouldn't have any more trouble with this guy snooping around."

Marina felt the hairs on the back of her neck begin to tingle again. Was this what Wesley had been so secretive about lately? "A message?"

"He'll know. Business stuff. You don't have to be concerned about it." He reached into his bag and took out a piece of cake, which he started eating right there. Marina moved to the side to avoid his crumbs, watching as he carelessly dropped some of the confectioner's sugar onto his shirt.

"Any other details?"

"Nope."

"Okay then." She paused. "Just one question, why would you trust me to tell him this if he asked you to do it? I mean, you said you work with him all the time, then you must know how particular my husband can be about the details?"

He shrugged. "Like I said, no big deal. And you *are* his

wife." He laughed slightly, using the cake in his hand to point in her direction. Marina cringed, shrinking back to avoid his hand. "He and your father speak so highly of you all the time, I don't think he would mind, right?" He pushed the last morsel of cake into his mouth and licked his fingers. "I envy him. You guys must have the perfect marriage."

Marina sighed. "No, I guess he wouldn't mind. You take care." *He probably talks about me so much so you would think he lives in paradise.* Wesley was so much about appearances. She turned and walked away.

Chapter 11

Cody drove silently, without the radio to distract him. He was so lost in his thoughts that much of the route had been a blur. He looked around. The neighborhood changed immediately on this side of the highway, reminding him of home. The wood frame houses were smaller, but varied, and most of the streets were lined with small, concrete sidewalks.

He was supposed to meet Barry at 5:30, but he was a few minutes late. That could not be helped. At the last minute he'd been asked to stay at work a little late to finish a project. Originally, Cody and Barry had planned to ride to the barbershop together. Barry had wanted to drive so that Cody would be a captive; he would have to go where Barry wanted. He'd told Barry to go ahead of him so that he could hold them a place in the inevitably long line. Green's Barbershop was one of the more popular ones, and there was no such thing as an appointment there. Everybody waited.

Cody was glad for the solitude; his thought had vacillated all day between wondering why Marina had treated him like she had and trying to plan his next step with Claudia. Marina had suddenly turned cold. They had remained friends, up to and through the wedding, and then the thing

that should have had them working together had totally
pushed them apart. Cody tried hard to put Marina out of his
mind, but it was more difficult than he thought. Since get-
ting the letter about his kids, he couldn't help thinking
about her and wondering what would have happened if she
had done as he'd wanted and left her husband so they could
be together, at least to raise their kids. Or he could have
raised them alone and *she* could have paid child support.

Barry was right, they were a bad match anyway; he was
passionate about everything he did, including falling in
love, and it was obvious that the only thing Marina cared
about was herself.

He shook his head and blinked, trying to dispel the sense
of melancholy that had come over him during the short
drive. He had to get himself together before he saw Barry.
No matter what he said or did, Barry had always been able
to read him like a book. Barry already thought he was a lit-
tle unbalanced, and he was in no mood for lectures. Nor
was he ready to share any information about Claudia. The
time was not right.

The parking near Green's Barbershop was notoriously
bad. Cody rubbed the back of his neck as he pulled onto the
street. The stress was mounting, and he expected most of
the spots to be taken. Thursday and Friday were tradition-
ally the most popular days for haircuts, but Green's was
sure to be packed any day of the week. Cody moved his
head from side to side and stretched his neck muscles.
Barry would be there already, waiting, probably annoyed
with him. He was always on time, even though he had
nowhere in particular to be anymore, not since he'd left cor-
porate America. The small start-up had gone public in a
short time, and Barry had cashed out at the right moment.

Why couldn't I ever get involved in deals like that? Cody won-
dered. With his luck, he would have gotten caught in a dot-
com bust. He always seemed to be at the wrong place at the
wrong time, and no matter what, either he just missed the
boat or he was one step behind, playing catch-up. Barry
was one lucky SOB. Cody teased him about it often. His
friend's good fortune was one of his favorite things to joke
about, but if Barry played his cards right and was conser-
vative, he would not have to work for the rest of his life.

Cody circled the block once, finally finding a parking
space right out in front. He eased his car into the space, just
fitting between two sport utility vehicles. Before he'd moved
to Austin, he had never seen so many people driving trucks
in his life. The funny thing was, there were so many big cars
and nowhere for them to park; it seemed as if all the park-
ing spaces were for compact cars. Cody chuckled—that was
a metaphor for the story of his life; things just did not seem
to fit.

Cody quickly made his way to the barbershop and
opened the door, appreciating the old-fashioned jingle the
door chime made as he entered. The room smelled like a
barbershop, the kind from years past. Memories of visiting
similar barbershops when he was small immediately
flooded his mind, which welcomed the smell of aftershave
and cigar smoke. He smiled. He still remembered having to
sit on a booster seat so he would be high enough to have his
hair cut. Most of all, he remembered looking forward to
going with his father: That would be their day, away from
his sisters and his mother, the only time when one of them
could not steal him away from his father, when his father
would have to concentrate on him alone.

His dad had been a good man, an upstanding father, and

wonderful husband. Cody frowned as he remembered the way his father doted on his "girls," as he called Cody's mother and sisters. His father had treated his mother like a queen most of the time, and his sisters like princesses, pampering them without end. They'd taken all of the attention, and Cody was not sure that even his mother could reciprocate. Unfortunately, that had never left much room for Cody. He had always felt ignored as a child, or at the very least, like an ugly and unwanted stepchild. His father seemed to resent him, and he'd never been able to figure out why. They'd always clashed, especially when he was a teenager. The thought of some of their fights still brought a bitter taste to his mouth.

It was ironic that in the end it was just the two of them. After his mother died, his sisters moved away and didn't even send money to help with their father's care. Justice is a funny thing. When he was a kid, his father had no time for him. Then, at the end of his life, Cody was all he had.

Barry was sitting in the back of the small store, his large frame impossible to miss. The room was packed with people who had come from all over town to get their hair cut. Each of the three barbers had at least four customers waiting for him. Cody looked around the room and tensed, remembering why he'd let Barry cut his hair for so long rather than coming here. From the looks of the number of people in the room, he knew he was in for at least an hour's wait.

There was a small area in the back that contained three small leather love seat couches. These were old-fashioned too, made of tough leather and studded on the front trim. Two of the three had small cuts in the seats. They were arranged in a U shape, convenient for conversation or for focusing on the small black-and-white TV.

There were several other men there. Cody attempted to smile as Barry signaled to him, motioning for him to join them. He hopped out of his seat like a schoolkid. As always, he stood a little too tall and motioned a little too frantically. Cody shook his head. As far back as he could remember, Barry had been the goofy one. He always went a little over the top, but Cody loved him anyway. Unlike Cody, Barry never seemed to care that he didn't quite fit in. It was almost as if he accepted his misfit status and it did not bother him one bit. He was comfortable with himself.

Cody forced a smile and strode over to his friend quickly, hoping to stop him from making a fool out of himself. If he took too long to acknowledge him, he knew that Barry would shout at him across the small room, embarrassing him for sure then.

"Do you even move loud?" he sighed and slid into a seat on the love seat across from his friend. A few of the other men nodded a greeting.

Barry grinned widely, exposing the slight gap between his front teeth. He knew that his friend was embarrassed by him sometimes. "You need to get over yourself. Don't nobody care about how I wave at you. Can't you ever loosen up?"

"How long a wait do we have?" Cody glanced at his watch. He did not plan on taking all night to get a haircut.

"You know there is no telling." Barry shrugged. "Just relax and enjoy all this beautiful male bonding going on here. You walked in here looking all serious. What could be that bad?"

"Male bonding?" Cody let out a half-laugh, amused by his friend's remarks. "It's time for you to get a job. You've been watching too many of those daytime talk shows." He shook his head. "I wasn't serious, just pensive. I have a lot on my mind. Some of us have things to worry about. I think I have heard everything. This is a barbershop. You come here and sit on folding chairs while you wait, hoping and praying that the guy taking a razor to your head has had a good day."

"I suppose you want it to be a more *efficient* process?"

"It wouldn't hurt. And it would probably help business. More people would come here instead of trying to have a friend butcher their heads. You know, efficiency and order do have their place."

Barry laughed, rubbing his hands along his thighs. "This is a tradition. This is the way we do it. Not everything has a science to it, you know. That is what is wrong with you—"

"Before you get up on your soapbox and go into my faults and tell me the problem with the way I see the world, could you say hello? I mean, what is that about?" Cody knew that it would not take long for Barry to start preaching at him about something. He rolled his eyes the way his sisters used to.

Two of the other men sitting with them in the small sitting area hushed them. The news was on, and they leaned closer to the small television. Cody sank back into his couch. The front door jingled as another man entered.

"I'm not getting on any soapbox. Just calm yourself. But have you ever noticed that lately nothing is ever good enough for you? You are getting more and more critical as you age." Barry lowered his voice but raised his eyebrows. "I was just trying to offer you some advice." He picked up a newspaper that was lying on the floor and opened it. He shook it, trying to shake out the wrinkles as he turned the pages.

Barry just had no idea. If his life looked like Cody's did,

he would be critical too. Cody counted to ten so that he wouldn't yell, then licked his lips instead. "That is easy for you to say. You are Mr. Hakuna Matata himself. Everything *you* touch turns to gold. That doesn't happen for me." He reached up and moved the paper that Barry had placed between them. His head began to pound, and he rubbed it. Barry could not begin to understand half of his problems from where he was standing.

"That's because you try too hard sometimes. I am no smarter than the next guy, but you, you are always too much in a hurry for things to happen for you. You need to learn to accept that some things are just *fate*. You can't make them happen the way you want."

"Whatever. I didn't think you would understand. I just feel like it has to be my turn soon. Must you turn everything into a sermon?"

Their discourse was interrupted as the man in the barber chair closest to them prepared to stand up. The barber removed the drape that was on him and snapped it, shaking freshly cut hair onto the floor and stopping their conversation. Both Cody and Barry jumped in response. They were silent, anticipating, watching, like the other customers, while the barber swept the floor around his chair. His strokes were slow and deliberate, giving no hint of the number of people who were waiting for their turn in the chair. He had no reason to rush. The man who vacated the seat made his way to the front of the store, stopping at the cash register. The barber signaled to Barry, and conversations began again in the small alcove.

Barry moved to the chair and sat down. The barber pushed on the foot pump two times, lowering the chair so he could reach the top of Barry's head. He draped him with a fresh gray cape and stood back, looking at his hair as one might look at a blank canvas before beginning to paint.

"So, you met any new women yet?" Barry spoke to Cody while looking at him through the mirrors.

Cody narrowed his eyes. What did Barry know? How was he always able to tell what was going on in his mind that way? He shrugged. "Almost."

"Either you have or you haven't. How do you *almost* meet someone?"

"I met her. She just doesn't know that we are destined for a relationship yet." Cody's mouth felt dry, and he licked his lips. There was only so much he wanted to share right now, and he was not in the mood to get Barry started; Barry would find a way to find fault with everything Cody said.

Barry sighed. "I see. You know, it does take two to have a relationship. She has to be attracted to you too."

"She will be."

"And just how do you know this? Has she given you any indication that there is even a remote possibility that—"

"Look, I will let you know when something happens, okay? Why do you always have to ask me so many questions and treat me like I don't know what I am doing? You are not my daddy."

"I never said I was." Barry shook his head. "I'm just trying to make conversation. There is no need for you to be so snappy."

"Well, make conversation about something else. My love life is not your business." Cody felt exposed. The four men sitting in the small area seemed to have stopped talking. *Are they listening? None of this is any of their business either.* Although no one turned around, they did not seem to really be paying attention to the TV anymore. Cody moved away from them, closer to Barry's barber chair. The barber also seemed to not be paying attention to anything in particular, but Cody was sure that behind his humming he was really tuning in on their conversation.

Barry ignored him. "So what is her name? Where did you meet her?"

"Did I not say that was none of your business yet? Because that is next." Cody fidgeted. This joint haircut excursion was turning out to be more stressful than it was worth. Barry was just too good at making him feel as if he was living his life incorrectly.

"Fine. I won't give you my advice then. Just don't come running to me when your heart is broken. Again." Barry snapped his paper for emphasis and crossed his legs under the barber drape.

Cody rolled his eyes, looking up at the ceiling. Barry could just not help himself. "I wasn't aware that I asked for any advice. Last I recalled, you are no expert on women at all. Not with your record. Look how you got together with your woman. You did nothing. She wanted you. She got you. Period. Do you think it was an accident that she claimed to be locked out of her place and needed to stay with you? Yeah, right, how many times does that happen? You never even questioned it, and she just never went home."

Barry flicked the cape, and some of his dark brown hair floated to the floor. "We are not talking about me." His voice was clipped as he spoke through his teeth, now clenched tightly together. He knew that Cody had never approved of how he'd met his wife, and to this day he felt as if his friend was merely tolerating her, almost as if she were a momentary distraction, rather than the woman he had chosen to be his life partner. "Trust me, when you know, you know. Obviously you have not experienced that yet."

"No, I forgot. You and your transgressions are a taboo subject. You never want me to talk about her. What did you know about her? Nothing other than her amazing ability to suck a golf ball through a garden hose. Am I right?"

The barber flinched and sucked in his breath.

"I'm going to ignore that and assume that you are just being an asshole today." They were still for a split second. "Who is on the soapbox now? You sound like a jealous girl-friend. I am not going to have you speak about my wife that way." Barry's nose flared as he struggled to regain his composure. "I know how you are, so I am going to just let that one pass, okay? I am not the one trying to be hurtful or nasty." Barry paused, hoping that Cody would get the picture. Cody was really good at hitting below the belt, and the people in the barbershop certainly did not need to know his business. "All I'm saying is that sometimes Grandma's advice IS right. You got to love the person that loves you instead of going to look for love where it doesn't exist. I'm pretty happy with myself today. How about you? I don't think you can say that."

Cody didn't answer. It wasn't that he was unhappy, he wasn't. He just sometimes felt as if he wasn't as happy as he could be.

"Uhm-huh. That is what I am talking about."

"Again, I say you are misled. Matters of the heart—the whole thing is like a game of chess. A strategy game. I treat it as such, not like a silly game of checkers—"

Barry held up his hand, signaling to Cody that he had had enough of his snide remarks. "I don't know what happened to you to make you so twisted. This is *life* we are talking about."

The barber next to Barry wiped off his now empty chair and signaled. He tapped his chair, and Cody slid into it, briefly making eye contact with the man on the other side and nodding a greeting. The barber draped him and spun him around. He was glad for that; he would no longer have to make conversation with Barry. He didn't like the direction they were going anyway. Instead, he listened to the drone from the television in the back of the room, and began to catch snippets of the various conversations that were going on around the shop.

The barber working on him wore a name tag that said his name was Malcolm, but he did not try to talk with Cody. Cody made sure that his body language sent the message loud and clear that he was in no mood for conversation. Barry sure knew how to kill a good mood.

He sat in the chair so stiffly that everyone, not just the man cutting his hair, could sense that he was tense. Malcolm worked in silence.

The barber in the chair next to him, however, seemed to know his client quite well. They chattered on, and they nodded and laughed together every few minutes. Cody was good at listening, and he could not help but hear what they were saying, particularly after hearing the barber ask his client about someone named Claudia. He held his breath for a minute, straining to hear their conversation.

"She still working at that same place?" the barber asked. He spun the man around again, stopping the moving chair to snip at his hair.

"Yeah, she is."

The man in the chair had a sudden change of mood as his smile disappeared from his face.

"So did you set a date? You two have been going strong

for awhile now. Did you know that I have known her and her family since she was a girl? Yup, they used to live right across from us. You can't do no better than her. She was always the belle of the neighborhood. A princess. And always with that Pam girl, too. Those two have been thick as thieves since they were little. She—"

"We broke up."

The barber spun him around. "What? You ain't dating someone else, are you? You are crazy if you are. That girl is fine. A gem. The best family. All that hair. And well formed in all the right places. . . ." He waved his clippers in the air.

"Nothing like that." His deep voice was curt. "I want to get married, she doesn't. *She* is the one who is not ready."

Malcolm turned his chair around, and Cody could now get a good view of the man in the next chair. From the way his knees stuck out, Cody could tell that he was very tall, and of medium build. Cody remembered that he was very well dressed under that drape, in a brown, well-cut business suit. He had a small, neatly trimmed goatee and very long eyelashes. His otherwise clean-cut face appeared ashen, and he was obviously not happy about the situation with his Claudia person. What were the chances they were talking about the same Claudia? His Claudia? Cody smirked. Given the size of Austin, the chances were probably very good. It had to be the same woman. She *did* have lots of hair. And she was from Austin, not many people were, he was finding out. And her friend. Cody wasn't sure what her name was yet, but it had to be her. Although the man was obviously not happy about his breakup, this was nothing but good news for Cody.

He looked up, out through the pane glass storefront. The day looked brighter to him than it did before. He smiled openly now. His job just got easier. He knew that Claudia wore an engagement ring, a nice one at that. But that looked like it would no longer be a problem for him. Claudia had kicked Mr. Wrong to the curb, and a good thing too. Cody could step up his plan. One man's loss could be his gain. And why not? There was one less pawn for him to worry about. It was about time things started to go his way.

Chapter 12

The garage door opener was broken again. Claudia swore under her breath as she climbed the long, concrete stairway that led to the front door she almost never used. She counted the cracks as she climbed and remembered thinking that when she'd first purchased her house, the long steps had added what her real estate agent had called "curb appeal" to the town house. Now they were just adding unwanted sweat to her forehead. She breathed heavily at the top of the steps, wiping the sweat away with the back of her hand.

She was obviously going to have to buy a new garage door opener whether she wanted to or not—this was the third time in as many months that she'd had to enter her own home as a guest, rather than come through the garage like almost everyone else on the street. Another thing for her growing "to-do" list, and she had no idea even where to begin looking. Where, exactly, did you find someone to change lightbulbs that you did not want to change and to fix garage door openers? She frowned. There was no more Jackson to take care of these little problems or even call a proper repair company for her. He might not be the handyman type, but he sure knew his way around a phone book and a phone. She used to be able to count on him to at least get these types of things taken care of. Now she was going to have to get used to doing them for herself.

The front door opened easily, swinging inward. Claudia was startled; she had not even had to use her key. Normally, the door was left bolted, but the tumbler indicated otherwise. It opened with only one rotation of the knob. She stopped at the door and searched her memory; she was generally pretty careful about things like locking doors and turning off the stove. No one was perfect; she had probably forgotten to lock it last time she opened it, but she still peered into the front hallway cautiously. After all, a girl never could be too careful, especially a girl who lived alone. Really alone. Isn't that what her mother always told her? Jackson was around quite a bit, but news traveled fast. Who knew how many people knew about their breakup by now?

The sound of the small television she kept on her kitchen counter drifted to her ears. She knew she had not left that on, she never did. Someone was in her house. Her stomach tightened; Claudia was suddenly afraid, and for a moment considered reclosing the door and going next door to call the police. Her lips went dry, and she licked them. Why had she chosen this time to break up with her boyfriend? Under normal conditions, she could have gone back to her car and called, and he would have come faster than she could say "Penelope Pittstop." Rescuing a damsel in distress had been Jackson's forte. She almost smiled as she thought about the satisfaction he seemed to get from helping her, or any other female that needed help. Although she hated to admit it, her feelings were hurt about the breakup, so there was no way in hell she would call him now.

The door swung fully open, and she very nearly tumbled

into the hallway—she had been leaning against the door with it slightly cracked open, trying to figure out what to do.

"I was wondering when you would be here. I hoped you wouldn't be working too late."

Claudia caught herself on the entryway table and stood up, pursing her lips. Her feelings of relief were quickly replaced by annoyance. Henrietta had made good on her promise. Here she was, in Claudia's house, and Claudia had no doubt that she had made herself at home already. As usual, her mother looked fabulous. Her clothes were impeccably chosen and hopelessly stylish. Claudia scowled as she looked at her, and she could not remember a day that she had seen her mother without full makeup, eye shadow matching her clothes and all. Today, as her mother would say, it was a lovely shade of mauve. The rest of the family joked that she woke up that way every day, perfect and ready to go. No one who knew Claudia well would ever believe that Henrietta was her mother.

Claudia shifted uncomfortably. "Mom, what are you doing here? I thought I told you not to come." Claudia looked down, trying not to let her mother see the emotions that danced across her face. She dropped her bag and headed toward the kitchen, talking over her shoulder. "You scared the hell out of me. You should have at least called me and told me you were in my house."

"Since when do you use that kind of language with me, and since when do I listen to you? I thought I was the mother. Stop fussing and come see what I have been cooking."

Henrietta Barrett pooh-poohed her daughter's concerns as if they did not matter. Claudia felt her anxiety level rise. She hated when her mother treated her as if she were still a child. Unfortunately, she was very good at condescension, and she practiced it often. It was almost as if she was frozen as a ten-year-old in her mother's head. Claudia figured she would stay that way until she produced a grandchild. Getting Claudia to procreate seemed to have become Henrietta's number one priority long since she passed her twenty-third birthday. It was what her mother lived for now, and she never missed an opportunity to talk about this friend or that one's grandchildren.

"I'm sorry, Ma. I'm just a little tense today."

"Uh-huh. You're not too big for a spanking, you know."

They moved down the small hallway toward the kitchen, as her mother commanded. Every time her mother came to visit, she would cook, even if she was only staying for a few hours. It was almost as if she believed that Claudia did not eat without her around. And it was always something extra fattening. Not that she had to worry; Henrietta was as thin as the day she was married, her svelte figure showing no signs of childbearing or aging whatsoever—another thing that annoyed Claudia.

Cooking like she did, it was a wonder that her mother could stay so thin. Every cook tasted what they made, they had to, but her mother had always been a perfect size six. The family curse of being extra curvy seemed to have slipped right by her and landed on Claudia. Her mother looked as good as she ever had, stylishly clad in a beige pantsuit. She had even brought her own matching apron with her.

This time was no different. The kitchen smelled wonderful, and Claudia's mouth began to water in response, even before her mother opened the large pot now sitting on top of the stove, simmering away.

"Ma, you know I am on a diet. I can't eat—"

"Nonsense. How can you say that when you don't even know what it is? Why are you on a diet anyway? You are fine just the way you are. Men don't like scrawny women. You gotta have some booty."

Claudia raised her eyebrows. Her mother was thin, almost scrawny herself by some standards, and all heads still turned when she walked into a room at nearly sixty years old. How did she explain that? "I want to stay that way, too. And I have never been scrawny. I'll take scrawny over plump any day."

"Don't be silly. You know you are perfect."

Then why did she always find something to pick at?

Claudia kicked off her shoes and sat at her table, rubbing her feet. She could smell the cheese and herb biscuits that were her mother's specialty. "How long are you staying, Ma?" Each day could equate to a pound added. Claudia ticked them away in her head, wondering if her mother purposely tried to sabotage the plans for the diet she always seemed to be on.

"Not too long. Like I told you on the phone, your dad went out of town with a few of his buddies. After all these years he decided that he plays golf, of all things." She waved her hand in the air, replacing the top on the stockpot simmering on the stove.

Claudia bit her lip and tried not to look too disappointed. "Not too long" was relative and could mean anything from a day or so to a few weeks. "Well, I told you it might not be the best of times for you to come. I can't entertain you or anything. I am going to be very busy. Even tonight, I am only going to be home for a few minutes. I am supposed to meet Pam—"

"You *should* be meeting Jackson." She paused. "How is that fine man of yours doing? Did you set a date? I am so ready to start planning the wedding of my only daughter. You know I am not getting any younger." She paused again, stirring her pot as only she could do, making it look glamorous, as usual. "Your dad isn't either. We want to live to see grandchildren."

Claudia felt her stomach tighten at the mention of Jackson's name. It never took long for her mother to get to talking about Jackson, always trying to be in her business. She bit her lip. Her mother would be heartbroken if she knew they had broken up. She liked Jackson so much that you would think she had handpicked him for Claudia herself. She even already called him "Son" sometimes.

"Claudia, are you listening to me?" Her mother stood, facing her with her hands on her hips.

"Huh?" Now was the time her mother would begin to talk about Jackson's so-called people-gree, which is what her mother called his family background and education, as if he were a purebred dog instead of a man.

"I said, you told me you were going to set a date. What did you two decide on? A man like Jackson won't keep waiting forever, you know. He is quite a catch. There aren't many like him anymore. People don't seem to care about the same things like they used to. His family—"

"—is well respected and he graduated from Harvard. I know." Claudia rolled her eyes. What about her? Wasn't she a good catch too? People were just people, but Claudia had had that argument many a time with her mother and was in no mood for it now. The best thing to do would be to just nod and go along with the program.

"Don't be fresh, girl. Not to mention that he is good looking enough that you wouldn't have to worry about having ugly babies."

"Mother, that is not necessarily true. Cousin Samantha and her husband are both very good looking people. Look at their kids. You said yourself that they look like zoo animals." Claudia could not keep a grin from spreading across her face. She loved to show her mother the flaws in her logic, especially when it came to her all-too-perfect cousins, the bane of her mother's existence.

"Stop it. They just have to dress those kids up and they will be just fine. Keep in mind that your cousin's husband makes very good money. It won't matter much what those kids look like. You rest assured they will get everything they need anyway. Money makes you better looking. Look at how Oprah gets better with age." She waved her wooden spoon in the air for emphasis.

Claudia looked at the steam rising off the spoon and tried to suppress the feelings of hunger that were beginning to nag at her. Whatever was in that pot was definitely not on The Zone Diet, so none of it was going to cross her lips. She knew her mother would refer to Oprah sooner or later. According to Henrietta, that woman was next to God himself and seemed to have an answer to or an opinion about everything and anything.

"I hope you are not planning a summer wedding. You know how hot it can be here in the summertime. The fall is by far the best and prettiest time to get married, if you ask me."

Claudia held back the urge to tell her mother that she had not asked her. She closed her eyes. *One, two, three.* She counted to herself and then breathed in, then out. It would do no good to make her mother too angry. That could lead to nothing but a lecture. She licked her lips and measured her words. She knew that if she set Henrietta off now, she would never get out of the house. "Mom, we can talk about all this later, okay? I really have to go meet Pam. I promised her." Claudia stood up. Her mother certainly did not need to know the details behind their getting together. "You are going to have to eat your dinner by yourself. Or go and visit some of your friends, okay?" Claudia started back toward her bedroom. She felt a twinge of guilt but pushed it away. That food would do better on her mother's thighs than hers anyway.

Her mother yelled after her. "You take care of your business, but I do hope you are going to talk about wedding stuff. You can fill me in on all the details later."

Claudia did not answer. Instead she waved over her shoulder in the general direction of the kitchen, where she had left her mother standing. The day had been long and emotionally draining, and she did not feel like discussing her future with her mother. She could not, for the life of her, figure out why her mother was forever trying to be in her business. It was above and beyond normal motherdom, or so it seemed. Her mother's insistence on her getting married and meddling in her life had gotten worse since her parents had moved away, not better, as she'd imagined it would. She shook her head. The day just seemed to get worse as it went on.

PF Chang's was crowded. Several people stood outside on the curb, talking on cell phones as they waited. The valet parking attendants had sweat running down their backs and through their shirts as they ran back and forth, trying to keep up with the demand. No one, including Claudia, wanted to bother with parking themselves. Downtown was a mess with all the construction in the area, so the possibil-

ity of finding a meter within a reasonable walking distance
was slim. Claudia dropped her keys into the hand of the
valet parking attendant without a second thought.

Claudia knew that she would get to the restaurant before
Pam. It was just written that way somewhere. Claudia first,
then Pam, that is just how it was, for everything, except, of
course, getting married. Pam had had to go and do that
first, and after five years, Claudia still found herself playing
catch-up. She sighed as she thought of her mother and the
way she threw that little tidbit up in her face every chance
she got. Normally, Henrietta would not be overly fond of
Pam, but on the subject of marriage she could do no wrong.
According to Claudia's mother, Pam was just a little crazy,
so she was extra lucky to have corralled such a *good* man.
Although it had been a big issue when they'd first gotten
married, it was no longer an issue that he was, as her
mother would say, a bit on the beige side. Her husband
might not be rich or black, but he was hardworking and a
good provider. And he made pretty kids. That counted for
a lot in Henrietta's world.

Claudia put her name on the list, hoping that Pam would
make it before the fifteen-minute wait was up. She knew
there was no telling if this was a day when her friend would
be only a little late or a lot. She had been known to be as
much as a whole hour late, but the way Claudia was feel-
ing, she was not willing to wait that long. She glanced at her
watch, setting her limit at twenty minutes max. She was
quickly lost in mulling over the day's events; her breakup,
her hectic workday, and the unexpected visit from her
mother. She barely noticed the other people in the waiting
area and was only vaguely aware of the ruckus they were
making.

Pam finally erupted onto the scene, scurrying over to Claudia with a fake apologetic look on her face. Every eye in the small waiting area turned to look at Pam. She looked fabulous—glowing even. She was expertly dressed in a light-colored knit pantsuit that hugged her every curve. Claudia checked her out; knowing her friend, that pantsuit was probably St. John. Her shoes and coordinated bag were just what her outfit needed to set it off. Even her jewelry, understated but expensive, was just right for an early dinner with a girlfriend. Her clothes made you want to look but did not necessarily announce that she was available. Henrietta would approve, Claudia knew, and she immediately felt just a little dowdy for the second time since she left work. She was wearing a pair of khakis from last year with a worn summer sweater. She carried her regular old Nine West purse, the one she carried almost every day with every outfit. She slid the worn black bag, now gray in some places, behind her hip and stood up just as Pam made eye contact with her. At least her shoes were fabulous. As usual, Pam was bubbling over with smiles.

"I am so sorry that I am late. I just got so caught up." Pam opened her bag and dropped her sunglasses, just as fashionable as the rest of her, inside it. She snapped it shut with her expertly manicured fingernails.

"I am afraid to ask with what," Claudia murmured as she raised her eyebrows. She could only guess what Pam had been doing. She was always "caught up" with something, but any woman with a smile on her face like the one Pam was wearing had to have just finished having sex.

Pam opened her mouth to speak but was interrupted by the maitre d' motioning for them to follow. The table was ready. They were led to a table near the back of the restaurant, near a window. They both slid into their seats without a sound, although Claudia imagined that Pam did it just a little bit more gracefully than she did. She had never noticed just how graceful her friend really was. They had been friends for years, and it was almost an unspoken rule that they not talk in the presence of a waitress, just in case she might be listening in on some of the knowledge they were sure to impart to each other, as if they were that knowledgeable of the important.

They unfolded their napkins, placing them on their laps. Pam looked around, scanning the room. PF Chang's was one of the new hot spots in town. It was very trendy, with wood floors; colossal statues of lionlike creatures sat on either end of the black granite bar that ran the length of the restaurant. Large canisters of fresh flowers were placed throughout the room. The place was always full, overly so at lunchtime, and known as the place to be if you wanted to see "anyone who was anyone" or get a glimpse of a local celebrity, what few there were in town.

"I like this place so much." Pam scanned the room like a tourist seeing an urban skyscraper for the first time. It was one of Pam's favorite places.

"Tell me why I am friends with you again?" Claudia asked half-jokingly. "You look great for no reason, and then come in late with a look on your face that screams you had sex at noon. What is the deal?"

Pam smiled. "What are you talking about? You could look like this too. Isn't that why we are meeting? To come up with a plan of attack?" She licked her lips and smiled coyly. "And if you did, Jackson would be giving it to ya right regular."

"Right regular? There you go, talking that trailer park

slang again. What the hell does that mean?" Claudia's feelings smarted underneath her calm veneer. She was not quite ready to begin talking about Jackson just yet.

"Now you know that my family has not inhabited a trailer park for at least a generation." Pam smiled. She was used to Claudia and her biting sarcasm. "What is wrong with you? You only treat me like this when something is wrong. Maybe it's that handbag." She motioned. "A bad handbag day will do it to me every time. I say we start with that."

"My handbag is just fine, missy. Leave it alone."

"I'm sorry. Carrying a suitcase is your prerogative. Why are you so snippy? Did you have a bad day at work, or are you just jealous that I got some and you didn't? Would you like to tell me what happened so you can feel better about it?"

Claudia sighed, fighting back the tears that wanted to come to her eyes. Pam was as good a person as any to tell about how rotten her day had become. In fact, she was the only person she could tell. She was not only her closest friend but also the only one of her group that would put up with her being scarce all of the time due to the unrelenting work schedule she set for herself. "Well," she sniffled and used her napkin to dab at her nose, "it seems I am not going to need that makeover after all."

They paused as the waiter came, placing two iced teas on the table.

"Jackson broke up with me."

Claudia blurted the words out all at once, as if she were in a hurry. She figured that perhaps if she said it out loud, she would feel better, and the weight that seemed to be resting on her head would lift.

Taking a sip of her tea, Pam almost choked. She sputtered, attempting to clear her throat. "What do you mean? You are getting married. I can't believe it. We were going to be two married people, together, like in the movies. Old friends with husbands that are friends. Our kids are supposed to be friends. We are supposed to borrow sugar from each other."

Claudia blinked with surprise at Pam's extreme reaction. You would have thought she was the one breaking up, not Claudia. "Believe it. Jackson said that I am obviously not ready to get married, so he doesn't want to wait for me any more. How do you like that?" She set all the way back in her chair and sipped her tea. She set the heavy glass down on the table a little too hard, and the tea splashed onto the white tablecloth.

The look on Pam's face changed from one of astonishment to one of anger, the normal paleness of her skin changing from yellow-pink to deep red. "That bastard! How dare he? I don't know what he thinks this is when he can just pass up a woman like you. You have been around for years. He can't just throw you away like that. He is going to be hard-pressed to replace you." Her head shot up. "Do you think he is seeing someone else?"

Claudia had not thought of that before. What if she had already been replaced? Was he cheating on her and she had no idea? She had been so self-absorbed lately that the thought of unfaithfulness on his part had not even crossed her mind. Her stomach churned and sank, and she rubbed it gently. The thought of being one of those women who had no idea what was going on in her boyfriend's life was more than she could take. Her eyes stung briefly, as if she might cry. She struggled to maintain her composure.

"I don't think so. That would not be his style." She shook

her head. She was not about to admit it if it was. "But you can calm down. I was going to break up with him anyway." She watched Pam's face. She knew her friend did not believe her. "But that is not the half of it. Guess who is in town for a little surprise visit? My mother. And of course she wants to know the wedding date."

"She could have called you on the phone for that."

"I know, but you know how she is. And I just couldn't tell her there isn't going to be a wedding." Claudia stared down at the table, nervously playing with her silverware. Her mouth suddenly felt dry. "Did we order? I don't remember ordering. Where is the waiter?"

Pam looked at her friend, mouth agape. She could not remember the last time she'd seen Claudia, the original Miss In Control, looking so helpless. She immediately felt sorry for her and reached over and rubbed the back of her hand, smiling. "Well, we can handle this. She doesn't have to know anything. Not yet. I guess you really are going to need that makeover, then. You *will* be like a new woman when I am done."

"What are you talking about? Didn't you hear what I just said? There is no longer a need for a makeover, I don't have anyone to impress, seduce, or undress for anymore."

"Yes, I heard you loud and clear, dearie. What I heard you say was you need a new man now, and you want your mother to think it's business as usual until you are ready to tell her, right? So why can't we get you all together and then just replace Jackson with a bigger and better model? You don't need a makeover, you need a Ms. Pamela Special." She grinned and winked, her false eyelashes fluttering. "You have to think of this as a beginning as opposed to an ending." Pam lifted her menu and hummed while she scanned it.

Claudia narrowed her eyes, her brain whirring. Pam always could turn a negative into a positive. If she were to tell her mother she had a new man, it would soften the blow of there not being an imminent wedding. Besides what better way to make Jackson eat his words?

"You might have a point. I didn't need him anyway. That bastard is going to rue the day he left me. I want to look good, good, good." She slapped the table with each good. "I hope you know that is different from *cheap*, right?"

"Do I ever look cheap? Raunchy, yes, but cheap?"

"No comment."

Pam cut her eyes at Claudia, a smirk playing at the corners of her mouth.

"But where am I going to meet a new someone fast? I know lots of single women who are having the hardest time just finding a date."

"Well, I am not saying we are going to be planning a wedding again real soon, but I know a few places you can go to meet people. If nothing else, we can have some fun and perhaps the word will get back to Jackson, accidentally-on-purpose. This town isn't that big. He will come running back so fast—"

Claudia held up her hand. "Wait. I never said I wanted him back. I just want him replaced, or at least I want him to have second thoughts about what he did. I think."

"Uh-huh. Whatever you say. I am just going to make you look good in the process. That way you will have the option of turning him down when he comes running back, and you won't have to be so humiliated in your mother's eyes. Okay?"

Claudia paused again. What did she have to lose? Pam was happily married most of the time, but she sure got her share of passes. She always had. It was like she was a magnet, the way she attracted people. Right now, all Claudia had was work, and that was starting to feel more lonely every day. She had always thought that she did not really need a man. And that was still true, but she was not ready to be a modern-day spinster. She pictured herself alone at night, surrounded by her *People* magazines, and her stomach quivered. She craved some excitement.

"Okay, you win. What did you have in mind? I have no idea where to begin."

Pam nodded. She had been waiting and trying for years to get Claudia to spice up her look. "You just stick with me. We have work to do." Pam raised her glass in toast fashion and Claudia followed suit, their glasses touching.

"To the new you, girlfriend."

Chapter 13

Marina slid her yellow gloves over her manicured hands and donned the wide-brimmed hat she reserved for gardening. She breathed a sigh of relief as she took in the summer fragrances wafting from her small haven. Her backyard gave the illusion that she lived in a peaceful neighborhood, instead of an area filled with semi-nice houses on too-small lots. Her parents had lived in this neighborhood back when it was built in the 1940s. It had been peaceful then, before the city had engulfed it. Marina remembered her father's stories of living here as a small child, when Queens was considered far outside the city. She smiled as she reminisced over his describing how he would dig for worms in the backyard with his father to go fishing out in the Rockaways. He'd given that up when his business had taken off the way it had. Nowadays, you would be a fool to eat fish that came from those waters anyway, she thought.

The small plot of land behind the house was neatly rimmed on three sides by tall, clipped hedges. They helped block out the hints of the neighbors that were not too far away. When she was a child there had been no chain-link fences between the houses. Back then, Marina and the neighborhood children would run freely through all of the backyards. It would make her mother so upset; they'd had virtually no respect for any of her plants or bushes. Nowadays, Marina could sit or work quietly in the yard and listen to the conversations of the people on either side of her. Today, no one was around, and she was glad; there would be no stray conversation to grab her attention and keep her from her thoughts.

The rosebushes Marina tended were her pride and joy. Her mother had been a rosarian, and she had passed that love on to Marina. Sometimes she would spend hours pruning and feeding her bushes for no other reason than the simple enjoyment of the reward of their blooms. Marina knew that her husband could not stand to sweat, nor could he tolerate the bugs, so her garden was one place where she was assured of her solitude. Her brow furrowed as she approached the first bush. She thought of Dominic and his cryptic message. What had Wesley been up to? That had hardly sounded like business. More like some kind of mischief on the side, she thought. Who had been snooping around, and what had they been looking for?

Hopefully, Wesley was a smart man and was not involved in anything illegal. That was something she knew her father would not tolerate. He would never allow anyone to muddy the name of the business that he'd worked so hard to build over the years. Chivers Technologies was small but well known in the information technology field. The company and her father were both well respected. It would not matter that Wesley was married to his only daughter. If he was doing anything crooked, he would be finished.

Marina shrugged and thought about how secretive Wes-

ley had become. When they first got together, she had been
the one with the secrets. Marina had not been in love with
Wesley and had only started dating him because it had
been what her father had wanted, and she hadn't broken up
with Cody immediately. She'd tried, but it had been hard.
He never did take no for an answer and had kept coming
around. That last time they were together sexually had been
the first time in months, and it had only happened in a mo-
ment of weakness on her part.

Wesley had tried to be so open about everything, or so
he'd said. But then, naturally, that had all stopped with the
pregnancy. A thorn pricked Marina's hand through her gar-
dening glove and she winced, but did not stop working.
She thought about how he'd assured her that he would
stand by her. He'd believed that she would grow to love
him and would tire of Cody eventually.

Wesley and her father had persuaded Marina that the
best thing for her to do was to stay married, and they'd told
Cody together. Wesley had even stood by her while she'd
cried. It turned out that when Cody found out about the
pregnancy, he didn't want anything to do with her or the
children. Wesley had taken care of everything for her. Tears
came to her eyes as she thought about the long hours that
Wesley had spent in his office after that. He'd withdrawn
from her. It had been torture, but she'd deserved it. Al-
though he'd said in counseling that he could forgive her,
he'd had silently exacted his own private punishment. He
even locked the office door for awhile.

Her thoughts came at her like lightning bolts. Why
hadn't she thought of this before? The answer to all of Wes-
ley's secretiveness and dealings she knew nothing about
were in his study. Even though she knew he had long since

stopped locking the door, she'd never started to go in there again, even when Wesley sometimes stayed inside the small room overnight. She had been so busy feeling as if she wore a scarlet letter on her chest that she had overlooked the obvious.

Marina quickly made her way to the back porch, removing her apron and gloves as she went. She dusted off her hands and rubbed the dirt from the knees of her pants. Once inside the house, she stood silently for a minute, willing her ears to pick up any sound. She glanced at the clock. Wesley would not usually be home this time of day, but she had to make sure. Snooping around in his office would surely piss him off. His schedule had become unpredictable as of late. The only sound that her ears could pick up was her grandfather's cuckoo clock ticking loudly in the living room.

Her footsteps held a new determination as she headed for the small study. She took one last glance around as she turned the doorknob and stepped inside the small, dimly lit room. It was located at the front of the house, so the shades were drawn in an attempt to keep out the midday sun. The room was stuffy, and as Marina waited for her eyes to adjust, she felt the trickle of sweat begin to roll down her sides, under her arms.

Her eyes quickly located the filing cabinet, set back into a recessed corner of the room. The small, two-drawer cabinet was gray, and she remembered that Wesley insisted that it be fire safe. The delivery men had cursed out loud, without apology, as they'd struggled with its weight, up the front steps and into the house.

Marina licked her lips as she tugged on the top drawer, hoping that it would not be locked. The drawer did not open, and she fumed as one of her acrylic nails broke in two.

She sat down in Wesley's executive chair and spun around, sucking on her finger. She would have to hurry; the longer she stayed in the room, the greater her chances of being caught there. Wesley was very organized, so she tried to look through his drawers for the key without moving too many things. If just one sheet was out of place, he would notice immediately. Finally, she found what she was looking for in the last drawer she looked into. She grabbed the key and paused to rub her stomach in an attempt to quiet it.

Marina turned the key in the lock on the small cabinetry, and the drawers released immediately. She smiled as she opened the top drawer. It couldn't have been any easier. Just as she expected, Wesley had each file expertly labeled. She thumbed through the tops of the manila folder system. He was generally pretty predictable; he was still using the same system she'd helped him set up two years before. Most of the file folders were in exactly the same order she remembered. At first, nothing seemed out of place, then suddenly, at the back of the second drawer, one unlabeled file caught her eye. She knew that this file was the one she was looking for.

Sweat was beginning to make her T-shirt wet. Her makeup was starting to run from the heat, so she grabbed a tissue from the box that Wesley kept on his desk and wiped off what was left of her makeup.

The papers in the file were stiff, as if they had once been wet. She touched them gingerly. What she saw did not make sense to her at first. Maybe she was overreacting, she thought. There did not appear to be anything in the folder but a series of receipts for bank transfers. Her mind whirred. These transfers appeared to be coming from an account number that she did not recognize, one that did not

have her name on it. The receiving account was not famil-
iar at all.

When they first got married, Wesley had insisted on joint
everything, even to the point of becoming irate when she'd
suggested they have separate accounts. Now here he was,
with a bank account she knew nothing about, making large
transfers to some bank in Austin, Texas, that she also knew
nothing about. She did not recognize the name of the recip-
ient either. The transfers just named a bank.

A car passed close to the house, and Marina jumped. She
snapped her head up and quickly closed the folder, putting
it back into its place in the back of the drawer. In one swift
move, she closed and locked the file cabinet. She straight-
ened a few items on the desk and, not thinking, threw her
tissues into the wastebasket at the side. As she exited the
room, she glanced around to make sure that it did not look
disturbed. She would need more information before she
could confront Wesley. A couple of bank transfers told her
nothing. But at least she would have a place to start. Maybe
the answer to some of Wesley's secret dealings could be
found down in Austin. She could feel it; this was somehow
connected to Cody. It was time she made a few secret phone
calls of her own.

Chapter 14

Hoover's stood at the corner of Manor Road like a sentinel, guarding the entryway to the east side of Austin. It was almost dark, and the parking lot was still full. There was no visible line from the outside, but Cody knew that the place was busy. It always was. It was a favorite of the locals and the few white folk who ventured there to eat during the workday. East Austin was becoming a trendy place, and restaurants and businesses catering to the politicians and downtowners were popping up all over that side of town.

The modest-looking building encased one of Barry and Cody's favorite places to get old-fashioned comfort food that reminded them of home—the kind of food their grandmothers would serve up. Cody had suggested they go there after getting their haircuts; a plate full of buffalo wings and macaroni and cheese was just what he needed to help him think things through.

The inside of the restaurant was not that large, and Cody was able to spot Barry easily before the hostess could offer to seat them. He was already sitting at what had become their favorite table, at the far side of the restaurant, away from the windows, right at the end of the short, brown bar. Cody strode over and joined his friend. Barry's head was down as he perused the menu. Cody slapped him on the back as he passed, quickly sitting down in the sturdy, no-frills wooden chair. He rubbed his hands together as if to warm them up; he was ready to eat.

"*You* are in a good mood." Barry jumped but did not look up.

Cody grinned. He sure was. Barry had no idea how good. "The menu hasn't changed since last week. I don't know why you bother to look. You should have ordered for us already."

Barry waved Cody's comments away, although what he said was true; he always ordered the same thing, and in fact had only ever had one thing on the menu—the buffalo wings that the place was known for. They had become his favorite since moving to Austin. His thick lips curved into a smile as he brushed his newly trimmed, jaw-length locks away from his face. He signaled to the waiter over Cody's shoulder so that he would bring out their usual.

"You got a problem sitting still? Or do you have to go to the bathroom? What is eating you, man? I have never seen anyone so happy about a simple haircut."

Cody momentarily stopped the fidgeting he had been doing since he joined Barry at the table. "I can't help it. I think I am in love."

"In love? Since leaving Green's? How did that happen? You could not have possibly met anyone that quickly. A few minutes ago you didn't want to talk about it."

"True dat, I didn't. I just haven't really told you about her." Ever since the whole incident with Marina, Cody knew that Barry was overly cautious with him when it came to women. As if he could control what his heart did or something.

"So, is this the same woman that has you into running at ungodly hours all of a sudden? Would I be wrong to suspect that?"

The waiter slid two large glasses of iced tea in front of them. Cody took a sip of his and grimaced before answering. He shook his head. "One and the same. You were right. But this woman is so fine, I have no problem running after her."

Barry pursed his lips but did not speak. He could feel danger coming. He leaned across the table, and Cody leaned in in response, drawing closer. Barry's voice was hushed. "Don't get upset if I ask you this. But is she married, engaged, or otherwise attached?"

"For your information, she is very single." A smile spread across Cody's face. "At least now she is. I think she was engaged, but that is all over now." He nodded his head. "Yup, she is as available as they come."

Barry leaned back in his chair and exhaled heavily. "That is a relief. I'm happy for you, man. It's about time you moved on. In my opinion, you need a woman in your life. Someone to make you do right. You aren't getting any younger. You need to settle down."

"Oh, like you settled down and started getting gray hair, right? Don't act like I don't know you dye your hair. That woman is driving you crazy. I wasn't the one who was the playa among us. I have had one real girlfriend my entire dating life."

Barry was not exactly the poster child for marriage. He'd married someone he didn't know well, gained forty pounds, and gotten gray hair, which he colored frequently.

"Yes, unfortunately, she was going to marry someone else."

Barry cleared his throat as he added sugar to his tea. If he knew Cody, there was probably so much more to the Marina story than his friend Cody had ever let on.

"Anyway. That was all the past. I need you to help me. I want to do this right. This one is different."

Barry's mouth dropped open. Was he hearing right? "Let me get this straight. You want me to help you get a woman's attention? I can't believe it. You wouldn't even talk to me before."

"You were always the ladies' man between the two of us, right? And she is special. This one is a professional woman. I need to be smooth."

Barry rubbed his chin. "Hmm. I see." His friend must really be sprung to ask his advice. Cody was not the ask-for-help type. "You say she is a professional? A professional what? That could mean—"

"I'm serious. Could you put your jokes to rest for once? Yes, she is a few years older than me. A beautiful, beautiful, lady. And she is an executive at my job."

"Okay, hold on. Didn't you ever hear the saying that you don't shit where you eat? Romance at work just is not cool. You don't work for her or anything, do you?" Visions of Cody going overboard danced in Barry's head. Cody could be a little obsessive when it came to things he wanted.

"No, nothing like that. I am not trying to romance her at work. We work in totally different departments. I'm just trying to figure out the best way to approach her."

They stopped talking momentarily as the waiter arrived with a steaming plate of buffalo wings. Cody's mouth began to water as the smell of hot sauce hit his nose. They both placed their napkins on their laps at almost the same time.

"Well, I would say to make her an expert." He waved a wing in the air as he talked, licking his fingers between bites. "Everyone likes to feel as if they are an expert on something."

Cody raised his eyebrows.

"It's just like getting a job interview with an acquaintance. Ask her for help with a work project or something. Even if you don't really need it. That is the easiest way to get close to her, get the door open."

"And then it will be up to me to make the transition—"

"—from business to taking care of business."

Cody nodded his head. What Barry was saying made sense to him. That approach was sure a lot easier than what he had been doing; although the surveillance he had been conducting was useful, he knew he was bordering on stalking the woman. Some people might take that the wrong way. All he had to do was get Claudia to meet with him one time, and then he could segue to a more intimate setting. Once Claudia got close to him, there would be no way she could overlook his charm.

"So, you say you think she just broke it off with her fiancé? Who did the breaking up? Do you know?"

"That isn't quite clear to me yet. Why?"

"Well, simple. If he broke up with her, chances are she is feeling a little miffed. There might be an opening there for you. She may need some reassurance. It might be a little easier for you to get in the door. But there are those who say being part of a rebound romance isn't such a good deal."

Cody paused for a minute as he thought about it. He certainly did not want to miss his window of opportunity. He had to move fast. He shook his head. "I don't care about that. In is in."

And *in* was where he planned to be.

Chapter 15

Claudia smiled as she pulled her car into the parking lot at Austin's small Saks Fifth Avenue. Pam always had a way of making her feel better about everything and anything. She had just been dumped, but after talking to Pam she was looking at the bright side of being a manless old maid. That was better than the alternative. If she had not met Pam for dinner, she would probably be at home, with her mother, wallowing in self-pity as she listened to a barrage of "I told you sos," packing the pounds onto her thighs, and shoving food into her mouth.

Pam clicked her longer-than-professional nails on Claudia's driver-side window. Claudia jumped at the unexpected sight of her friend's brightly colored talons, and she glanced at her watch. Saks would only be open another hour or so, and she knew that made Pam impatient. Shopping was an urgent matter with her. Pam was already dancing anxiously, as if she'd been waiting for Claudia to arrive for hours instead of having just followed her there.

Claudia closed her visor mirror and blotted the nude lipstick she had just applied. She opened her door to follow Pam, who was already making a beeline for the store's brightly lit entryway. She panted as she ran to catch up.

Any other day, Pam would whine if you said run. She was moving faster than Claudia had ever seen her go.

"Maybe I should shout 'Shop' at the beginning of our next run?"

"I'm trying to help you, Miss Smarty-pants."

"Do you have a game plan here, or do you plan on just having me shop willy-nilly?" Claudia asked, frowning. Pam was already carried away and she had not even asked Claudia what she wanted to spend. The concepts of budget and restraint could be alien to Pam, and in her mind she probably was enjoying being able to shop with someone else's money.

"Yes, I have a plan, a very simple one actually, but re-member you said you would let me mold you." Pam chuck-led as she made modeling motions in the air.

"I was just checking. I know how you are about shop-ping, especially when it comes to my pockets. And I don't remember exactly using the *mold* word. You just remember that I am not you, nor do I want to look like a mini-you." A picture of Pam's hair on her head flashed in Claudia's mind, and she cringed. Claudia preferred a more toned-down approach. She wasn't sure that Pam did not know that sexy and loud were not necessarily synonymous, but bland old her obviously wasn't working.

The inside of Saks was clean and bright, and various smells engulfed Claudia and Pam as they passed the makeup counters cluttered near the front of the store. Clau-dia blinked in the artificial light, and they paused just in-side the door.

"Well, we are going to start in the back and come toward the front, okay? That always works for me. I have to have a system when I come shopping. I called ahead on the way over here, and my friend in the salon had just enough time to take care of your hair."

"You didn't say anything about my hair." A sinking feeling hit Claudia's stomach. "You know how I am about that. I like my style." She smoothed her slightly fuzzy chignon.

Pam reached out and put her hand on Claudia's shoulder. "Look, I am only saying this because you are my friend and I love you. You *have* no style. You wear your hair in a perpetual ponytail or bun, and that does not count. Tell me what the point is of having all that hair if you don't do anything with it."

"But I don't want—"

"Don't worry, we are not going to relax it or anything." She made a face. Pam did not want to hear one of Claudia's long tirades about the evils of chemical processing. "We are just going to arrange it a bit and comb it. He is going to show you how to spruce it up. You have been wearing it the same way since high school. Besides, your hair is part of the package. It should be your crowning glory, not an afterthought."

Claudia bit her lip, suddenly wondering what she had gotten herself into. "And I don't want Texas big hair either. I have to maintain my professional image, and I don't want my hair taking center stage instead of what I am saying. People should pay attention to my brains at work, not how I look."

This was going to be harder than Pam thought. Did Claudia really think that she didn't know her? They had only been friends forever. "You don't trust me."

"No, it's not that. It's just . . . I will say one word—Rio."

"C'mon, I am not doing anything myself this time. We are running out of time. I am not going to totally change your image, just test your limits a bit." She rolled her eyes.

"Trust me, there is not that much time in the world. All you really need are a few tweaks here and there. Just follow me. I am going to pick out a few outfits for you while the hair salon takes care of the rest. You can just park it in the salon and let these good people work their magic."

The wisdom of listening to Pam was doubtful as they made their way to the back of the store and then upstairs. Claudia shuddered as the not-too-pleasant memories washed over her. What was she doing? Every other time she'd listened to Pam it had backfired. In high school, she'd let Pam convince her to relax her hair. She'd sat in her mother's kitchen while Pam had experimented on her head, and she'd cried when they'd ended up with a sink full of dissolved mush and a short, uneven crop where her hair used to be.

Then there was RIO. The magic potion, supposedly all natural, had been advertised on television, guaranteed to make your mane luxurious without the harshness of chemicals. Pam had talked her into that too. She remembered thinking that it had to be safe, people ate it. That was before it had turned her fingernails green and her hair had started hitting the bathroom floor in chunks. She'd worn a weave for two years as she'd waited for her hair to grow back and for the class action lawsuit to be settled. The seventy-five dollars she'd collected after the company filed bankruptcy had barely paid for one trip to the hair dresser. And here she was, being led by her very own kitchen beautician, once again, like a lamb to the slaughter.

The salon was in the very back of the upstairs part of the building. Claudia felt immediately wary. The last time she'd gone to a salon this white, a disaster had remained on top of her head where her previously acceptable hair had been. Pam had been responsible for that too. Claudia had had to wash her hair three times to get it back to normal. She looked around cautiously without speaking. The gray walls were all the same, punctuated here and there with the obscure art and neoclassical-looking department store furniture. It was separated from the rest of the customer service area next to it by smoked glass partitions, and the smell of hair chemicals and spray assaulted them before they even reached the top of the stairs.

There were three people in the salon, and they all seemed to pause in midsentence as Claudia and Pam entered. Claudia shifted as they waited, feeling immediately uncomfortable and unwelcome. She knew that it was more her than them as sweat began to trickle down her underarms. One woman lifted her chin as if to ask, "Can I help you?" without moving her lips. The phone was pressed to her ear, and she didn't even bother to remove it. Pam spoke first.

"Hi, I called. My friend is here to see Eric." The three people in the room let out a collective sigh, as if they were glad that Pam and Claudia were not there to see any of them so close to closing time. The woman who had almost greeted them glanced at the clock. The rest immediately went back to what they were doing, which did not look like much to Claudia.

One man, whom Claudia assumed to be the famous Eric, sashayed out from behind yet another partition. Claudia narrowed her eyes slightly as she took him in. Pam talked nonstop about the wonders that Eric worked for her. According to her, he worked numerous beauty miracles weekly, ranging from hair to nails to eyebrows. You name it, Eric did it.

He was small, almost wiry, and dressed in Saks chic all

black. His pants were tight-fitting polyester with a mock turtleneck that was exactly the same shade. His hair was neat and arranged in perfectly measured short twists. His hairdo was accented by two perfectly round gold hoops, one in each ear. He extended his hand to Pam almost as if he expected her to kiss it. Claudia watched, amused as they touched fingertips as if they were going to shake hands, and then embraced instead. He let out various exclamations as he kissed Pam on each cheek, as if she were a long lost friend rather than a customer he saw weekly. Claudia smiled inside. It was amazing how nice people would be to you when they knew they could get your money.

Unable to stand them fawning over each other anymore, Claudia cleared her throat.

"Oh, Eric, this is Claudia. The one I called you about. My friend."

Eric raised one eyebrow. Claudia stood silently as he looked her over. She arranged her shirt as she felt his eyes galloping over her body. He was examining her as if she were produce or a prized calf, as opposed to a person.

"We need a makeover. Something daring, but not too. Can you help? Oh, and no chemicals to the hair. She doesn't do that."

Eric rolled his eyes. Claudia noticed that he had on more eyeliner than any of the women present. "We can do that. It is going to take some creativity, but that is why you come to me." He circled around Claudia like a vulture above a half-dead meal.

She shuddered, and her face darkened as she crossed her arms in front of her. How dare he look at her like that. He was working on no tip. "Yes, I am sure that is why you get paid the way you do too." Claudia's face began to get hot. It annoyed her to be spoken about as if she were a child or not present. "I just need a new hairdo. How hard can that be?"

"It is not about the difficulty. A new hairstyle is a very intricate process." He waved his hands in the air dramatically, drawing out his words as he spoke. "I want to make sure that all of my customers have hairstyles that fit their personalities. Or at least the personality they are trying to project. And according to Pam you want to look like a new woman, right?"

Claudia looked from Eric to Pam. Her friend stood behind her, grinning from ear to ear, like a child that had just discovered their favorite candy hidden in the back of a candy store. She acted as if it were alright that she had revealed all of Claudia's personal business to this obviously whacked-out stranger. She was apparently really into this Eric guy. She talked about him like he was her beauty guru, and she was now hanging on his every word. You might even believe that she was the one getting the makeover. She didn't answer, she just nodded. It could only get better, right?

Pam clapped her hands and jumped up and down, startling Claudia.

"Good, we can get started."

"And you can calm down." Claudia could not help scowling at her friend's enthusiasm. "I'm here now, so I might as well."

"Good, I am going to pick out some outfits for you and have them wrapped up for you to take home. Eric is going to take care of your makeup too, and I will get some of that for you as well."

Claudia grabbed Pam's arm as she attempted to dart away.

"Okay so, after I am a magical new me, then what?"

"You are not only going to be magical, you are going to have new duds right down to your undies. Then, my dear, I have a surprise for you. We are going to try out your new look in a few days at a party I found for you."

"Just for me, huh?" Claudia looked at Pam questioningly. "What did you do, throw together a little coming-out shindig or something?"

"Again with the sarcasm." Pam pushed on Claudia's shoulder playfully. "It's just an opening that you would have skipped. One of those socialite things you hate so much."

"Oh, joy. I can't wait."

Pam ran off gleefully into the bowels of the department store, leaving Claudia to follow Eric into the back of the salon. Silently, she slipped into the black smock he offered and took the place he pointed out in the salon chair. She may as well utilize the idle time productively. If nothing else, she would have some time to think about what she was going to tell her mother. She closed her eyes and sat back.

Chapter 16

Jackson wasn't there. Claudia stood poised, ready to drop her keys in their normal spot on her hallway table, when she remembered her breakup, and all of the joy she had been feeling went out of her. New hair and a bag full of new clothing made her feel good, although she hated to admit that Pam had been right. Almost all the way home, she had smiled to herself. She'd kept flipping down her visor to stare at her hair and makeover, wondering how in the world she was going to re-create it. She ran her fingers through her newly behaving hair time and time again. She was not in love with it yet, but she definitely loved the way it felt. And that Eric sure knew how to wash a mean head of hair. He had massaged her head so thoroughly that it had almost been sexual. Another minute of his fingers on her scalp and she would have been searching for new underwear, too. When Eric was done, Claudia had automatically thought of Jackson. Normally, if he wasn't already at her place, she would call him to share things smaller than this. Chills ran down Claudia's spine as she imagined Jackson, walking around her checking her out thoroughly.

He would probably say something like, "Oh, looky here now," or something equally as corny, Claudia imagined.

For a short minute, she missed him. And then the loneliness set in.

The lonely feeling was interrupted by her mother's shrill voice. Claudia cringed, and her shoulders immediately tensed as some of the stress Eric had washed away returned.

"I didn't think you were coming back. And what time is it? Don't you have to work tomorrow?"

Claudia had almost forgotten about her mother too. As usual, she started in with her scolding. Couldn't she talk to Claudia in any other tone of voice? It was as if she were still eight years old, being reprimanded for yet another something she did not do exactly as her mother wanted.

Growing up, Claudia remembered her father always asking her mother not to yell, and her mother always insisting that she wasn't, that the high pitch she used so often was her normal tone of voice. Well, one of them certainly had a hearing problem, and Claudia was coming to realize that it had definitely NOT been her father. No wonder he was off with his friends.

Her mother flicked on the lights that Claudia had purposely left off, without so much as a break in her sentence.

"What are you doing here in the dark?"

Claudia did not answer as her mother yammered on. "I thought you were kidding when you said I would be eating alone. What am I supposed to do with all that—" She cut her sentence off midstream and stood with her perfectly lipsticked mouth agape. Even late at night, her mother would not be seen without her makeup. She had on her nighttime face. Claudia knew it by heart from all the years of watching her mother's routine as a girl—light moisturizer, and an almost nude lipstick with just a hint of color. She sniffed, smelling for her mother's signature scent. She must have stock in the company that produced Chanel No. 5.

Claudia rolled her eyes. She kicked off her shoes. "You can close your mouth, Ma." She did not expect any positive comments. Her mother's favorite pastime had always been finding fault with Claudia. "And could you lower your voice just a little? I don't want to disturb the neighbors."

"You *have* been busy. What is the occasion? You look so . . . daring. I mean, I am so used to you—"

"—Being what? Dowdy? Conservative? What other not positive word can you think of to describe me, Ma?"

"I have never used a negative word when I talked about you, girl. I just like to make sure you are always your best. Wouldn't you rather I point out your flaws than someone else? You know people can be so cruel sometimes. And you always look *nice*. I just wasn't expecting you to look so different than when you left here. Would you mind telling me what is going on?" She didn't wait for an answer.

Claudia watched as her mother did not stop to catch her breath, her hands motioning in the air as she spoke in her usual, animated style.

"I like it, though. The hair is you. The makeup, well, that is nice too, just a little too much eyeliner for my taste. Are they still wearing that stuff?"

Claudia sighed. There was no use in her even explaining to her mother. She knew she would never be able to please her, no matter what she did. Just once, she wished that her mother were someone else, a mother she could confide in and who would comfort her, tell her it would be alright. But she had not ever been that growing up, and she certainly wasn't going to start doing that now. You can't teach an old dog new tricks. Isn't that what they said? It had always been that way between them, even when she was a small child. When Claudia brought home a B, Henrietta would ask, "Where is the A?" An A would get, "Oh, I expect no less"—not a "Good job" like the other kids got. Claudia shook her head. The sad thing was, her mother didn't even realize she was doing it.

Claudia yawned, then stretched. "I'm kinda tired, Ma. How about you?"

"Tired? Why should I be tired? I was here resting while I waited for you to come home. Don't you have to work tomorrow? You were out traipsing the streets all hours of the night like you don't have to work or something. What does Jackson have to say about his fiancée being out like that?"

"I don't answer to him or any other man. You know that."

Her mother waved her hand in the air, as if dismissing Claudia's comment. "Did you go shopping too? Do you have bags?" She made a beeline for the still open garage door. "Let me get them for you."

There was no use fighting. Claudia made her way to the kitchen as her mother went through her car, removing her purchases. Claudia knew that she really did not want to be helpful; she wanted to be nosey. Claudia would let Henrietta look at her things. She wouldn't like anything Pam picked out, Claudia was sure of that. She would probably tell her everything was too tight or too loud.

The sounds from the garage let Claudia know that her mother was doing a thorough examination of the bags. She shrugged. Oh well. She put the kettle on for her nightly cup of tea, wondering how much longer she was going to have to endure her mother. Every time Henrietta visited, she changed her mind about how long she would stay, and the time would usually be longer than she'd said it would in the beginning. Claudia would prefer it if she did not have to tell her mother about Jackson, but she knew she would find out eventually. It would be obvious. Jackson would usually have dinner with her mother at least once. He made it a point to butter her up regularly. Henrietta would be sure to notice a difference, even if Claudia did not mention a word about their breakup.

The garage door banged against the door stop with a thud as her mother returned from the garage. Claudia jumped, almost burning her hand with the hot water she was pouring.

"Ma, do you think it's possible for you to do anything quietly?" Claudia was starting to miss the peace and quiet she had come to take for granted.

"Lots of bags here. But what is this?"

Claudia had completely forgotten about the box from work. She had been preoccupied with the outsourcing rumor and had never gotten to it. It was still in the backseat, where she had thrown it when she'd left.

"It is really pretty paper. Very unusual. You don't see pressed flowers that much anymore. Where did you have it wrapped?"

"I didn't. It's from work. It's probably something HR dreamed up, some development tool or something. They are always coming up with these ideas to make us feel like the training that no one wants to attend is a privilege." Claudia took the package from her mother and began to unwrap it. Her mother watched intently, forgetting about the other shopping bags.

Claudia opened the box. It was stuffed with mainly tissue, but in the center was another, smaller box. She fingered it gently as she examined it thoroughly. It was very pretty, made of some kind of stone, and it was hand painted in gold lacquer with a gray-and-black diamond pattern. Her mother cleared her throat.

"Well, they sure spend a lot of money on training. What a waste. I sure need to sell my stock. That has to catch up to them eventually. Did you make me some tea too?"

Claudia nodded, suddenly tense. This box was not from human resources. It was too elaborate, almost beautiful. She turned her back, not wanting her mother to see its contents. She handed her mother the natural sugar she liked so much and wetted her lips. She could hear her heart beat inside her head.

"Mom, why don't you take a look at the clothes I bought." She steered her mother in the direction of her bags, wanting her to forget about the mysterious box. "I'm trying to be a little less conservative. I want to change my image a little."

"Really? And you say Pam is helping you with that? Do you think that is a wise decision? She will have you looking like the neighborhood sleaze. Next she will be taking you to a strip club or something to try and teach you how to seduce a man."

Claudia ignored her mother's last comment. It was really the best thing to do, the only way they could reach some semblance of peace. "Okay, Mom, just take them into the living room. I will bring your tea. Maybe I will model them for you." She smiled a fake smile, remembering as a child how her mother would make her try on every stitch of new clothing as soon as she got home from shopping.

As soon as Henrietta left the kitchen, Claudia carefully opened the top of the box. It was filled with rose petals surrounding a note. She lifted it up carefully, admiring this paper as much as she had the wrapping paper. It was handmade and delicate and now softly scented by the roses that had surrounded it. It had only one line.

You motivate me in your specialness.

"That from Jackson?"

Claudia jumped as her mother squawked in her ear.

"I told you that man was special. Does he send you notes often?" She shook her head. "He is a keeper."

Claudia had not even heard her mother return to the kitchen.

"Did anyone ever tell you that reading over someone's shoulder is rude?" Her face flushed and felt hot.

"I'm sorry, I didn't realize it was a secret. You act like you two just started dating or something. It's sweet that he does those things after five years. I just came back for my tea. You know I like it steaming hot."

Claudia bit her tongue. She was pretty sure that the package was not from Jackson; he had not one romantic bone in his body. But who would leave her such a thing? At work? Whoever it was obviously knew things about her, like when she was at work and when she wasn't. They also obviously knew that she liked little boxes and that roses were her favorite. Or maybe not—those things could be a coincidence.

Her mother nudged her. "I said, I had no idea Jackson was such a romantic. Your father used to be that way when we first got married. But you know what they say, a man is at his best when he is in the dating phase. It is only downhill from there. You better enjoy it now."

Claudia smiled weakly. "Yeah, he is very romantic." She lied as her mother droned on. Part of her was scared. Someone was watching her. At the same time, she felt her stomach flip. She was confused and excited all at the same time. She was thirty years old, but it felt like high school all over again. She had a secret admirer.

Chapter 17

Damn! Marina swore under her breath. Every time she dialed a long-distance number she had to do it more than once. She promised herself she would cut her nails; she kept pressing more keys than she wanted to. A chill ran down her spine as she sat in her semi-dark basement. She was running out of time. Before she knew it, Wesley would be breathing down her neck. The clock ticked loudly as she waited for someone to answer the phone. It seemed as if an eternity passed before she finally got through.

Asking the right questions would be easy. She knew now to be extra friendly, posing as if she didn't remember making the bank transfer from her account. She would start talking before the woman did, answering her security questions easily. Phone banking was a wonderful thing. She knew all of Wesley's identifying information, and thanks to those slips, she knew the bank account number too. She had personally never heard of a woman named Wesley, but she didn't doubt that there was at least one somewhere.

She crossed her fingers, hoping she would get a male on the phone. She thought it might be easier for her if she did.

"Thank you for calling Bank of America. How may I help you today?"

Marina smiled; the voice on the phone was a deep one, just as she wanted. Young sounding too. Even better.

"I am having such a stressful day, I hope yours is better." She laughed her best tired-sounding laugh, almost a giggle. "I was going through my statements and I see a transaction I don't recognize. Can you help me with that?" Marina's voice was full of saccharine as she tried her best not to sound nervous. She gave the account number and her husband's identifying information. Just as she expected, the young-sounding man on the phone responded to her bait.

"Well, let's see if I can make it any better for you. That looks like it was a fed fund transfer. Do you remember making it?"

Marina sighed heavily. "Well, let me see. I make so many. Maybe if you tell me the receiver it will jog my memory. Can you see that on your screen?"

Marina held her breath as the person on the phone paused. She had a few tricks of her own up her sleeve and thoroughly believed that she could find out the information she wanted if she just asked the correct questions.

"Just a minute. I can see a routing number, but I can't see the benefit account. I think you are going to have to go into a branch for that."

"Are you sure? Is there any more information here that might be helpful? I am not sure I authorized this. Would the bank let someone wire money from my account without verifying their identity? That doesn't seem right. It's a large sum of money too. Seems like they would be more careful."

The teller cleared his throat. Marina could tell that what she had said had made him nervous, just as she knew it would.

"Now don't be too hasty, I'm not done. It looks like that transfer was made to a Bank of America Branch in Austin. I can't see a name, but it looks like it established a new account for someone. I'm sorry. Is there anything else I can help you with?"

Marina's heart sank. "No, thanks." She hung up the phone, feeling disappointed that she hadn't gotten more information. She was just going to have to go back into Wesley's office again.

Marina was pensive as she sat with her husband eating the dinner she'd prepared. What was the big secret? Not knowing was killing her. She knew in her gut that whatever it was that Wesley was involved in was something that she needed to know about. Her ears rang as her thoughts drowned out the sounds of Wesley's words. He was attempting to carry on their usual evening conversation, usually something she cared nothing about that happened to him during the day.

He banged his fist on the table, making all the dishes chatter.

"Are you even listening to me?" His face had darkened, and the now shrill sound of his voice was enough to draw Marina back.

She jumped. "I'm sorry, honey. I was somewhere else." Marina attempted a wan smile.

"Well, that is obvious. What is going on? I thought the purpose of us sitting down to eat dinner as a family was so we could get to spend some time together, perhaps talk about our day. What is so important that you can't carry on a conversation with me?" He paused, drumming his fingers on the table as he waited for her answer.

Marina jumped and placed her hand on her trembling stomach. Wesley hated to be ignored. He pushed his chair back from the Italian mahogany dining table and slowly walked over to her chair, placing his hands on her shoulders as if to massage her.

"Let me guess." Marina tensed as he rubbed her shoulders, his artificially sweet voice dripping with sarcasm. "You are deep in thought about how much you love me, right? Why are you so tense, honey?"

His grip became tighter on her shoulders. Marina didn't answer. She did not get the sense that she was supposed to.

"Or maybe you are thinking about your secrets, right? Or maybe my secrets? Tell me, is that why you were snooping in my office?" Wesley suddenly stopped massaging her thin shoulders, instead gripping them as he interrogated her. She pictured the new bruises that would surely appear there tomorrow. Again.

"Why the hell were you in my office, Marina? You know I don't like you to go in there. I don't snoop around in your things."

Spinning around, Marina tore herself from his grip. She scurried to get away from him. "What do you mean?" Her eyes were wide with fear. How had he known?

"Don't play stupid with me. I know you were in there. You tried to put everything back where it had come from, but you made one mistake. You left tissues in my wastebasket. Did you think I wouldn't see them? We have been together a long time, I know what your lipstick looks like. And there certainly hasn't been any other woman in this house, so don't try to deny it."

Her mind whirred. She closed her eyes and then opened them again as sweat began to form on her brow. How could she have been so stupid? But she was not the one with the secrets, and she refused to be made into the villain.

"You can't make me feel as if I am the one doing wrong, Wesley." Marina's voice became venomous. "Why don't you tell me about the mysterious bank account you have? What happened to share and share alike? Why are you hiding money from me? While you are at it, why don't you tell me about the wire transfers? What about those? Was that money you sent to a girlfriend somewhere or something? Someone you don't want me to know about? You better not be involved in anything illegal."

By now, Marina had walked around to the other side of the table, and she stood with her hands on the back of a chair, directly facing Wesley, who was doing the same. Her chest heaved from her anger. If she was going to question him, she wanted to be a safe distance away. She knew that he would not have a positive reaction to her talking back; it was so out of character for her.

Wesley's eyes shined with hatred. His face was beet-red. The table between them was her saving grace; she could sense that he would reach out and grab her if he could, he had done it so many times before.

His fingers blanched as he gripped the back of the chair tensely. His thin lips trembled as he struggled to get out his words.

"Have you lost your mind? Since when do you question me and what I do? I am the man of this house." Wesley hit his chest for emphasis.

Marina jumped.

"Who have you been talking to?"

Marina felt herself become even more furious than Wesley looked. For a minute, she thought she was experiencing déjà vu, a flashback of her own father and mother. Marina could never remember her mother speaking up for herself, and the one time she had, her father had practically beaten her senseless while Marina had watched. She was not about to let that happen to her.

"I'm tired of this. I have a mind of my own. You want to know who I have been talking to? Nobody, that's who, that is, if you don't count your little friend who asked me to relay a message to you. Your 'problem' has been taken care of. What problem could he mean?" She paused, but he did not answer. "You treat me as if I don't matter. I gave up my life for you because my father thought you were the best choice for me. I deserve to be treated like an equal partner in this relationship." Marina blinked to try and stop the tears she knew were surely going to come now; they always did when she was angry. And right now, she was pissed.

Wesley's face was covered with shock. He had never heard Marina talk to him as she was right now. His usually large frame appeared shrunken. He handled things the best he knew, and now they were falling apart. He took a deep breath. "You lost the equal partner privilege—"

Marina held up her hand to stop him. "This is about you, not me. I will not continually serve penance for something you said you could forgive me for, no matter what my father thinks."

The couple paused, glaring at each other. The clock ferociously ticked away the minutes. For a minute, neither one of them spoke. Finally, Marina cleared her throat.

"You know, I should have followed my heart and never married you. At least I would have been loved."

Wesley's mouth dropped open. How dare she. "Maybe you should go to him if you feel that way. But you couldn't find him if you tried. Your father and I made sure of that. You want to know the truth? Your lover wasn't as true as you thought. We offered him money and he snatched it and ran like a thief in the night."

Marina's mouth dropped open. It was her turn to look shocked. What in the world—?

Wesley pulled out his chair and sat down. He reached for the brown cigar box on the table. He removed a cigar and snipped off the end. "That's right. It wasn't like I said. We bought him, your father and I. We offered him a clean, debt-free slate. And he took it. He virtually sold those bastard kids of yours too. We just added a few more dollars, and that was all it took. Some love, huh? He sold you like chattel." Wesley licked his cigar and laughed a deep belly laugh. "So you go to him if you want to. That's who is in Austin. But I would be careful if I were you, and think long and hard about your decision, because there will be no turning back. Your father will cut you off too. And think twice before you throw it all away for someone like that. He obviously likes money so much that he might have you turning tricks for him soon." Wesley chortled as he watched Marina crumble and break into tears. He lit his cigar and puffed on it. He felt no remorse. She'd asked for the truth and gotten it.

Marina's chest heaved. The pain she felt was unimaginable. She could not believe that what Wesley was saying was true. She'd had no idea that he could be so heartless and cruel, nor could she believe that her father was involved in all of this. She sat down heavily and hung her head in her hands. This was not to be believed. How could Cody possibly accept money in exchange for their relationship? If she'd had any idea that he'd wanted her, she would have never agreed to the adoption of her children, but apparently it was worse than she'd thought.

Wesley finished his cigar and stood up from the table. He was glad that Marina was back in her place. She loved her comfortable life and her money. It didn't matter if she knew the truth. She would never leave all of this behind for that scum Cody.

"I'm going to my office. You make sure you stay out of there in the future." He looked around the dining room table. "Clean up the dinner dishes."

Marina lifted her head. There was no way in hell she was going to become her mother. But she had to think about things; she needed a plan. She sniffed and wiped her face, watching from the corner of her eye as Wesley strode away. He was a bastard. He obviously thought he had broken her, like a wild horse. But it wasn't over. Marina was going to find Cody, and her children. Wesley had won a battle, but the war was not over yet. It was only just beginning.

Chapter 18

Cody arrived at his rock earlier than normal. He let the light mist that was falling wet his face. He enjoyed the warm wetness, not bothering to wipe it dry. He did not even bother to use his telescope this morning, and he had skipped his morning coffee. He didn't need it. Today was the day he would make his move.

He waited patiently for Claudia, watching the ducks that swam in the lake. He'd even left his book at home. It was not necessary for him to fake reading it. Today he really was going to run.

He inhaled the pleasant smell that came off the water. It was beautiful here, even on an overcast day. He had not eaten breakfast, but he was not hungry. His stomach was grumbling, but not from hunger. He was excited. Claudia was now a free woman. There was one less thing standing in the way of them being together, so the time had come for him to get on with it.

He could not understand the effect that she had on him. Ever since he'd overheard her ex talking about her in the barbershop, he could not get her off his mind. He thought about her even more than he had before. He wanted to run his hands through her mounds of hair. He imagined kissing her over and over with no guilt.

He glanced at his watch and stood up to begin stretching. He had to at least make his attempt at running look believable. He did not think Claudia was the type to be impressed if he could not at least keep up with her. He lifted his head and his breath stopped for a moment. She was coming. He smiled to himself, then frowned, noticing that she looked different today, although every bit as delicious as usual. She was also alone, that was good. He would not have to be nice to her friend. Instead, he could just cut right to the chase.

She ran right by Cody, and the pounding sound her running shoes made on the packed gravel was like music to his ears. Just as she passed, he fell into stride behind her. He let her rhythm become his own, but he tripped as he started out, swearing under his breath. That was just like him. He quickly regained his balance and took off, not wanting Claudia to get too far ahead.

Cody ran slightly faster than Claudia did, passing her. As soon as he got a few feet ahead, he looked over his shoulder and tried to look as surprised as possible.

"Hey, Claudia. What a surprise." He smiled warmly and fell into step beside her. Although he had rehearsed what he planned to say, he could not remember any of it.

She nodded but kept running, exhaling heavily through her mouth.

"I didn't know you were a runner, too. It is such a small world." Cody's lips twitched.

Claudia smiled as much as possible through panting, and she reached up to move the hair that had fallen into her face. She brushed it back, annoyed that she'd let Eric cut it so short. It hadn't been twenty-four hours, and she missed her ponytail already. Worse yet, she hoped she didn't sweat it out or she would surely have a good, old-fashioned Afro the likes of which Austin had not seen in a long time.

She knew she should recognize the man that was talking to her, but it took her a minute to place his face. "I try to get out here as often as I can," she said. Her breath came in spurts. Without Pam to slow her down, she had been running hard for quite a while. She wanted to push herself. New hair, new clothes, may as well get a new body too.

"I should have known, the way you look. You look like you try to keep things together." Cody smiled to himself. Life was too short to beat around the bush. Claudia was fine as hell and he wanted her to know it. He liked his women with ample meat on their bones, and this one fit the bill perfectly.

His comment immediately sparked her memory. This was the guy from the supermarket, the flirt. "You don't ever quit, do you? It seems like every time I see you, you try to flirt with me. What is it you want really?"

"I don't want anything. Like I said, I just appreciate women. Did you change your hair? It is very becoming, even while you are running. It makes you look younger." He paused. "You cut it, right?"

Claudia's face softened. Okay, so what if he was flirting? He sure knew what to say to a woman. And he wasn't that bad-looking either. She decided he could do her no harm. He was handsome enough, with his caramel-colored skin and pretty smile. And who couldn't like a man with a dimple? Her stomach flip-flopped, surprising her. It had been a long time since she had had that reaction to any male. Her mind had been so tied up in work that she hadn't had time to think about her love life, and with Jackson waiting in the wings, she'd had no reason to before. And look where that had gotten her.

She nodded, and the two of them continued down the path in silence.

Cody's mind whirled as he ran beside her. He let her set the pace, and it was a tough one. He knew that her run was almost over. He'd purposely joined her in the later half of the path he knew she took almost every other morning. It was a good thing too; he didn't want to chance passing out before he'd had time to get her attention properly.

He admired Claudia as they ran. She was definitely a beautiful woman. Too bad about the hair, but it could grow back. Although it was shorter than he liked, there was still lots of it for him to dig his hands into.

Cody struggled to get his breathing together. He felt as if his lungs were being squeezed. Just as he thought that he could not take it anymore, she slowed the pace to a fast walk, breathing heavily.

"That was pretty impressive. You must run a lot." Claudia had purposely sped up when Cody had joined her. She'd wanted to see what he was made of. He had passed the test. She smiled, placing her hand on her chest. She did not realize how much time she and Pam spent talking instead of running normally, and she was feeling it now. Her heart rate was too fast, and there was pounding in her ears. A wake-up call. And if she didn't know better, she would think that he was suffering just a tiny bit too in the aftermath of their little run.

They reached the crossover near the new pedestrian bridge. She stopped, stretching one of her legs up and leaning into the steps, beginning her normal after-run stretch routine. She sighed but did not speak, savoring the release she felt in her legs. Stretching was her favorite part of the run.

Cody imitated her as best he could. "I try. Unfortunately I get so tied up in my work that I don't get out here as often as I like."

"That's right. You work for Pittsford too. How is that coming for you? I never see you around."

"Well, you know how it is. I want to be promoted, so I can be Big Willy, like you. Or should I say, Big Wilhelmina?" he grinned.

Claudia chuckled. "I wouldn't go that far. But you are on the right track. Hard work is the way to do it. Eventually it will all pay off, in this company or the next."

"So, am I hearing you say that you don't see a life for yourself there? Don't you want to retire from Pittsford?"

"I was talking about you. And the days of working for one company for thirty years are gone. Corporate America is like chess. You have to make the right moves at the right time to win the game."

You got that right, Cody thought to himself. The right time had certainly come for him to throw caution to the wind and make some moves in Ms. Claudia's direction. They finished stretching, and Claudia started walking toward her car. "I'm parked over by Bread Alone. You over there, too?"

He shook his head. "I walked. It adds a little something extra to my workout. I actually don't live too far." He took a deep breath. "You know, I sure would like to pick your brain some time. There are so few people to talk to about work. So many of the folks at your level are just not approachable. I mean, if you wouldn't mind. Maybe we can have lunch or something? I would appreciate it. You really seem to know what you are doing."

Claudia paused. *What would it hurt, lunch with this young guy?* She could hear the office gossip now. She pursed her lips. "My schedule is kind of tight the next few days." It would be no good to make it too easy for him.

"No rush. I wouldn't want to inconvenience you. We could go at your leisure, whatever works best for you." Cody's heart was beating so hard that he was sure she could hear it. "Maybe we could have a working lunch. I have a project I am working on that I would love to bend your ear about." He hoped that Claudia wanted to be an expert as much as Barry said.

Claudia rubbed her forehead. A working lunch she could do. He may have seemed like a flirt, but he really seemed considerate of her time. She ran her eyes over him, admiring the way his sweat suit draped over his body. There were obviously some muscles under there. She flashed her best Pam-like smile. And he still smelled good even though he had just run just as hard as she had.

"That seems fine. Just shoot me an e-mail, and we can get it on my calendar. Does that work for you? You know how to reach me, right?"

Cody grinned. He sure did. He knew more about Claudia than she cared to imagine. Things were going more smoothly than he'd thought they would. If Claudia had reservations because of just getting out of a relationship, he sure couldn't tell. Maybe there was something to what Barry said—she needed to feel special after being dumped. Who could blame her for that? His life was finally looking up.

Chapter 19

The office was already buzzing when Claudia arrived. She let the door slam behind her as she rushed in, cursing Pam under her breath. Although she had to admit that her new hair made her feel good, it had taken too long for her to get it together, and now her normal schedule was way off. She glanced down at her watch and hurried even more. She had ten minutes to get to her meeting, and she still had to print out her presentation. Not to mention the fact that she felt a little uncomfortable in her clothes. Her skirt was shorter than she normally liked it, hitting her just above her knees. She and Pam had argued about the skirt, but in the end, she'd let Pam win. Pam had always known what to say to get Claudia to do what she wanted, convincing Claudia that the short pencil skirt looked good on her, telling her that her legs were her best feature, which they were, if Claudia could say so herself.

This was just what Claudia needed to hear; she could still hear her mother's words when she was sixteen, calling her knobby-kneed. It had stayed with her over the years until she almost never bought a skirt or dress that did not cover them up. She stuck to pants and pantsuits. Now, as she was about to make her debut in this new outfit, she was having second thoughts. Not only was it too short but the outfit was also bright, a funny color of burnt orange, and her knees were cold, even in the summer heat.

Mary met her at her desk, her eyes immediately widening as she took in Claudia's new look.

"Don't you look nice. You have been busy. You even got new hair. Wow." Mary circled Claudia to check her out. "Do we have a new beau or something?"

"Nope, just felt like a change. It was time." Claudia feigned a smile and ground her teeth together. The mention of the word *beau* made her cringe.

Mary touched her own hair. "I haven't changed my hair in years."

Claudia did not look up. No change for Mary was not a good thing; she was not exactly the most admired woman in the office when it came to her hair and clothes. God forbid that people put her in the same category as frumpy Mary, although she had not worn a bow on her butt since the third grade. But she was not in the mood to discuss it. Her love life was no business of Miss Busy Body anyway.

"I need to get my presentation printed on transparencies for the marketing meeting this morning." Claudia was suddenly conscience of the sound her panty hose made as she walked. Was that her thighs rubbing together?

"It is printing as we speak."

At that moment, her eyes were drawn to the corner of her cubicle by a large bouquet of flowers. They sat back in a large, clear glass vase. Claudia frowned.

"Do you know anything about those?" She waved her hand in the direction of the flowers. Inside she smiled, but she tried to act as if they were no big deal.

"You mean, other than they delivered them very early

this morning? No. But you might read the card. I could hardly wait for you to get here so you could fill me in." Mary grinned so big one might think that she was the one receiving flowers.

Claudia glared. "And I would do that because . . ." Mary always seemed to have some quip up her sleeve, which she doled out without mercy. Claudia gave her one of her best none-of-your-business looks as she reached around to the back of the bouquet. She removed the card as Mary watched.

Claudia paused, peering out of her cubicle in the direction of her boss's office.

"He here yet?" she asked.

Mary shrugged.

"Do you need some work to do? Could you go and check on the transparencies? We wouldn't want them to get stuck in the printer." Claudia toyed with the envelope. She didn't need an audience and had no desire to be the talk of the administrative pool.

Mary left reluctantly. The bodice of her old-fashioned flowered dress filled up with air with her abrupt turn. Claudia smirked. She turned her back to the cubicle opening. Her stomach quivered with anticipation. *What has gotten into me?* she thought. *They are just flowers.*

She loved flowers. They made her feel good and reminded her of being a little girl, but her reaction made her realize how long it had been since she had received any from someone else. Sure, she bought fresh flowers from the market all the time, but there was nothing like someone buying them for her. And receiving them when you didn't expect them? Now that was special.

When she was a child, her father would always bring her

a flower or two for her birthday or other special occasions. He would say she was his "best girl." She thought of Jackson and frowned. He used to buy her flowers when they first started dating, but that had stopped a long time ago, along with most of the other romantic things they used to do. That should have been her clue about the direction their relationship was going; he had started treating her like an old married woman before they'd even made that trip down the aisle. Mother was right; she'd waited too long. Maybe if she had paid attention to the signs, she wouldn't have wasted the last five years of her life.

Claudia turned the card over in her hand. It was not signed. All it said was, "You make me smile." That was strange. She had no idea who'd sent them. Just like the little box. She stepped fully out of her cubicle and looked around, even though she knew whoever had sent the flowers was long gone and probably had not even delivered them personally. There was not a soul in the hallway, although she could hear the *click-click* sounds of computer keyboards from all over the office and the murmur of a few people talking over the phone. The office was almost never empty. Someone had to have seen something. After her meeting, she would have to have a chat with security. Whoever had left her the package and the flowers sure had a handle on being mysterious. Her face felt warm. Claudia raised her hand to her cheek, then covered her mouth, which was spreading into a wide grin. The mystery excited her.

Just then, Claudia spied her boss's door. It was open. No matter what time she arrived, he seemed to already be in. *That's why he's the boss.* She dropped the card into an open desk drawer, closing it firmly, then shimmied as she straightened her skirt. Claudia headed toward the open door. She wanted to catch him before he headed off to his next meeting. He stayed out of his office more than he did in it.

Her work space was at the head of cubicle row and was double the size of those around her. David Roscoe was her direct superior, and he rated an actual office, one with a door and a window view. She was cautious as she peeked into the office, knocking softly.

"Got a minute?" she asked, smiling.

He looked up and motioned her in.

She stepped inside.

His eyes swept over her, then looked into hers. He didn't comment.

Claudia drew herself up before speaking. "I was wondering if you could clarify something I heard on the office grapevine."

"Such as?"

"Such as, I heard that there has been some talk of outsourcing my customer service units. That could directly affect me. Any truth to this?"

"Your job is secure." He placed his fingertips on the desk.

"So you are saying that it is true?"

He nodded, glancing at his watch.

"It makes sense to me that I would be involved in the discussion. Most of those folks work for me, right? I am one of the few people who have insight into what the customer thinks of this type of thing. Instead, it almost sounds like I am one of the last to know. I mean, I heard about it on an elevator—"

He held up his hand. "As I said, your job is secure. But if it makes you feel better, we'll bring you in. We were going to do it anyway, but we were trying to keep things under wraps. You know, talk about eliminating jobs can be touchy. But it looks like the cat is already out of the bag." His weak smile lacked warmth.

"But India? Has anyone investigated what the customer thinks?"

"Who do you think is driving this?" David picked up several files from his desk. "I really am in a hurry. Why don't you get Mary to schedule us some one-on-one time—"

"Really? That is surprising. All the data show that end users are not as satisfied with foreign call centers. Some of our competitors are even closing theirs, right?"

He paused, nodding. "You are going to go far." He started toward the door. "Chivers Technologies—"

"They are not even one of our biggest clients—"

"That may be so, but they have started a coalition to drive down costs in the industry, and it has picked up a lot of momentum. We can talk about this later. Get on my calendar." He strode away, leaving Claudia standing in the doorway with an open mouth. Her star status had lasted less than a week. If she was hearing him right, she had been left out of the loop on a major company decision that would impact her directly. First her love life, now her job. Couldn't any part of her life stay in order?

Chapter 20

Marina had a bad night. She spent most of it alternating between staring at the ceiling and tossing and turning, dreaming those weird dreams that come to you in the twilight of sleep. Somewhere in the middle of that, she realized that she had to go and talk to her father and find out about his part in all of this.

She had always known that Wesley was driven, but when had he crossed the line to ruthless? First, she couldn't believe that he had actually done what he'd said—paid Cody to leave her and the babies. That alone made it clear to her that Wesley was crazy. Who in their right mind would do such a thing? It was obvious that he would do anything to get what he wanted. But did he think she would never find out about it?

Even harder to believe was the idea that her father, the same man that had been so wonderful to her growing up, claiming he only wanted the best for his precious daughter, was in cahoots with Wesley. That, more than anything, cut her deep. She had spent a whole year or more feeling that she had been betrayed by the man who had professed his undying love for her since childhood, and now she knew that she had been betrayed not once but three times—by virtually every man in her life. Marina wanted answers.

When morning finally arrived, she stayed in bed feigning sleep until after Wesley was dressed and gone. She did not even react when he tried to kiss her good-bye. What would even make him think that she wanted him to kiss her, anyway? That should be reserved for someone who actually cared about her, and it was obvious that the only person Wesley cared about was himself.

He leaned over her, and she cringed as she held her eyes tightly shut. If it weren't for the fact that she wanted him to go about his day as usual, thinking she had heeded his warnings like a good little wife, she would have lashed out and smacked that handsome face that he was so proud of.

As soon as she heard the front door slam, she dragged herself from the bed, rubbing first her eyes, then her temples. Her head felt tight as it always did when she didn't get enough sleep. Marina went to the window in her bedroom and moved the drapes aside. She watched Wesley as he stepped into the car that was waiting, and she kept watching until it turned the corner and disappeared. Up until now she had not been sure what the feeling that was hiding in the corner of her heart was, but now she knew. Her mother had been wrong; she had not grown to love Wesley as she'd said she would. Instead, she hated him.

The real question that had haunted her all night was about her father and his involvement in Wesley's scheme. Marina jumped into her sweats. She grabbed a towel and wet it with cold water, dabbing at her eyes before she put on her makeup. For months, her father had been talking more to her husband than to her. It was almost as if she didn't matter anymore. He used to talk to her when she was a teen, but now that she was married, it was almost as if he had relegated her to second-class status. It was true that Wesley worked with him, but she was still his daughter.

The city slipped by her as she drove, heading toward Jersey City, where her father's offices were located. When she arrived, she sat, numb, in the parking lot of the small building. She rubbed her steering wheel, hesitating. She could not believe the mess her life had become simply because she had trusted her father. She'd blindly let him make major decisions about her life, and now she realized that the choices hadn't all been good. He controlled her as if she were still nine years old. They hardly talked anymore. Since her mother had died right after she'd gotten married, he'd thrown himself into his work even more.

The security guard nodded and signed her in without speaking. Although she had not been to the offices in some time, Marina was sure that everyone knew who she was. Her father normally kept a variety of family pictures on his desk, which showcased her at every age. She spent many weekends and summers with these same people. He often talked about his company as a "family" company, although his own family life was often a mess. Marina had never really thought about the hypocrisy until now.

The fourth floor was abuzz with activity. It hit Marina in the face like a wall of water as soon as the elevator doors opened. Although the elevator was between two glass doors, she could feel the vibration of people moving around. The lights were brighter here and the marble tile on the floors looked shinier. She remembered that Wesley had helped her father refurbish the whole floor not too many months earlier, almost right after they'd moved to this location. He had been engrossed in the project for some time.

The contrast to the dark elevator jolted her and cut into her thoughts.

The door did not move when she pulled it. It was heavier than she thought. Marina jerked it back, causing it to swing open quickly. It slammed against the doorstop behind it, and the people scuttling by on the other side jumped. A few glared at her, annoyed at her intruding. A receptionist sat inside the door, and she dropped the paper she held in her hands as she forced the smile Marina knew she had been trained to give. Her father would never tolerate rude employees. She knew from experience. As a teenager, when the company was much smaller, she had worked as a receptionist for a summer. For a minute, she missed knowing so much about, and being a part of, her father's world.

"Can I help you?" she asked. Her voice squeaked. She didn't look much older than high school age herself.

"Yes, I am here to see my father—"

"Marina, what brings you here?"

For a big man, Mario Chivers was graceful. He appeared behind Marina without her even hearing him approach. The receptionist put down the phone that was already in her hand and smiled warmly at him. It was obvious that he was well liked in the office. Her father was that kind of boss. When he unleashed his charisma on people, they usually felt obligated to do as he wanted.

Mario was wide around the middle with skinny legs. He reminded Marina of a weeble because he almost wobbled instead of walked. It seemed his chicken legs got thinner every time she saw him. The lines in his face made him look more and more distinguished, and the temples that he'd let go gray only added to the effect. He put his arm around

Marina and guided her, gently but firmly, to his office. Marina let herself feel comforted by her father, in spite of the sinking feeling in the pit of her stomach. She needed to be comforted. He smiled, and she took in the familiar smell of his aftershave, the same one he had worn as long as she could remember. Wesley had to be lying, she thought to herself. There was no way her father could ever be involved in anything so hateful as what Wesley had described. He loved her; why would he seem to be protecting Wesley's interests rather than hers?

Mario closed the door behind the two of them and released Marina, his smile vanishing. He walked around his massive mahogany desk and opened his top drawer. His movements were brusque, and Marina once again felt the invisible wall that had grown between them over the years. She jumped, and some of the water that trickled in his desktop fountain splashed on the desk.

"What brings you here, Marina?" he asked. "As if you couldn't tell, I am a very busy person, and today is a particularly bad day. We are in the middle of a major deal, and I do not need distractions right now." He continued to rifle through his desk.

Marina narrowed her eyes, her nose stinging. She was a distraction now. Her father still had the power to make her feel the same as he had when she'd misbehaved as a small child. She could feel tears fighting to get out, but she didn't want to cry. She was all grown up now and wanted to ask her father honest questions and hopefully get honest, adult answers. "I need to know something, Daddy. I know you know how rough a time Wesley and I have been having, right?"

Mario nodded, barely raising his head from whatever he was looking for in his desk.

She swallowed. "Well, he has told me some things that are very disturbing, and I need to know the truth." She wiped at her eyes with her index finger. "He says you helped him buy off Cody. You paid him to move away."

Mario shut his desk drawer hard. A few of the papers piled on top slid onto the floor. He raised his head, his eyes meeting his daughter's.

"I know this is ridiculous, but I need to hear it from you." She cleared her throat, her eyes widening as she waited for her father's answer.

"I want you to understand that what I did, I did in your best interest. I did not want you to endure any more pain as a result of a bad decision."

"And what makes you think that I am incapable of making decisions on my own? I do not see why it is necessary for you or anyone else to try and manipulate me or try to change the course of my life." Marina's voice was getting increasingly louder, bordering on shrill. Tears were streaming down her face.

"Remember where you are and remember who you are talking to." Mario's jaw clenched. "It's not that I think you are not capable of good decisions, but why should you have to make such hard ones? Those type of things are best left to the men, don't you think?"

Marina could not believe what she was hearing. "Do you think this is the dark ages, or what? Why did you bother to raise me to think for myself if you were going to do it for me? The sad thing is, Wesley is just like you. It's more like he is your son than I am your daughter. I can't believe you." She paced back and forth, clenching her fists. "You think you can control everybody, but I am tired of it." She stopped in front of his desk and looked her father in the eye. "I want you to tell me the truth. Now. Do you know where Cody is? What about my children?"

"I don't want you to forget that I am your father and the head of this family. Don't think you can threaten me. I still run this family. And for your information, I had no direct hand in whatever your husband did. I gave him suggestions, but no specific instructions. He did whatever he did on his own. So, no, I do not know where they are. And it's best you leave it at that. Are you trying to ruin your life? This family?"

"You don't care about me or my life. All you care about is how it will look on you. What your friends will say. I am a grown woman now, and my life is my life." Marina pounded on the desk. Her breath came in spurts. She was so angry that she almost could not breathe.

"I know from experience what kind of trouble and grief this kind of thing can bring. You see, I have been there myself—"

"What are you saying?" Marina asked. She was now sobbing, tears running down her face and into her mouth.

Mario pulled some tissues from a box on his credenza and handed them to Marina. He walked over to the two leather seats in the sitting area inside his office, motioning for Marina to follow. "You were never supposed to know about this, but I had an affair after your brother was born. When he was little. I never meant for anything to come of it, but your mother was spending so much time with your brother, it just happened. I was so young and immature. There was no way I could expect to make a life with the woman, the two of us were too different. Your mother was who I had chosen, who my family had chosen. I couldn't have illegitimate children running around. So my father took care of it. In much the same way I advised Cody to."

Marina was not surprised. There were several times that the family had speculated about her father's indiscretions, but there had never been any proof of them.

"Lots of men have children out of wedlock, Daddy. What do you mean, you took care of it? What are you saying?"

"I'm saying that he did the same thing Wesley and I did. He made sure that the woman and her children could have a comfortable life without having to bother me again. He made sure she was no longer a temptation to me so your mother and I could go on and continue to build the life we'd planned. It was for the best. It got us through when we lost your brother. And guess what? My father was right, just as I am right now. Your mother was the best partner and support I could have imagined."

Marina flinched at the mention of the brother she barely remembered. He died before she was five years old. "But I am not you, Daddy. It's not the same." Her father thought he was comforting her, but as he talked, he was actually diminishing himself in Marina's eyes. He reached out to touch her, and she recoiled. She could not believe what she was hearing, but she could tell that he really believed what he was telling her. It was sick. Marina knew there was a point in every woman's life when she saw her parents as human and not infallible. Her father had always been perfect to her. Not anymore.

"Didn't you ever wonder what happened to them?"

"No. I couldn't. I made the best choice. What was the use of looking back? As for you, it would only cause you grief and stress, and heaven knows I do not need any more of that." He rubbed his hand across his furrowed brow. "Why don't you get yourself together and go home to your husband? Wesley loves you. And you need to let yourself love him. Trust me on that. A man needs his wife."

That was the last thing that Marina wanted to do. What about what a woman needed? She thought about it as she used the tissues her father gave her to wipe her eyes. Marina had no intention of being either a Stepford daughter or a Stepford wife. What was the sense of having your own mind if you didn't use it? And something was telling her that she needed to follow her heart. She didn't want to go home, and she didn't want to be part of this family anymore—as if she had a choice. However, Marina did not think her father or Wesley would let her just walk away—if that had been the case, they would have just cut her off when the incident with the twins had first come up. She needed a plan.

Marina remembered her mother and how tired she had been in the end, how time and her father had worn her down. She had always looked so much older than she really was, no matter how much makeup she had worn. No wonder. She'd had to live with an asshole for so many years, keeping it all inside. Marina knew now she couldn't do that; the past year had taken so much of her energy. There was no way she could live the same lies that her father had, just to keep other people happy. She couldn't be like him.

She cut her eyes at her father. "You are right, Dad. It is time for me to go now."

He smiled at her. "Let's not talk about this again, okay? I know what is best."

Marina nodded and walked out of the office. She was going to have a busy afternoon. Her father and Wesley might think they had her under control, but Marina knew she had to get away from them and do the right thing. If she didn't, she would be miserable the rest of her life.

Chapter 21

Cody skipped back to his building, oblivious to the people around him. It had been a long time since he had experienced anything or anyone like Claudia. It was wonderful to get to talk to someone with no one, like a husband, impeding the process. For as long as he could remember, there had been something in the way with Marina. First, it was the other people they went to school with. Then her parents, and finally her husband. He could not remember a time when they could just go to lunch without some kind of hassle, people protesting or pointing fingers at the mixed-race, forbidden couple. It was going to be different with Claudia.

He smiled, mumbling under his breath. A few passersby scurried out of his way. He thought about his father and how he would have described this feeling. His father could be crude, but sometimes he hit the nail right on the head. In the words of his father, Cody was "happier than a pig in shit."

Almost home. Cody stopped at the corner to make a call. He was so happy about Claudia's positive response that he was forgetting one of the things he preached about all the time. Romance was the key to any relationship. How often had he told Barry that very thing when he was trying to figure out how to keep his wife happy and off his back? He usually laughed in response. After all, Barry was the ladies' man between them, or had been. Cody could tell that Claudia definitely was a woman who liked romance. And she probably would appreciate it right about now. Almost all women did, right? He ordered up another nice bouquet for Claudia and sent them to her job. Might as well have her start her day feeling as good as he did, and what better than flowers to do the job? All of the other women in the office would make a big deal out of them, too. That would make her feel even that more special.

Claudia's reaction to him had been mild, but Cody knew she would eventually warm up. He understood that it was important for her to maintain appearances. She was that type of woman. It wouldn't do for her to jump up and down and scream that she would be delighted to go out with him at the top of her lungs. That was okay; he could tell from the way she looked at him that she wanted him too. And why not? Who could resist him? He was as charming as they came, right? He just couldn't help it. Cody flicked his phone closed, grinning again from ear to ear.

He whistled as he turned the corner into the narrow entryway to his building. Out of nowhere, he was snatched backwards, and his whistling was cut short by a large arm around his neck. Panic flashed through his mind; although he had never been mugged, he'd often imagined what it would feel like every time he heard about one on the news. He'd been so busy thinking about Claudia that he had not even seen it coming.

Things moved in slow motion. Something hard was jabbed into his side. He did not know if it was a gun or a knife, but he knew that he did not want to find out. All of the happiness and elation that he had been feeling moments earlier quickly disappeared.

"What do you want?" His throat constricted and his voice was hoarse, almost a whisper.

"You broke a promise." The voice that answered him was very deep and gruff.

Cody recognized the smell of cigar smoke. This was no ordinary thug.

"What are you talking about?" He asked the question, although he already knew the answer. He had thought the minor investigating he'd done about the twins had not been enough to raise any flags. Apparently he'd been wrong. Someone was very pissed off.

"You know. You have been probing around where you have no business. I am just a messenger, and I do not want to hurt you any more than is necessary." The man tightened his grip around Cody's neck. "Stop what you have been doing. Now. Understand me?"

Cody nodded and licked his now dry lips. Maybe someone would walk by and see his dilemma before things got out of hand. He hoped they would. Where was Barry when he needed him?

"Let sleeping dogs lie. You have a new, stress-free life that you should enjoy. You made a deal that can't be broken. Leave it that way."

The arm tightened around Cody's neck, and he gasped. He pulled at the arm to no avail; whoever was holding him was strong as hell, the type of person that Cody did not want to cross. He saw white things floating before his eyes, and his situation was suddenly funny. He realized that he was seeing stars. Although he wanted to laugh, he didn't;

he'd imagined that when you saw stars, they were really stars, not white specks floating around in your head.

In a sudden burst of energy, Cody whipped around, hoping to free himself. He hated the feeling of someone else being in control of his life. If he could just see who had a hold of him, he could size up his opponent. The man struggled, backing into a wall. Cody heard him grunt.

"Not a good idea," the man said, but he did not let go. He only tightened his grip on Cody's neck. Cody could feel the man's hot breath as he struggled to keep his hold.

Cody attempted to struggle once again, and the floaters came back. He blinked as they swam in front of him. For a split second, he saw Marina's face. It changed into Claudia's, then everything went white.

He woke up in his apartment. Barry was standing over him, talking on the phone. Cody could see that he looked concerned, but at first he could not make out any of the words that were spewing from his mouth. He tried to clear his throat to speak, but it hurt.

"I think he is waking up now. I will call you later." Barry hung up the phone and walked over to Cody.

Cody leaned forward, attempting to sit up. What had just happened? His head hurt, and he rubbed it. He'd had no idea that Wesley was that much of a crook, that he would call out his goons to come all the way to Texas to threaten him. This thug had done more than that—he had almost strangled him.

"Are you okay? I was worried for a while."

"Who were you talking to?" Cody rubbed his neck, wondering if he was bruised.

"My wife. She talked me through the whole thing. Told

me how to make sure you weren't dead or anything. You mind telling me what is going on? Why you were laying in the alley? Did you pass out from running or something?"

Cody contemplated telling Barry the truth but realized that was not much of an option. Barry would blow the whole thing out of proportion and feed him a whole bunch of "I told you sos." He was such a believer in justice that he would probably want Cody to call in the police. He already knew that wouldn't work; Wesley obviously had his own network of law enforcement wrapped around that pinky finger, and what would he tell them, anyway?

"I didn't pass out from running. You know I am in better shape than that. I think I was mugged. Did you find my wallet?"

Barry raised his hand. "Right here," he said. "You might want to check that everything is there. Were you being followed or anything? Did you see who did it?"

Cody's head pounded. "No, I didn't see or notice anything."

"That isn't like you. You are always so aware. Do you want to call the cops?"

"What good would that do? They didn't take anything."

"Except your dignity. You were assaulted." Barry raised his voice. He pointed at Cody for emphasis. "You always have to be so macho. What is that about? What does it get you? They could at least have someone watch your place for awhile. It's a good thing I came when I did. The guy downstairs helped me get you up here."

Cody stood up from the sofa and glanced at his watch. It was almost noon. He opened his wallet and checked it. Not one thing was out of place. "How long was I out? I am going to get fired for sure." He reached for the phone, thinking about what explanation could possibly be good enough this late in the day.

"Don't trip. I called in for you. Just so you know, you hurt yourself exercising. I almost took you to the hospital." Barry paced the room. "You seem awfully calm for someone who just got knocked on their ass. You mind telling me what you have gotten yourself into this time?" He knew it was something. Cody had always been into something; ever since they were teenagers, he'd walked just shy of the wrong side of the law or pissing off the wrong people. Barry did not expect it to be any different now that they were adults.

"What do you mean? I was mugged. Happens all the time."

"Umh-huh. Obviously. And knocked out, too."

Cody walked toward his kitchen, holding onto the counters for support. Why was Barry prying? "Don't you have somewhere to be? I'm going to have some coffee."

"Yes, it happens all the time in New York. This is Austin. And muggers generally don't take the time to pop open door locks along with mugging people. And even the dumb ones remember the wallet."

Cody paused with the coffee carafe in his hand. "My door was open?" he asked. He felt naked.

"Yes, it was. I couldn't see anything out of place in most of the apartment when I came in. I walked through to make sure there was no one in here before I dragged you inside. Then I saw your office. It is a mess. All of the stuff in your drawers is now on the floor. They were looking for something." Barry paused, eyeing his friend. "I feel like I am in a spy movie. You sure you don't know what is going on?"

Cody shook his head and moved to his office door. He

knew what they wanted. They were looking for any information he had found out about the twins. He hoped they'd gotten what they were looking for. He hadn't found much. Wesley had been too thorough. He looked around the room. Paper was everywhere. He shrugged, to no one in particular. A neat thug would have been too much to ask for.

Barry cleared his throat. "You sure you don't want to call the police?"

"Whatever it is, it is behind me now. I have to get to the office. I missed an important appointment." He tried to put on his best, innocent-looking poker face. "No police. No hospitals. I'll be fine. I'm made of tough stuff."

Hopefully, that would be enough for Barry. Besides, he did not think they would be back. He was tired of dead ends and had moved on to his new life. All that mess with Marina was behind him. He hoped.

Chapter 22

From the moment she'd sat down, Claudia had been working nonstop. She ran her hand across her furrowed brow. Instead of feeling tired, she still felt good in spite of the fact that she was worried about her discussion with her boss. Pam had been right; if you looked good, you would feel good. She smiled as she pressed the Send button on yet another e-mail. It sure helped that she had been fielding compliments all day. People really seemed to notice her change. It was almost as if the sharp, new look of her clothing had somehow changed her attitude too.

Her last meeting of the day started in twenty minutes. Claudia glanced at her watch. She had been waiting for a break so she could call Pam. She picked up the phone, humming as she dialed. Pam answered her cell phone almost immediately.

"Guess what? I think I have a secret admirer." Claudia's voice sounded almost like a teenager's again. "I got a beautiful bouquet of flowers again today and a note inside a lacquer box the other day. And you know how I am about boxes."

"Everyone does. They are all over your desk. And don't you sound chipper. Was the note signed? You must have some idea who is sending you this stuff."

"Nope. Nothing identifying. It is sort of exciting, but I have no clue whatsoever whom they could be from."

"Well, it looks like my little handiwork is already doing its job." Pam chuckled.

"Don't flatter yourself. I think I have something to do with it. And did you ever stop to think that whoever it is may have liked me the way I was before?"

"I'm sure you did have a little something to do with it. You told me yourself that the men were just swimming around you before, right?" She laughed. "Seriously, though. I would be careful. People are crazy nowadays. That stuff could be from some mad stalker or something. I mean, why can't whoever is sending the stuff just approach you upfront? This isn't high school. Did you ever think of that?"

Claudia pursed her lips. "Well, that would be less romantic." The thought of a lunatic stalking her had crossed her mind when she'd opened the first package, but she was not about to tell Pam that. This thing with Jackson was so negative, she just wanted to hold onto the idea that having a secret admirer was romantic, as opposed to dangerous. And she'd thought that Pam wanted to help her. She should be glad that Claudia was getting some attention for a change.

"I thought I was the pessimistic one. I think it is probably from someone I know. Maybe even Jackson. Maybe he misses me already." Claudia knew that couldn't possibly be true. It was pretty obvious that Jackson didn't miss her. He hadn't even called to check on her or anything.

Pam paused for a minute. "Maybe so. But listen, I got a sitter for tomorrow. We are going out like I promised. Be prepared and wear that other new outfit. The *new* Claudia is going to make her debut."

Claudia glanced at her watch. "You sure? I thought we could wait awhile before—"

"Before what? You grow old and crusty? You are not in mourning. He didn't die, he dumped you." She paused. "You better be ready. I will let you know where to meet me."

Pam anticipated Claudia's next words. She could tell her friend would try to find a way out if she could. "And no, you don't have a choice."

He might as well be dead, Claudia thought as she hung up the phone. She started to gather the things she would need for her meeting; her good mood was semi-squashed as a new sense of insecurity began to set in. She was just beginning to feel comfortable in her new self, and Pam was already parading her around town. It wasn't like she was desperate. At least not yet.

Being without a man hasn't been that bad so far, Claudia thought. Pam acted like being single was some type of high crime or something. It was true that Claudia had worked so much over the past few years that it had almost been like being without a man anyway. Sometimes she and Jackson had been like ships passing in the night, they'd seen each other in daylight so little. Even when they had been together, most of the time she'd just slept. That was annoying, she had to admit. And she was often a little peeved when Pam showed up bouncing around and all happy, the way only morning sex could make a woman feel. But all that had been her choice, so it wasn't Pam's fault, right?

Claudia glanced at her computer screen. A dozen new messages had come through to her e-mail inbox during the few minutes she'd talked with Pam on the phone. More than a few of them had a red Urgent flag next to them. Why was it that e-mail was supposed to be a step up from the old-fashioned inbox days, but she just felt like it made more work, at least for her.

Claudia sighed. She hated to go home and leave things hanging. That just made the next day more hectic. She was just going to have to check in remotely, on her notebook computer, later. If she let herself, she could stay in the office forever. But that was the old Claudia.

She stood up to go to her meeting with the area vice president, and her phone rang. Claudia glanced at the screen. Her home phone number was displayed, meaning that the call was from her mother.

What could she want? Against her better judgment, Claudia answered it.

"Yes, Ma. I was just on my way to a meeting. Is everything okay?"

"I wanted to talk to you for a minute."

Claudia noted the unusual nervousness in her mother's voice. "Could it wait until I got home?" she asked. She tried to hide the annoyance in her voice. "I'm really in a hurry."

"No, it can't, not really. I need to be truthful with you. I think you should know this."

Any other time, Claudia would pooh-pooh her mother, finding some way to put things off until it was more convenient for her. But something in her mother's voice told her that today was not the day to do that. She glanced at her watch again. She hated to be late. But more than that, she knew that if she didn't at least appear concerned about her mother's latest crisis, then she would have an impossible time once she finally got home. On top of whatever it was that was bothering her, her mother would whine forever about how Claudia couldn't find time for her. Although Henrietta usually appeared so composed, hysterics were not beyond her. "Okay," Claudia said. "Could I please have the short version?" She shifted her weight to the side, tapping her foot impatiently on the floor.

"I've left your father." Henrietta blurted the words out without pausing.

Claudia was speechless as she sat back down in her chair, dropping her portfolio folder onto the floor. Her mind whirled. She should have known that there was more to her mother's coming to visit than originally claimed. But what had happened? Her parents were the perfect couple, or so it seemed. They were supposed to grow old together.

"Are you there? I know this is a surprise, but I thought you should know. I wanted to tell you before he did."

"I'm here," Claudia said. "But I don't understand—"

"I didn't think you would. But I feel a lot better now that I have told you. I'm just glad that I don't have to hide it anymore."

Claudia rubbed her hand across her face in an attempt to recover from her shock. She had expected a lot of things from her mother, but never this. "Are you okay?" she asked.

"I'm fine. I tried to tell you before, but you were always so busy and I didn't want to bother you with my problems. We can talk about it more when you get home, okay?"

"I'm sorry, Ma. I had no idea." Claudia felt guilty for only worrying about her problems. It never occurred to her that her mother had come to visit her for some reason other than to meddle in her life. She hung up the phone, and her stomach churned with confusion. All her life she had looked to her parents as the model couple, even if her mother had been a little hard to get along with sometimes. Everything was crazy; it was almost as if her foundation was pulled out from under her. Her parents had been together forever. Theirs had been the candle by which she had measured all the relationships in her life. If they couldn't make it, then who could? There was certainly no hope for her.

Chapter 23

The hard edges of Mario's face returned as soon as his daughter left his office. He watched her go. If she only knew how much she'd grown to be like her mother. He'd never thought he would have to tell Marina the truth about the past, but she apparently had too much of her mother in her, God rest her soul. It was hard to believe that she'd never figured out that the woman who had raised her had not been her natural mother. It was even harder to believe that his wife had kept her promise about that until the day she died. She'd been reluctant at first; what woman wouldn't be reluctant to raise another woman's child? But she had wanted, more than life itself, to keep Mario happy. And in his mind, she should have. Hadn't he provided her with all the money she could have ever wanted and a comfortable home? That was one step up from the Chelsea housing project where she'd lived when they'd met.

He hadn't exactly told Marina the truth, but what good would that do now? Sure he'd had a child out of wedlock, but that child had been Marina. His father, God rest his soul, had made her biological mother disappear somewhere, and he'd taken that information with him to his grave. Mario had never asked how or why, she'd just gone away. He and his wife had raised Marina, and he still believed that had been the right thing to do, especially after they'd lost their own child. They'd never let her know the truth, and eventually, it had become too late to do so. They'd raised her in a seemingly normal, Italian American family. But his sins had been no worse than anyone else's. They had done what they had had to do.

Mario snatched the phone off the hook and called Wesley on his cell phone. Of all the days for him to pick to be visiting customers, he had to pick the day his wife would choose to be getting out of line. Wesley had a lot to learn yet. It was hard, but Mario was trying his best to teach it to him. Young men dismissed the old ways, but in his day, men had been men, not wimps who kowtowed to some woman.

"Wesley," he said. "We have a problem. You apparently screwed up again."

Wesley took in the gruff voice of his father-in-law. He was used to it. What had he done now? he wondered. He had already practically given the man blood. What more could he want?

"I'll fix whatever I need to, Pop," he answered.

"Well, you had better fix this, and fast. You apparently told Marina all the things we agreed were better left in the past. And she is pissed. I tried to calm her down, but she has a stubborn streak a mile long. You better put her back in her place before things get out of hand and more family secrets come tumbling out of the closet."

"She talked to you?" Wesley said.

"Talked to me? She was here, you imbecile. How could you let her get that angry at you and then get behind the wheel of a car? She wasn't rational. I had to humiliate myself and practically tell her about the unfortunate circumstances with her mother. I never wanted her to know that. The truth already drove my wife to an early death. I love Marina more than life itself. If she does anything crazy, I am holding you personally responsible. You understand me?"

Wesley understood all too well. He understood that by marrying Marina he had practically sold his soul to the devil. He had a father-in-law who was stuck in another era. If it weren't for the good lifestyle he could now provide for his own mother, he would think it was almost too much. Who would have known that any one family could have so many skeletons in the closet? "Pop, I'm sure she is just talking. What did she say she was going to do? I am sure we understood each other last time I had a talk with her."

"It's not what she said that worries me. It is what she didn't say. I think she might go looking for that boy. The one down in Austin. You take care of it and control your wife, you hear me? And I don't have to tell you that it all ends for you if you are not married to my daughter, right? The only reason you are where you are today is because I expect you to be able to keep my baby in the manner to which she is accustomed."

Wesley had heard those same words so many times now that he cringed. He didn't doubt Mario meant it. He was such a son of a bitch. Wesley wanted to tell him where he could go, but he didn't. He couldn't. "I hear you," he said. "I will make sure she can't go anywhere or do anything without asking me first, okay?"

Determination took on a new meaning for Marina. She carefully laid out her plan as she sat in traffic waiting to get back home. She was leaving. The past may have left too many scars for her and Cody to reconcile now, but she felt the need to at least talk to him and hear from his lips how he felt about her.

She arrived home, parked the car, and went straight to her bedroom, where she pulled a small suitcase from the closet. She wouldn't take much, just a few necessities. Marina knew that both Wesley and her father would be furious, but she would deal with them later. She could work through a lot of things, but she was not sure that she could continue to stomach Wesley's ruthlessness. And her father, well, either he would learn to accept her or he wouldn't. As strong as Mario was normally, it was hard for Marina to imagine him just accepting some edict from his father, one that kept him away from his own flesh and blood. Hadn't he even been curious about his children, she wondered?

As she gathered her things, she realized how much she let the two of them control her life. She even went to the supermarket on the day that Wesley had decreed as supermarket day. She almost had no life of her own. She had almost become one of the very women she looked down on at the yoga studio. She didn't brag about her husband or discuss his job as if it were her own, but she lived her life around his constantly and couldn't remember one time he'd made any real sacrifices for her in return.

She thought about her father. She was like him too. She rubbed her forehead. The realization hit her like a bullet between the eyes. It occurred to her that her father was so regimented and unyielding because he was afraid of not being successful, of failing. He didn't take chances on anything. He always ate the same things, went to work at the same time, and he expected everyone in his life to do the same. He didn't believe in taking chances. Just as it had been comfortable for Marina to sit back and let Wesley tell her what to do, it had been comfortable for her father to go about his business as usual too.

A chill ran down her spine, and she shivered, even though it was close to ninety degrees. If she never took any chances, she would never know. And that frightened Marina more than anything. Safe was nice, but it was boring. What if she had passed up the love of her life when she'd let Cody just walk away? She would probably never know now.

She zipped her bag closed and headed across the hall to the small room that served as her office. It was a small bedroom, really, but she used it to store whatever project she was working on at the time, as well as her computer. She opened her browser and typed in the address for the travel site she used occasionally. Normally, Wesley's secretary would book any travel she asked her to, but she doubted that would be a good move this time. The woman probably okayed everything with Wesley, and she doubted he would be approving this trip too fast.

Marina found a flight to Austin without too much difficulty. Her fingers flew across the keyboard as she typed in all of the required information. The faster she got there, the faster she could track down Cody. If she knew him as well as she thought she did, he would have taken Wesley's hush money, but that would only keep him quiet so long. He might have been able to walk away from her, but there was no way he could walk away from his own children. Chances were that he had been trying to track them down all along. Perhaps he had even found them already.

The browser stopped working, and Marina just stared at the message it displayed. There was a problem with her credit card. Although she knew the numbers to all of their cards by heart, she input it again. Perhaps she had inadvertently reversed two numbers or something. That had to be the answer; Wesley was a nut about paying the bills and paying them on time, so that could be the only answer. The same message appeared again. She tried one more time, and then switched cards, only to have the same thing happen.

What was going on? she wondered. She grabbed the nearby phone to call the credit card company. There had to be a mistake somewhere. The only thing was, she was in too much of a hurry for mistakes.

"I'm sorry, ma'am. Your account was closed earlier today."

"Excuse me. How could that be? I didn't close it," Marina said. She was indignant. Sometimes customer service people could be so incompetent. "Is there a supervisor I could talk to?"

"If you wish. But it says here that the account was closed by a Mr. Wesley Piscato. He was the primary account holder. Is that your husband? Perhaps you should talk with him."

Speechless, Marina hung up. She knew that she would get the same answer from all of the other credit card companies. Obviously her father had talked to Wesley already. They were playing hardball. She glanced at her watch. It was 2:00. Thank goodness she had heeded her mother's words. Marina could hear her mother's voice in her head almost as if she were standing right next to her. "A woman should have something of her own," she would say. In Marina's case, that something was a credit card. The only problem was that she kept it locked in a safe-deposit box at the bank. And she only had an hour to get there. Hopefully she would beat Wesley to the punch; perhaps he had not had time to close the bank accounts yet. No doubt that was his intention. If he hadn't, she would withdraw all of the money she could and open another account. She grabbed her bag and keys and ran down the steps to her car. The flight left at 11:00 P.M. She could make it if she made the bank. Perhaps she could have the last laugh for a change.

Chapter 24

The computer whirred and clicked, taking forever to power up. Cody ignored the whispers he heard from the other side of his cubicle. He knew they were talking about him. He could tell from the stares he'd gotten as he'd made his way to the cube. He tapped on the computer, as if the tapping would make it process faster. It continued to make working noises, seemingly oblivious to Cody's need for speed.

He dared one of them to say anything to him about getting to work as late as he had. He was there, wasn't he? How many other people would get mugged and still come to work? Probably not a one of them. He stretched, his back beginning to ache. Cody had not bothered to become friendly with any of his coworkers. When he'd first arrived, he'd still been too bitter in the aftermath of his ordeal with Wesley and Marina. Then he was always with Barry. He was glad that he hadn't; he did not need any extra people to explain to, but he knew that he was the odd man out in the office for it.

The Windows splash screen finally appeared, and Cody sighed as he clicked on the icon for his e-mail. If nothing else got done today, he was going to invite Claudia out to lunch. He didn't give a damn about the other fifty or so e-mails in his inbox. He knew none of them was important. At least they weren't to him.

He composed his e-mail carefully. He didn't want to seem too forward. That might scare her away. It took three tries for him to get the perfect wording, then, as an after-thought, he added his personal phone number. He reread it one last time and smiled. It was about time things went his way. She *would* call when she read this, he knew she would. He pressed Send.

The work day drifted by in a blur. The highlight of Cody's day had been sending that invitation to lunch to Claudia, but he waited in vain for her to answer it. He knew he was being impatient; Claudia was a busy woman and had a lot going on in her day. Still, he could not resist check-ing his mail every two minutes. Finally, he closed and locked his terminal and prepared to head home. The ball was in her court now, and there was nothing he could do to rush her into accepting his invitation to lunch. Some things couldn't be hurried. She would answer on her own time.

Cody stood up to leave just as he heard his supervisor call his name. He cringed. The less he had to talk to the man, the better. Cody knew that his boss never spoke to the people who worked for him unless they did something wrong. He rarely wasted his time congratulating people. He had made it clear when he'd started that he expected a good job from everyone.

Jason Marlboro was standing at the end of the row of cu-bicles, waiting like a cat ready to pounce. He was standing outside the row of supervisors' offices along the wall of the building. He ran his hand through his blond hair, pushing it back from his face. Cody swore that the man wore almost the same outfit every day; khaki pants and a striped shirt, but then again, almost everyone in Austin seemed to wear the same thing. The only thing that varied was the color of their security badge, depending on where they worked. Cody forced a wan smile. Jason signaled to him.

"Can I see you in my office, please?" Jason didn't wait for an answer. He turned and headed into his office, expecting Cody to follow automatically in response to his thinly disguised demand.

Cody closed and then opened his eyes. He mumbled under his breath. He was not really in the mood to be scolded; Jason had a habit of talking down to people as if he were their father. He could feel the other people still sitting in their cubes hold their breath as he walked by. They, too, knew that if Jason summoned you, you might as well be a dead man walking.

The small office was as neat as a pin, as Cody knew it would be. The company had a "clean desk policy" meant to protect sensitive information, and Jason seemed the type to follow every rule to the letter. Most people had at least one personal trinket or two displayed, but Jason did not even have a picture. No matter what time Cody came in, Jason was always already there, and no matter what time Cody left, he would leave the man at the office. It was almost as if he didn't have a life. It was that way with all of the management, or so it seemed. You wanted to get ahead, you worked long hours, period.

Jason was waiting for Cody and closed the door behind him as soon as he stepped through. He didn't sit.

"You wanted to see me?" Cody focused his gaze through the window. He scanned the remaining cars in the parking lot so he would not have to make eye contact with Jason.

Jason nodded. "I did. You doing alright?" he asked. "You have seemed so distracted lately, and I keep finding mistakes in your reports."

"I'm fine." Cody narrowed his eyes and wondered what the meeting was really about. Everybody made mistakes. That was the nature of data entry. In all his time at the company, he did not remember anyone ever getting a personal meeting about it.

"Good. I'm glad, just watch the mistakes. You have to remember that someone depends on our accuracy. Oh—and I expect you to take half a personal day for this morning. I heard about your mishap in the gym, but if you can't be here on time, there are lots of other people who would want your job. Understand?"

Cody pursed his lips. He wanted to give Jason a New York–style tongue-lashing, but didn't. He had to keep it together. He hadn't told them about his mugging, instead he'd let them go with Barry's story about passing out in the gym. He nodded.

Jason smiled and slapped Cody on the back. "Although, I do understand how those gym injuries go. Sometimes it can feel as if someone has got you by the neck, huh?" He laughed.

Cody's eyes widened in surprise. He was dumbfounded. How could he know? he wondered.

Jason steered him out of the office. "You just keep doing the things you are supposed to and you will go far around here. You might even be the lead soon."

Cody left, and Jason smiled to himself. Some people were so easily intimidated. He sat at his desk and dialed his cousin in New York.

"I just wanted to let you know that I had a meeting with

your quiet friend and let him know, in a gentle way, of
course, that he had to stay in his place or he would be with-
out a job."

"Good. We sent him another message, too. Probably not
as gentle as yours." Wesley's laugh was piercing, causing
Jason to pull the phone away from his ear.

"I gathered that much. The guy is going to have to wear
makeup or something to cover up the bruises your guy left
on his face. He didn't say a word about it, though. I would
bet he didn't even file a police report. I'm not surprised, he
is a generally quiet guy," Jason said.

"No doubt. I think we got him by the balls."

"My guess is you had him by the balls all along. They just
needed a little yanking, that's all. He is no fool. He is well
paid for not much work. Everybody likes to be comfortable.
You probably won't have too much more trouble from
him."

"We better not."

If it weren't for the soreness that was starting to set in,
Cody would have forgotten the mess he'd left in his
apartment. After Barry had left this morning, Cody had
rushed out to the office so quickly that he had not had
time to clean up. The morning's events rushed at him as
he looked at the paper that was still strewn around the
floor. It would take him hours to get everything back to-
gether. At first he'd thought that whoever had dumped
everything out of his desk might have been looking for
something, but now he wasn't so sure. There didn't seem
to be any rhyme or reason to what they had done. It looked
as if everything had just been dumped out and mixed up.
They might have just been trying to send him a message,

make him think that they were dangerous and could make a bigger mess of his life.

Cody remembered Wesley telling him that he would pay if he didn't stick to his end of the bargain, which meant he was not to snoop and he was to stay away from Marina forever. Wesley had always tried to act so refined and better than Cody, but Cody knew a thug was a thug. Wesley was just a thug with access to money, so he was able to have others do his dirty work. Cody couldn't for the life of him figure out how Jason was involved, though. He had not given any indication of that before. But Cody should have known that there would be someone around connected to Wesley. The way they had gotten him this job, with no questions asked, was almost too good to be true.

In retrospect, he wished he had stood up to Wesley, at least demanded to know were the children were. He still could not believe that Marina had agreed to have her kids just given away like she had. They were her own flesh and blood, for goodness' sake.

Cody moaned as he bent down to pick up a handful of papers. He rubbed his thigh. It ached terribly, although he could not remember being hit there. The whole altercation in the alley was almost a non-memory. Things had just happened so fast. Just as they had that day when he'd talked with Wesley; the reality that Marina wanted nothing to do with him had rushed at him like a tidal wave, and before he knew it, he had accepted Wesley's hush money. It had seemed the right thing to do at the time. His creditors were calling him almost daily, and Marina had thrown him away like a piece of stale bread. She was getting a new life with her big-shot husband, so why shouldn't he? And just when he thought he was moving on, the past had come back to haunt him.

Cody pulled out his file on the twins. They had missed it. It was very easy to do; the manila folder was almost empty, save for a few letters that were evidence of the dead ends he kept hitting. Wesley apparently knew a lot of people. Everywhere Cody looked, files had been conveniently "lost" and medical records had been altered. The nuns down in Puerto Rico wouldn't even talk. The times he had called there, everyone seemed so afraid at the mention of the name Piscato. But sounding afraid did not give one a leg to stand on in any court of law. Cody would have shrugged his shoulders if they weren't so sore.

Whoever that guy was, he'd sure put a hurting on him. Cody could still feel the strength of the massive arm around his neck. He had wasted his energy, and Wesley had wasted his money. There was no need for any of that; Cody was done before that. He tore the file in his hand into pieces. He had to think about his future, which he hoped was with Claudia. He knew that she would stand for none of this nonsense. She seemed like the kind of person that would be gone as soon as she sensed anything as shady as his past.

Cody tried to get the room as clean as possible; he dumped some things back into drawers and others into the trash. He did not want to think about it. There was no use dwelling on things he couldn't change. He just wanted to get to a hot bathtub and soak a long time. His back, his leg, and his shoulder all hurt like hell. When and if Claudia called, he wanted to walk with confidence on their date rather than limp around like he had been hit by a train. He smiled and imagined lying in a warm, soft feather bed with

Claudia massaging him, nursing him back to health. That was the most pleasant thought he'd had all afternoon.

The phone rang and Cody jumped, startled. He was so lost in his fantasies that he'd forgotten that he'd been waiting for Claudia to call. She had not answered his e-mail before he'd left the office.

"Cody?" she asked. Claudia's voice was music to his ears.

He cleared his throat, trying not to sound as groggy as he had when he first picked up the phone.

"Are you asleep already? I'm sorry I called so late, but I ended up staying at the office later than I expected."

"No problem. I wasn't sleeping. Actually, I've been doing some cleaning." He hoped that she was not able to hear his heart pounding inside his chest.

"I'm not going to keep you. If you are anything like me, you need your rest. I can't meet you for lunch, but would you mind getting together for coffee? We can meet after the morning run. How does that work for you?"

He opened his mouth to agree, but his legs and shoulder protested; there was no way he was going to be able to run in the morning. If he was this sore, it was just going to get worse before it got better.

"Well, I had planned on taking a different route. I like to mix up the workout so I don't get bored. But I can meet you at Bread Alone at about seven? Does that work?"

"That's fine. I'll see you then."

Cody hung up the phone. He didn't feel like cleaning anymore. All this stuff could wait. All of the day's events were pushed to the back of his mind. He headed to the bathroom to take his bath and think about some legitimate-sounding questions to ask her just in case they ran out of things to talk about. But he doubted they would.

Chapter 25

The morning rain caressed Claudia's face. She didn't bother to wipe it away, instead she let it collect in the hopes that it would eventually run down her cheeks. The warm wetness was refreshing. It helped her to stay cool. She ran alone this morning, as any sign of bad weather was usually enough to keep Pam indoors.

The trail was lined with gravel in most places, but there were a few patches of mud along the way. Claudia ran around them when she could. Otherwise, she charged right through them, the muscles in her legs tightening to keep her from slipping.

When it rained, the bikers stayed away and there were very few other runners. Claudia enjoyed her solitude and the deserted feeling in the park. It was almost as if she had the whole trail to herself.

It was about ten minutes before she was supposed to meet Cody. She slowed her run and headed toward Bread Alone, the coffee shop side of Shlotzsky's, a popular fast-food deli. Even if he didn't show, she could have a cup of coffee by herself and surf the net; her morning was free of meetings for a change. After her mother's news, she needed a break.

On her way into the restaurant, Claudia grabbed a napkin from the counter, using it to dry the rain from her face. She looked around. This time of day, the building would normally be brimming with people who exercised at the lake. The place was large and open, its wooden floors coated with polyurethane to produce a look that mimicked fresh wax without the labor. It was divided into two, almost distinct, restaurants joined in the middle by one large seating area.

One side was mainly for bread, coffee, and pastries, and it was lined with old-fashioned-looking glass counters with everything on display. The other side was set up more for lunch, and deli sandwiches were served there. Claudia inhaled, taking in the smell of breakfast mixed with lunch; the aroma from the pastries mingled with the smell from the ovens as they baked the bread that would serve as buns for sandwiches later.

The coffee bar side had a long line, mostly people dressed in some sort of exercise attire. The baristas behind the counter buzzed around as they tried to avoid bumping into each other in the small space. They barked coffee orders back and forth as their customers waited. Claudia didn't smile as she joined the line; although she loved the smells, this was not one of her favorite places to buy coffee. The coffee always tasted burnt no matter how she ordered it, and the delicious-looking pastries on display were too tempting to resist. The one thing they had going for them was the free internet access and the sleek-looking flat-panel screens in the computer area. Plus it was a good, very public, place to meet Cody, perfect for an informal business meeting.

Claudia touched the brim of the baseball cap that she

pulled over her head, but she did not remove it. She barely had enough hair left to make a ponytail, and she knew that if she took it off, her hair would stand all over her head like Buckwheat from the Little Rascals. Hopefully the cap had kept her hair dry enough so that she wouldn't have to do too much work before getting dressed. It had been a few days, but the verdict was still out on the hair. So far it had only added more work to Claudia's morning ritual. Her ponytail might not have been particularly stylish, but it sure had been functional.

Claudia removed cash from her waist pack to pay for the latte she ordered and looked around the restaurant for Cody. He was probably still out on his run, if he was running today, she thought. If he was as persistent in his running as he was in flirting with her, he would not let a little rain deter him from his exercise.

There were two entrances, one on each side, and Claudia wanted a clear view of each. She chose a seat by the window so she could get a view of the room, wanting to see him easily when he came in.

When she'd finally read the message from Cody last night, Claudia had hesitated to call him. She knew full well that the meeting he requested had more to do with him wanting to get to know her than it did with him wanting her mentorship. How many people would flirt that hard with someone they wanted business advice from? And didn't he work in data entry? She had never even worked in his department, so what could she possibly help him with? She might be able to tell him about some of the company politics, but that was about it. And he really didn't need her for that, she thought. He seemed intelligent, and finding out who one shouldn't piss off was not really rocket science at Pittsford. All of the gossip was pretty much out on the table.

Claudia found the attention he gave her flattering. She smiled as she thought about it. Every woman needed to know that she was just a little attractive to someone, and she definitely appreciated knowing that right now.

Pam was pushing her to find a new man, but Cody really wasn't a possibility. He was at least three to four years younger than she was, and for a man in his twenties, that was not good. Younger men needed to ripen just a little bit more. And the biggest minus for Claudia was that they worked at the same place. That meant he was off limits in a big way.

She sipped her latte, licking the stray foam from the outside of the paper cup. Cody might be technically untouchable, but he did have a nice physique. Claudia began to imagine his arms wrapped around her and her face buried in his neck, taking in that Egyptian Musk she'd smelled that first time in the supermarket, but she stopped herself. Her hormones were obviously galloping free. They could produce chaos if she let them. Still, it wouldn't hurt to get to know him. Pam was right; the only way she was going to move on with her life was if she forced herself to go out and meet people. It didn't make any sense for her to sit around and mourn the loss of a dead relationship, especially a dead relationship where there had been very little sex lately.

The good part of meeting with Cody was that he probably had other attractive and older, available friends. She just hoped he left those phony lines at home and relaxed. The two times she had talked with him in person, he'd seemed so on edge, almost as if he had been trying too hard. And he seemed a little too old to be uncomfortable around women. He wasn't *that* young.

A hand on her shoulder caused her to jump, almost spilling her hot coffee. Claudia had been so lost in thought as she'd stared out the window and into the rain that she had not seen Cody come in as she'd planned.

"Hey, I didn't mean to scare you. I'm sorry I'm late. My pace was a little slow today." Cody slid into the chair opposite Claudia.

"No problem," Claudia said. She wiped the drop of coffee she felt on her bottom lip. Cody's all-black running outfit appeared slightly wet from the rain, and he walked with a limp. Her throat was suddenly dry. "I cleared my morning. I needed a break. I have had a very hard week. Did you pull something in your run?"

"I'm sorry about your week." He reached down and rubbed his leg. "No, I think I caught a cramp. It will be okay." Cody smiled and looked directly into Claudia's deep, brown eyes. They were the most beautiful eyes he had seen in a long time. Rebound or no, he intended to work her vulnerability to his advantage. "You are a busy woman, so I won't keep you long. I know how precious a few moments to yourself can be." He cleared his throat, ready to launch into the introduction he had rehearsed.

Claudia tried to listen intently as he talked, but her mind kept drifting away. She could not look past how cute Cody was. Other than the few scratches on his face, his butterscotch skin was flawless. She heard him say something about her being the best at what she did. Claudia's stomach flip-flopped. And something else about a broader picture. She tried harder to concentrate. He wasn't the kind of cute she needed to get herself in trouble over. A romance between them would not look good. He worked down in data entry, for goodness' sake. She could not date down. Damn those hormones.

"Don't worry about the time," she said. "It's no problem, really. How long have you been with the company?"

"Not long. I moved here a little over a year ago from New York."

"That's not long at all. It's never too early to start planning out your career. New York, huh? That is one of my favorite cities. All the museums. One of my favorite places to visit."

"I hear you, but you wouldn't want to live there, right?" Cody chuckled and took a sip of his water. "I miss that. But Austin has its own flavor. Some of the local galleries are very nice."

"Are you comparing the galleries here to the Met? You are kidding, right?"

"No, you obviously know there is no comparison. But I will say that I have a thing for admiring the beautiful." Cody smiled sheepishly and looked down at the table. He fiddled with his water bottle, beginning to tear the label.

The room seemed suddenly quieter. Claudia felt her face get hot in response to his comment. She cleared her throat and placed her right hand over her left in an attempt to cover the engagement ring that was no longer there. *What the hell is going on?* she wondered. *It isn't like I'm some schoolgirl or something.* It was amazing how your body could betray you when it was deprived, as she felt. She cursed under her breath, then she realized that what she was doing was what any other normal female would do. She was reacting to flattering comments from an attractive man.

"Admiring the beautiful, huh?" It was her turn to chuckle. "I appreciate fine art myself. I'm pretty partial to a lot of the impressionist art. I just don't have enough time to go and enjoy it as much as I would like."

Cody nodded. "I can understand that. It is so easy to just let life happen, and we get away from the things we love. We should always make time, even if it is just a little bit, to get away and enjoy some of the things you want to do without ignoring what you need to do. At least that is what I do." Cody lowered his voice, sitting forward in his chair. "For instance, today I found a few minutes to arrange this meeting with you when I really need to be back in the office."

"Sort of killing two birds with one stone, huh?"

"Something like that, yes," he said.

"Do you always do what you want?" Claudia's face felt flushed. She couldn't help herself. Her own flirt mechanism was on autopilot. Her nose flared as she spoke.

"No. But I am the one picking *your* brain. Do you never do what you want?" Cody smiled. He could tell that he was getting to her.

Claudia smiled a small, quick smile and then stopped. She drank the last of the coffee before answering. "I don't know about that. I never thought about it much." She glanced out the window. That was probably the truest thing she had said all week. She always did the things she was supposed to first. "This rain is letting up. I better get moving or I will never get to the office. Let me know if you need any specific advice, okay? I think you will be just fine at Pittsford. You seem to be a man who knows what he wants. You'll fit right in."

She smoothed her clothes as she stood up to leave. Cody rose too, wanting to be a perfect gentleman.

"Thank you for your time. I hope I didn't offend you in any way."

Claudia shook her head, blinking her eyes slowly, almost seductively. "I don't know how helpful I was. We hardly talked about business at all." She picked up her car keys. "And no, you didn't offend me. I actually think that was good for a first meeting. It is a good idea for us to get to know a little bit about one another, how we do things. How else am I supposed to give you advice?"

"I guess you are right about that. You *are* the expert."

Claudia pushed her chair away from the table and stood up. "But it is just getting to know each other, okay? I mean, that extra attention is flattering, but we work together, know what I mean?"

He nodded, searching her face.

Hopefully, he was not able to tell how embarrassed she was. She could not believe how much she had flirted with the man when that hadn't been the original purpose of the meeting at all. At least not on her end, it hadn't been. She waved good-bye as she walked past the window to her car.

Cody was still sitting there watching her. Claudia was suddenly self-conscious, taking extra care to walk slowly so her butt wouldn't jiggle too much with him watching. What had her life come to? she wondered as she started her car. Although a romance with someone who worked at the same place was something she would normally never consider, her body was making a strong case on behalf of Mr. Cody. Maybe it had turned over a new leaf too.

Chapter 26

Any other day, Marina would walk or take the bus just because she knew that Wesley wanted her to take a car. Not today. She was already standing outside waiting when the black sedan from the livery service arrived, and she threw her small bag into the back of the sedan with her. The driver didn't even have a chance to get out, if he was so inclined. Marina was glad to see that the driver was not one she knew, and even more thankful that he was not in a talkative mood. She closed the door herself and prayed for minimal traffic on Queens Boulevard. It was getting toward rush hour, and things could get sticky.

Marina had done her banking at the same bank as long as she could remember, but never had she been so happy to see the round building come into view. A sense of relief washed over her as she jumped from the car and sprinted into the building. Hers was probably one of the few banks that still shut their doors at 3:00 P.M. instead of staying open until five.

Many of the longtime workers knew her well, and now they knew Wesley too. She had added his name to all her accounts when they'd married. She could kick herself for that now. Thank goodness she had one credit card, even though she only had that through a fluke.

It was an airline Visa; she had applied for it because they had offered her extra airline miles when she had. She had only used the darn thing one time and then decided to keep it. Thank goodness for small miracles.

The bank was not as crowded as Marina expected. She tapped her foot impatiently as she waited to be led back to her safe-deposit box. Finally the vault attendant called her name, and Marina stood up fast. She followed on the man's heels so closely that he kept looking over his shoulder. Marina didn't care. She was on a mission.

The short hall seemed longer than it ever had. Although the front of the bank had recently been redone, this area had not. The old-fashioned green paint on the walls made the hallways seem narrow and creepy. The fluorescent lighting was dim, and it smelled of ink. The only thing back here was the safe-deposit box area. Marina had walked this hall many times; as a child she would come here often with her father.

An even more old-fashioned metal door beckoned the way. As usual, it was left open during business hours. A glass security door had been installed just outside the room since the last time Marina visited. She jiggled impatiently as she waited for her escort to swipe his identification badge in the scanner so they could get through.

Where was his sense of urgency? He checked her driver's license and made her sign in as he should, but he moved slower than pancake syrup that had been stored in the freezer. The flight she planned to catch did not leave until eleven, but Marina still had to purchase the tickets before all the seats were gone. She did not want to chance being on standby; her mind was made up—she was getting the hell out of New York and away from Wesley and his madness.

Tonight. If she waited or planned any longer, she might change her mind, and there was no telling how long it would be before Wesley realized what was happening.

She thought about him coming home. He would probably realize first that he did not smell any cooking. His stomach would be the first thing that would send him in search of her. He would probably call her on her cell or storm through the house looking for her. Dinner on the table was one of the rules he must have learned from her father. Her mother might have stayed in her housedress all day, but come three o'clock, she would bathe, perfume herself, fix her hair, and get dressed. After she was dressed, she would tie on an apron that had been starched and pressed, and proceed to cook dinner. No matter what time her father had come in, dinner had been hot and waiting. Catherine had been a regular June Cleaver.

Marina had figured out early in her marriage that Wesley had to eat three times a day, whether he was hungry or not, and he expected her to make it happen. Feeding him was supposed to be the highlight of the day.

The man that led her into the vault cleared his throat as they stood in the small room. The room had the same industrial green walls as the hallway. The smell that Marina thought was ink earlier was stronger here; she recognized that it was some type of strong cleaner, probably something they used to clean the fingerprints from the boxes. They all looked as if they had been buffed to a high shine. The room had boxes on three walls. There was a large, plain clock on the fourth. It was getting close to three o'clock.

She removed the contents of her box and dropped it into her waiting Louis Vuitton bag. She smiled at him as he looked at her and then looked away. Her hands trembled as she shut the box and jiggled the key. The small room seemed extra quiet as she struggled. Marina paused, closing and then reopening her eyes as she willed herself to relax.

"Everything okay, ma'am?" he asked. He tapped his foot on the floor behind Marina. His wing-tipped shoes hit the old stone floor with the regularity of a metronome, and the noise made her acutely aware of how little time she had.

"Yes, everything is fine," she said as she gave one last tug on her key. It came out of the hole so quickly that she was thrown off balance and almost bumped into him.

He steadied her, and sweat began to run from her underarms and down her sides beneath her clothes. "I need to see a manager. I know you will be closing in a few minutes, but I need to open an account."

"They may be all tied up. Would it be possible for you to come back tomorrow?" His face strained and his nose flared as he glanced at the clock over Marina's shoulder.

She spun around, squinting to make out the name on the man's nametag. "No, *James*, it would not be possible. How would you know that they were all tied up if you never even bothered to ask?" Marina forced a smile, looking more like she was baring her teeth like a wolf before the kill. "I need to see a manager *today*, and it would behoove you to make it happen. You just tell them that Marina Chivers Piscato wants to open another account right now. If that is a problem, we can take our business elsewhere. All of it."

James's businesslike smile was replaced by a look of frustration. She knew that she was providing a less-than-perfect ending to his day, but she didn't care. She watched him switch his slim hips as he walked away. She was through with pleasing other people, at least for now. There were some things she needed to make happen.

*   *   *

Just as she thought, opening the new account was no prob-
lem. The teller who'd led her into the vault scurried away
when he saw that she meant business. They even locked the
door with her inside the bank filling out the final paper-
work. They wanted her business. No wonder her family
had banked here for so long.

Thank goodness that Wesley had not thought to remove
her from the accounts. For the first time in awhile, Marina
was glad she was her father's daughter. He had taught her
to think fast, be quick on her feet. Still, she didn't suck Wes-
ley dry. She left a few thousand dollars in the account, tak-
ing enough for her to get away with without raising too
many red flags. She might even decide to stay permanently
gone. And Wesley might decide to do some banking from
home tonight. A totally empty account might send up a red
flag before she could get her foot good and out of the door.

The livery driver was still waiting. The car was running,
right beside a hydrant in front of the bank. The driver was
looking down and smoking when Marina approached. He
spotted her and dropped his cigarette, stamping it out with
his foot.

Marina gripped her receipts in her hand and hopped
into the car without speaking. The driver walked around to
the other side, looking at her quizzically as he waited for
direction.

"Newark airport." Marina rechecked the receipts, fold-
ing them carefully. They were her ticket to a new life.

"Whoa, I'm not sure I'm authorized to cross the bridge.
No one said I would be going to Jersey today."

"I'll tip you big. It's covered."

"I should call—"

"Don't." She gripped the back of the front seat. The last thing she needed was for the dispatcher to call around the company to get authorization for a trip no one was cleared to take. She should have called a regular cab, but it was too late for that now. For whatever reason, there were more flights out of Newark than any of the other area airports. She lowered her voice. "I'll pay cash."

"I'll need round-trip tolls."

Marina nodded.

He shrugged and put the car in gear. "Going on a trip?" Marina glared at him but did not answer. What kind of asshole question was that? Wasn't that obvious? He'd waited for her for over twenty minutes; she knew that by now he would have seen her bag in the backseat. She folded her arms and stared out the window. She didn't have to answer to him. After today, she wouldn't have to answer to anyone else, either.

Chapter 27

If he could have danced, Cody would have. No way could he have imagined that Claudia would have reacted to him the way she had. Her relationship must have really been bad, because she had soaked up his compliments like a sponge. She was obviously starving for attention. This was going to be easier than he'd thought.

After she left Bread Alone, he sat in his chair and watched her walk to her car. She was beautiful and didn't even know it. That was rare nowadays. Maybe that was why he had not been particularly interested in anyone he'd met lately. Heaven knows how many women Barry had thrown at him over the past year. It wasn't that they hadn't been attractive, but nothing had clicked, there had been none of that "magic" they talked about on television so much. The women were all empty inside, lacking in substance, and that just didn't do it for him. But it was all different with Claudia. He had known the first day he'd seen her.

He had not been at Pittsford all that long, maybe a few weeks at most. Claudia had come to the main building for a meeting. He'd already been in the elevator when the door had opened, and there she'd been. He remembered exactly what she had worn that day, a dark gray single-breasted

pantsuit that fit her perfectly, very tailored and under-
stated. Her hair had been smoothed back in waves, coming
together in a neat chignon at the base of her head. She'd
smelled wonderful, as if she had just stepped from a long
shower. Cody had tried to inhale her scent in the elevator,
like it had been a drug he couldn't get enough of. It had
been like magic. And it had only gotten better from there.
He had been watching her ever since, doing what many
men never take the time to do; learning about his woman.

He'd found out about her habits, what she liked and
where she liked to go. He'd even gone to the supermarket
and smelled as many soaps as he could to try to found out
which one she'd smelled like that day. The more he found
out about her, the more he knew that she was the one for
him. And now it appeared that she liked him too, just as
he'd thought she would.

Cody hoped he'd made as good of an impression as he
thought he had. His insides got so tied up sometimes when
he was excited; he knew he could say goofy things. He was
just thankful that although she had noticed his limp, she
hadn't questioned him about it, or the scratches on his face.
It wasn't like she could have missed them, but she was too
polite to say anything. He noticed every little thing she had
changed about her. Once they were together, he was going
to have to talk to her about letting her hair grow back. He
couldn't understand why she had changed it in the first
place; there was no need to fix what wasn't broken.

The rain stopped as soon as he stepped outside. The heat
began to creep up slowly but steadily, and the air became
gradually heavier as he walked. Full of energy, Cody
started his walk back home. The soreness in his leg seemed
to dissipate a little. He crossed the street and flipped open

his phone. The message icon was lit. He scrolled through his call log and saw that Barry had called. Given the events of the past two days, Cody was surprised that he had only called once this morning. He pressed redial.

Barry picked up on the first ring. "Where have you been? I have been worried sick."

His voice had a familiar whining quality to it. Cody was used to him sounding that way when he was upset. When they were younger, people would tease him about it. "Calm down," he said. "I was out getting some exercise. I'm fine."

"Exercise? What is wrong with you, man? You were mugged, for goodness' sake. Head injuries are serious. You shouldn't be doing that by yourself. Something could happen. What if—"

"What if nothing." Cody rolled his eyes. "Why is it necessary to be so melodramatic? I needed to run off some soreness. And it wasn't a head injury. I was choked. I think."

"See, you can't even remember." Barry paused. "You do sound okay. Better than I have heard you sound in awhile. You going in to work this morning? The wife thinks I should come by and check on you."

"Yes, I am working. I have some things I want to share with you anyway. Why don't you come on by? I have about an hour before I leave." Cody just should not keep the news of Claudia totally to himself any more. He had only shared scant details with Barry, but Barry's advice on making her feel like an expert seemed to have worked. He wanted to share his good news.

"I'll meet you at your door." Cody closed his phone and quickened his pace. It wouldn't take Barry long to get there. That was one of the primary reasons he had chosen his apartment; it was virtually downtown, not really far from anything in Austin. Sure, Barry had been right when he'd said that it wasn't the safest neighborhood in the world, but he was a single man and safety wasn't all that important.

Hopefully Wesley and his thug friend were done with him and there would be no more surprise visits. Still, Cody couldn't be too careful. It wouldn't hurt to have Barry as backup just in case. He couldn't very well step to Claudia all beat up, now could he?

"So, tell me, what is the glow all about?" As promised, Barry was there, waiting, when Cody rounded the corner.

"Glow?" Cody broke into a grin, partly from relief and partly from the lingering happiness over his better-than-expected meeting with Claudia. He looked around the narrow entryway carefully.

"Don't get dumb on me. You know what I mean. You look too happy for someone who just got the shit kicked out of him just yesterday."

Cody sighed. Every time Barry brought it up, it sounded worse and worse. "Just come on." He put the key in his lock to open the door. "The way I see it, I only have two choices. Moan about it and tell everyone what happened, or move on. I have obviously chosen the latter."

He had made reasonable headway in cleaning up, and most of the apartment was back to normal. Cody had even removed the thin layer of dust that had been collecting for weeks. Barry followed him in and visually spot-checked for things out of place. Cody didn't understand why he tried to take inventory of his life almost every time they were together.

"Looks like you been doing some spring-cleaning. That

is good to see. Do I sense the old anal-retentive Cody com-
ing back? The one that used to iron his underwear?" He ran
his index finger across the top of the coffee table like a Jew-
ish grandmother visiting soon-to-be in-laws.

"Shut up. I had to pick things up anyway, so it was as
good a time as any to get rid of some of the dust."

"And some of the pictures too? I see you got rid of the
pictures of you-know-who." Barry whispered, as if her
name were a code word.

"You don't have to act all weird. I am over her. *You* are
the one who said I should move on with my life." Cody no-
ticed the voice messaging light blinking on his phone. He
pressed speaker phone to dial his voice mail.

"Do I sense that things are looking up with that new
woman in your life? The one you told me about? I was right
all along, wasn't I?" Barry danced back and forth like a kid
about to get some much-wanted candy.

Although he wanted to share his news with Barry, Cody
felt a twinge of annoyance creeping into the pit of his stom-
ach. Why did Barry have to be so annoying? Couldn't he let
things just come out normally and gradually? He was al-
ways walking on eggshells, as if Cody might break any
minute. Now he constantly prodded with question after
question, like Cody was still a child. "I'll tell you about
things when the time is right."

Cody picked up the pen he kept by the phone to take
messages. He stood, poised to write. He held up his index
finger of his other hand; if he didn't, Barry would just yam-
mer on, right through his messages. And he was not about
to let him steal his thunder; he would tell him more about
Claudia on his own time.

They both paused as the messages played. The first three

were hang ups. Whoever it was had left no message. The fourth was someone trying to sell him a newspaper.

Cody put the pen down and frowned. He scrolled the caller ID. He could not tell where the three hang-up calls had come from. Caller ID had gotten so much better in the past few months; usually, even if there was no name, there would at least be a number. He hoped it wasn't more of Wesley and his crew. He had heard his message, loud and clear.

"Well, someone didn't want to leave a message," Barry said.

"I guess." Cody looked at the floor, away from Barry. He was concerned about the calls, but Barry didn't need to know that. Cody forced himself to grin. He sat on the couch and prepared to fill Barry in about the new woman in his life.

The shower was rejuvenating. Cody stayed in the hot water longer than normal, hoping to remove the last remaining traces of soreness from his back and legs. When he was done, the walls of his bedroom dripped with water, and the bed felt slightly wet. He had left the door open and humidified the whole apartment. He dried himself, halfway expecting his neighbors to complain that he had used up all of the hot water in the building, but he didn't care. He was still feeling good from recounting the details of his meeting with Claudia.

He grabbed his things and headed out to work, but he paused to check his messages again. Something about the hang-up calls made him uneasy. He replayed the messages, straining to discern any details or noises in the background. Wesley would not catch him by surprise again—he would make sure he took the time to take in everything that could possibly give him any clues. Cody used to laugh at his father and the way he would make jokes at least twice a week about being alert. "Be alert," he would say. "The world needs more lerts." He would guffaw loudly every time, like it was the first time he'd ever made that tired statement. He might have sounded like a bad greeting card, but there was something to what he said. If Cody had paid attention, maybe he wouldn't be nursing his wounds now.

He strained to hear what he could in the empty messages. The phone was pressed against his ear so tightly that it created a suction cup. In the end, the only thing he knew was that whoever was calling was in a very noisy place.

It could very well be that the calls were honest wrong numbers. All the hairs on the back of Cody's neck stood at attention. Maybe he was being paranoid now, he thought. Somehow, he didn't think so.

Chapter 28

Airport security was a madhouse. Marina shook her head and tried her best not to be angry at the airport screeners; it wasn't their fault. She almost had to strip, but she waited patiently, barefoot, as they scanned her shoes. Normally, she would have been concerned about the sanitary conditions of the floor they had her standing on, but today that was the least of her worries.

The young man who was doing the scanning looked barely out of high school. He puffed up his chest in his crisp, newly ironed uniform, handing Marina her shoes. "Here you go, ma'am," he said. Marina could not tell if he was winking at her of if he had something in his eye.

She nodded, wanting to tell him that this was not the best place to pick up women, especially after he had annoyed her by searching every crevice of her carry-on bag, but she didn't. Instead she accepted her shoes silently and slid them onto her feet as if she were grateful instead of annoyed. Truth be told, Marina just wanted to get to her gate so she could sit down.

It would be hours before she would be able to board her plane. She didn't care. She was going to sit and wait as she tried to make heads or tails of the information she had taken from Wesley's office. Not actually expecting anything meaningful to still be there, she'd grabbed a whole file from his "forbidden" office. Somewhere in the file was the information she was looking for. Even if it was a small tidbit that could lead her in the right direction, that would be better than her showing up in a town she had never been to with no idea what she was going to do next.

The gate was crowded. The small waiting area brimmed over with weary-looking travelers, most of them dressed in business attire. Marina glanced at the monitors. One of the flights waiting to leave the area had been cancelled. She passed by crowds of people with stoic faces, some reading, others staring at the airport news blaring on the televisions suspended overhead.

Most of the gray seats were full. A few people took up more than one. Several were filled by someone else's bags. No one moved or noticed her as she tripped over a briefcase. Finally, Marina found a seat in the corner that no one wanted; the only other people in the row were a mother and her three small children. Two of them climbed over the seats, while the other crawled on the floor. The mother looked haggard and drawn, her face pinched as she reached for the smallest child to stop her from putting something in her mouth. She made eye contact with Marina, giving her a smile as she shooed her children out of the way.

Marina slid into the seat just as her phone rang. Her heartbeat quickened and she froze, almost surprised that it had taken Wesley this long to call her. She contemplated not answering, but at the last minute she pressed the button, her voice tentative.

"Yes."

"Hey. I just got here. Where are you?"

Marina could not sense any anger in his voice, not yet. "Um, running some errands." She strained to suppress the bitterness she felt welling up in the pit of her stomach. How dare he act like nothing at all was wrong? "I'll be home soon. I hope you don't mind, but I didn't cook. I'll pick something up on the way."

"That's fine." Wesley paused, his voice uncertain. "Marina? We are going to be okay if you let us. It really is all for the best."

Marina's mouth dropped open and then closed. She could not believe the condescension that was coming from him. What he wanted was the best for him, but she refused to live a lie any longer. He must think she was an idiot. "Okay. No problem, dear. I will be a little while. I had to go to the bank to get cash. For some reason, my credit card wouldn't work." She sweetened her voice. "But I will pick up your favorite on the way back. And with traffic so bad, I might be another hour and a half or so. Think you could wait that long?"

He would wait. That should give her some time before he figured it out. Hopefully he wouldn't be able to track down the driver she'd used. She sighed with relief. She had really taken a chance, but now she had her ticket and boarding pass in hand. With the new security procedures in the airport, even if Wesley did track her down, he would not be able to get to the gate without buying a ticket himself. A smile crossed Marina's face. She was on to the next challenge. Taking charge was feeling good.

Marina sifted through the information in the manila folder. It was thick and seemed mostly to be a collection of unrelated receipts, banking information, with a few other miscellaneous papers thrown in. Some of the papers were

crumpled, as if they had first been wadded up to be dis-
carded, and then flattened again as an afterthought. As she
studied the various papers, her phone rang again. The air-
port noises faded into the background. She didn't answer
or bother to glance at the caller ID, and she left her seat only
once to use the bathroom. Marina knew that it would only
be a matter of time before Wesley figured out that her story
about being late was only a delay tactic. He would, at the
very least, make one good attempt at getting her to come
back home, but chances are he would do more. If he knew
where she was headed, he would probably do much more.

Toward the back of the folder, the remains of a Post-it
note caught her eye. Like the papers it was sandwiched be-
tween, it was crumpled as if it had been crumbled into a
ball or, at the very least, folded tightly. There were numbers
written on it. They were smudged and barely legible. Ma-
rina stared at it, and chills ran down her spine. This num-
ber had to be a phone number.

She turned it over in her hand. There was no name, and
no other information. Without hesitating, she dug her
phone out of her purse and flipped it open. Her hands
trembled. She had to dial the number several times before
she got the phone to connect. Her chest rose and fell, almost
as if she were panting as she listened to the distant-
sounding ring. What would she say when the person an-
swered? What if it was Cody's number? That would be too
good to be true.

The calls dropped the first two times before anyone
could answer. Marina's stomach was in knots. Just when
you needed it, electronics failed you every time. Finally, the
third time, an answering machine picked up. Marina lis-
tened intently, but it was not Cody's voice; instead, all she

heard was a generic electronic voice announcing the number, but she would not be convinced. She had to know for sure. She would have to try again later. That piece of paper was the only thing in the file that she could make sense of. If it wasn't Cody's number, maybe it was someone that could lead her to him. It had to be a clue.

Chapter 29

The heels of Henrietta's shoes echoed on the tiled entry-way floor. Claudia barely looked up from her portable computer. She sat in the living room, finishing her e-mails from work. This was the first time she had seen her mother in almost forty-eight hours. Claudia bit her lip; her mother had a lot of nerve to drop a bombshell like she had and then virtually disappear, coming and going at all hours of the night.

"Well, don't you look nice? Is there a special occasion? You must have a date with Jackson."

"Hello to you, too, Ma. And you sound like a broken record." Claudia snapped the top of the computer closed. "Where have you been? I have been worried about you. I didn't know if you had gone home or what."

Henrietta stepped into the living room and plopped into a chair opposite Claudia, kicking off her shoes. She reached down to rub her instep. "Shopping is so hard on the feet," she said.

"It wouldn't be if you wore sensible shoes to do it in." Claudia shook her head. She could not believe her mother. "You look like you are dressed for a day at the office and you haven't worked for years."

"I beg your pardon. I have worked every day of the past thirty or so years that I have been married to your father. Every damn day. Being a wife is work, thank you very much." Her nose flared, and she set her feet down hard on the floor.

Claudia jumped at her mother's outburst. She was obviously more than just a bit touchy.

"So, where are you and Jackson going?" Henrietta asked.

"Since we are all being so candid about everything, you might as well know now. Jackson and I broke up. I'm going out with Pam." Claudia looked down at her nails, pretending to pick at them. The silence between them grew heavy.

"I see. So is that what this new look is about? When did this happen? You could have told me about it instead of having me asking about a wedding that isn't going to happen like an idiot. What did you do?"

It was obvious to Claudia that her mother didn't get it. "Yeah, I could have told you. Like you could have told me about you and Dad. I could ask you the same question." Claudia stood up, clenching her fists. "Why must you always assume that things are my fault? It would be nice for you to take my side for a change."

"There is no need for you to raise your voice. I'm sorry. You are right. But you could have told me. I would have understood. And I was going to tell you about your father in due time."

Claudia folded her arms, glaring. What did "in due time" mean? Things never changed, but she certainly did not feel like debating the point with her mother now. She counted to ten. Besides, she needed to finish her e-mails and then call Pam and find out where they were going to meet.

"So, the new clothes and hair . . . you trying to get him back? A good man like Jackson—"

"Was obviously not meant for me, Ma, so let's just drop it. I want to know about Dad."

"I'm sure you do," Henrietta said. "And you have a right to know. Your dad and I have been going downhill a long time." She leaned forward in her seat.

"Do you love him?"

"Of course. I never stopped loving him. But a marriage is about more than love. It's about consideration and give and take. And your father has always only known how to take."

Claudia's brow furrowed. "But I don't understand. You and Dad always seemed so happy. You always did so much for him."

"That's true. But that is because that is what I was raised to believe I was supposed to do, or at least what my mother and the other women of my generation wanted me to believe. But it just didn't work for me. I wanted more. I have been waiting many years to go my own way." She paused, searching Claudia's face for a reaction.

What was her mother saying? "What do you mean by more, Ma? You wanted a career? I don't remember Daddy ever saying you couldn't work. So many other Black women had to work to help make ends meet. Didn't you feel privileged?"

"C'mon, Claudia. Look at yourself and how much pleasure your job gives you. It isn't about making ends meet for you. You enjoy what you do, right? I wanted some of that too. And your father didn't tell me I couldn't work. Sure, selling Avon or something would have been fine for him, not taking away from those women who enjoy those types of things. But I wanted something more substantial, and he made it hard for me to get it. He gave lip service to the idea of supporting me, but when push came to shove, he made it hard for me to do anything that took any time away from the family, in a passive-aggressive kind of way. There was always another thing that he couldn't do and needed me to do it. And that being needed part was too hard to resist. I fell for it hook, line, and sinker."

The world that her mother was talking about was unfathomable to Claudia. It must have been like being in prison. How long had her mother lived that way? she wondered. Had she ever been happy? "But what I don't understand is why you are pushing me so hard to go and do the exact same thing. Why have you been lobbying so hard for me to marry Jackson?"

"Honey, I just want you to be happy, that's all. I wouldn't change anything that I did, because if I did, I wouldn't have had you. I apologize if you feel I was railroading you into something you didn't want. Marriage is a big decision, and I stick by you no matter what. But I do think that Jackson would make a good, supportive husband. And things are different nowadays. Men don't expect the same things. I just don't want you to let a good thing slip away, if that is what you really want, okay?"

Claudia nodded. The news about her parents left her feeling dizzy and confused. They had been her model for a perfect marriage for years, and now that image was shattered. "Are you okay with all this, Ma?" Claudia's voice quavered slightly. She was not sure whether she should cry or be happy for her mother.

"Oh, honey, I'm fine. I have never felt so free. I just needed some time on my own. As Henrietta. Not as Mrs. Claude Barrett."

"What about Dad?"

She waved her hand in Claudia's direction as if shooing

her away. "That man is fine, he really is off playing golf with his buddies. He is just glad I am not nagging him about staying on the golf course all weekend." She smiled.

Claudia stood up and picked up her laptop. The e-mail could wait. She needed to go think about it some more. "Okay then," she said. "I guess it is okay. I have to meet Pam." Claudia headed to her room to change. She shook her head. Her mother was truly unbelievable, but it was her life. At least the news about Jackson was off her chest. And her mother had not reacted the way she thought she would have at all. It hadn't hurt one bit.

Claudia slammed the phone back onto its base. That damned Pam had done it again. She'd neglected to mention that her husband would accompany them to this soiree they were attending tonight. Claudia plopped down on the bed. What if she was the only one there without a date? She bit her lip. More than anything, she hated being the third wheel. She imagined Pam and her husband looking at her through eyes full of pity. They would be thinking, *Poor Claudia, the old maid.* She shook her head. She wanted no part of that.

It only took a few minutes for Claudia to grab her laptop and power it on. She opened her e-mail, scanning for the one from Cody. He was her only option right now, and he had included his phone number in his tag. Maybe she was going out on a limb, but Claudia was sure that he would be willing to accompany her. He was attractive, younger, and he smelled good too. Those were all pluses in his favor. Men took women along as eye candy all the time, so why couldn't she? And she had already made it clear that it was not possible for them to have any relationship outside of a platonic one, so he was safe. Hopefully he didn't have any plans tonight.

"Yes." Cody's voice was gruff.

Claudia held the phone away from her ear. "Did I catch you at a bad time?" She had not expected him to yell the way he had and he sounded out of breath.

"I'm sorry. I have been getting hang-up calls, and I thought that this was going to be one of them." He lowered his voice. "This is a surprise. I wasn't expecting you to call me. And at home, at that."

"I know it is unusual, but I need a favor." Claudia closed her eyes. Pam would pay for this one.

"Oh?" he said. "Do you normally ask for favors from men you barely know?"

She gritted her teeth. "No, not normally. I just thought you might want to take advantage of a great opportunity to meet some of the movers and shakers in this town. You said you hadn't been here for too long. But if it's a problem—"

"No, okay. I was just kidding. What can I do for you?"

"I have to attend a small get-together this evening, and I would like you to accompany me. Can you fit it in?" She crossed her fingers. Now she knew why she and Jackson had stayed together for so long—there was always another opening, event, or cocktail reception where one or the other of them needed a date.

Chapter 30

Surprises never ended. Cody had thought that his coffee meeting with Claudia had gone well, but he had not expected her to call him up and ask him out so soon. He rubbed his hands together and slapped aftershave onto his face. He reveled in the slight sting and smiled. He knew he was good, but damn. She obviously wanted to get with him as much as he hoped she would.

There was no need to check the address, he knew where she lived. It was almost as if his car made its way cross town on autopilot. He had been to her house many times. It was silly, he knew; at least three of the times he had sat outside her house, hoping to catch a glimpse of her car sliding into her garage. He hadn't even been able to see her. Only two of the times had he actually approached the house. A twinge of guilt surfaced. *Was he obsessed?* He knew it was a felony to mess around with people's mail, but he hadn't been able to resist it. He'd had to know more about her, and who knew more about a woman than her mail delivery person? Besides, he hadn't actually stolen anything, just read the mail she'd gotten, and he had even returned the phone bills the next day. Some folks might think he was being obsessive, but he liked to think of it as being thorough, covering all bases.

Cody climbed the stairs in front of her house, his palms sweating. He loosened the vicelike grip he had on the bouquet of flowers he'd picked up on the way over. Hopefully, he had not broken any of the stems. He paused before ringing the bell and licked his lips. He inhaled and reached for the bell just as the door swung open.

"Oh," he said, glancing at his watch. Claudia opened the door. He ran his eyes over her green, sliplike dress. She looked beautiful. "Am I late?"

"No, no of course not. I wasn't sure you would be able to get here on time on such short notice," she said, blushing.

Cody shifted his weight from one foot to the other, clearing his throat. She had no idea that he had taken the fastest shower in history. He'd halfway expected his mother to burst into the bathroom any minute and scold him for not wetting his shoulders. "I told you that it wasn't a problem. These are for you." His hand trembled slightly as he handed her the small bouquet of flowers.

"Thank you," she said, smiling. The flowers were wrapped in the same paper as the ones she'd received at work. She opened her mouth to ask, but then closed it again. It was probably a coincidence. What reason would Cody have had to send her flowers? "C'mon in. We have to wait for my friend Pam. We are going with her and her husband."

Cody nodded and Claudia stepped aside, closing the door after him. He followed her into the living room.

The room was a stark contrast to Cody's haphazardly put-together apartment. Where he had secondhand or hand-built furniture, everything in Claudia's living room was perfectly coordinated. He glanced around.

"You have a lovely home," he said, immediately wishing

he could retract the statement. He did not want to sound too rehearsed. "I mean, it's so put-together and organized."

"No big deal," she answered. "I get that a lot. Trust me, I am not that talented. I just went to Rooms-to-Go, closed my eyes, pointed, and told them to give me that. Poof. I bought a whole room. Instant decoration." She waved her hands in the air above her head, wiggling her slender fingers. "I tend not to make a lot of time for things like that."

"It's all very nice." Cody nodded, looking around. "I don't make much time for domestic-type things either, so my place is a little more eclectic." He chuckled. "Before I moved here, I used to do a lot of things with my hands, like restoring old furniture or designing my own. But it is whatever hits me that day, so nothing really goes with anything else. Know what I mean?"

"You can have a seat if you want." She motioned toward a sofa set back against the wall. Cody sat down where she indicated and was immediately swallowed by the down pillows that lined the back. A twinge of soreness reminded him of his encounter, and he was immediately grateful for the softness and comfort the seat offered.

The doorbell rang, interrupting their conversation. Claudia exhaled as relief spread across her face. Pam was finally here. She headed for the door. Cody put his hands on his knees, tapping his fingers. From where he was sitting, he could hear Claudia open the door and exchange greetings with someone.

Pam erupted onto the scene, followed by a short white man that Cody assumed to be her husband. He stood up, surprised. He thought he knew everything about Claudia, but he had neglected to ascertain this piece of information about her best friend's husband. Obviously, snooping in the mail could only tell you so much. Not that he and Pam were so different looking. She was so light you almost had to look twice to see that she was a Black woman herself.

"Okay, I am so sorry we are late." Pam sounded as if she were talking to someone in another room, as opposed to Claudia, who was right next to her. Cody noticed that she was very animated, in a way reminding him of Barry. He doubted that she would be able to do anything quietly either. She was dressed nicely, also in a cocktail dress, only instead of being understated like Claudia's, Pam's dress was bright red, with shiny lines throughout.

"You know, I told the sitter fifteen minutes earlier than I really wanted and that girl was still late."

Her husband didn't speak. Cody watched as he and Claudia exchanged hugs that looked more cordial than friendly.

"Well, you are here now," Claudia said. "Let me grab my bag."

It was then that Pam noticed Cody. "Oh," she said. "Who is this? You didn't tell me you were bringing someone." She elongated her words, her eyebrows reaching toward the ceiling.

"And neither did you." Claudia made the introductions as Pam eyed Cody. Afterward, Claudia excused herself, guiding Pam into the kitchen.

"What is going on? You weren't supposed to have a date." Pam's whisper was heavy and loud.

"Keep your voice down. Neither were you. You neglected to tell me that you were bringing your husband until the last minute. You made it sound as if this was a *girl's* night out. I wasn't about to be a third wheel. You know how much I hate that."

"I know. I'm sorry. But he insisted on coming. He was having a jealous moment," she said. "Who is he, anyway?" Pam motioned toward the living room, where her husband and Cody seemed to be engaged in conversation.

"Someone from work. We had coffee this morning." Claudia opened her compact and began applying her lipstick.

"Oh. It's like that, huh? You didn't tell me there was anyone from work. I guess you didn't need my help after all. You sure didn't waste any time getting out there. What's it been, a week? He seems a little young, though."

"No need for sarcasm. You are the one that said I needed a replacement for Jackson."

"But what do you know about this man? Where is he from? Who are his people? I bet he didn't even do Jack & Jill or anything and didn't go to college." Pam referred to the social group for African American children that Claudia had belonged to growing up.

"What do you know about that? As I recall, you didn't do any of that either. The trailer park you came from is now the site of a convenience store. And you went to college, look where that got you. People are people. You and I are from two entirely different backgrounds and we have been friends longer than any of those other people I know with all the right credentials. And besides, we are not getting married, we are just going to a party together, that's all."

They looked up as Claudia's mother came into the kitchen. "What are you two in here whispering about? Hello, Miss Pam. How are you?" Henrietta held out her arms and embraced Pam. "You sure are all dolled up in that dress. How did you get it on?"

"I'm fine, Mrs. Barrett. You are looking younger and younger every time I see you."

Claudia rolled her eyes. "We can't keep them waiting."

"Who is that young thang in the living room with your husband? He sure is fine."

"That is Claudia's *date*." Pam stood with her hands on her hips. They both turned to look at Claudia. "I was taking her to a party so she could meet eligible singles, and she decided to bring one along instead."

"I see, this is gang-up-on-the-soon-to-be-old-maid day, huh? Cody and I work at the same place. There is nothing between us. He knows that. I know that."

"Does he now?" Pam said. "I wouldn't be too sure about that. He has the look of twitterpation in his eyes. You know, like Bambi in springtime."

"Oh—really?" Henrietta slapped Claudia on the shoulder lightly. "Don't you let Pam mess with you. I might go and get me some young thing too." They laughed.

Pam raised her eyebrows.

Claudia feigned covering her ears. "I don't want to hear this. Ma, I am not even used to the idea of you and Dad apart yet. Please."

Pam raised her eyebrows, looking from Claudia to her mother. This information about Claudia's parents was news to her. "I'm just concerned," Pam said. "She doesn't even know anything about him, I bet. She has never said a word about him to me. And I thought we were friends."

"That is because, as I have said, there is nothing to tell. I just didn't want to go solo. And he is nice enough. It will be fine."

Henrietta opened a bottle of aspirin. "You two have a good time. But from my experience, there isn't much to know. Men are all the same, they just change the faces so we can tell them apart." They all broke into laughter. "You have a good time."

Pam and Claudia watched as Henrietta left. "We had better go. This is rude. Cody and I will follow you there, okay?"

"That's fine." They headed toward the living room. "I am so surprised at your mother," Pam said. "I thought you said she would take the news about you and you-know-who hard."

Claudia shrugged. "I thought she would, but I guess I was wrong. But she has her own little drama going on. Stuff I never even realized."

"You never can tell about people nowadays," Pam said.

Claudia guided Pam and her husband to the door, locking it behind them. "No," she said as the four of them started down the steps. Cody offered his arm for support, and she took it. "I guess you can't."

Chapter 31

"What do you mean, she left?" Mario paced the floor in front of Wesley, his hands clasped behind his back. "A man is supposed to know where his wife is. What is wrong with you? You must have done something. I don't see my daughter being hotheaded, not under normal circumstances."

Wesley wiped the beads of perspiration that stung his forehead and folded his hands into his armpits. He did not want the sweat that was accumulating there to show through his white shirt. The small cuckoo clock in the living room showed that it was close to midnight. He took a deep breath, wanting to appear more relaxed than he was. His father-in-law was irate and didn't need to see how upset he was. He fed off that kind of thing.

"She told you about our little disagreement, right? Well, I did what you said. I closed the credit card accounts so she wouldn't get any ideas. I had no idea she would leave. I thought maybe she would just try and go on a shopping spree or something."

"So what you are saying is, my only daughter, the apple of my eye, is out there, with no money. And you don't know where? I need to sit down." He fell backward, plopping down in Wesley's armchair. "Do you have any idea where she is?"

"Not really." Wesley looked away. "Well, maybe. She took a file from my office. I think she is going to try and track down Cody."

"Okay, so what I am hearing you say is, you kept a file, after I told you to make this whole thing disappear, and she found it? Can't you do anything right? Have you harmed the boy?"

Wesley shook his head.

"You better not have. You were supposed to speak to him rationally, reason with him. If you did anything to him that points to me or even suggests that I was involved, you will be sorry. Do you understand me?"

Wesley understood loud and clear. He swallowed the large lump that was suspended in his throat.

"Seems like you are not as swift as I thought you were. I have no idea what you did to that man, or those kids, and you know what, I don't want to know. I am going to do you a favor and tell you what you are going to do now, okay? You are going to track down my daughter and bring her back. Fast. Period. You understand? Get me a beer." Mario waved his hand, dismissing Wesley as if he were a servant.

Wesley nodded and headed into the kitchen. He leaned against the refrigerator. Relieved, he listened as Mario barked orders into his cell phone. It could have been worse. He had no idea where Marina was right now, but he knew where she would end up eventually.

Chapter 32

The street was lined with small shops and a few galleries, many of which had been there for some time. During the day, this was a busy thoroughfare. Fifth Street was a heavily traveled route from West to East Austin, the way many people entered downtown from this side of the Colorado River. Now, in the early evening, it was quiet and the water was almost still, except for a slight rippling produced by a breeze too light to feel. The street was virtually deserted, other than the few people who were also attending the grand opening of the new office building, the only thing to change in the landscape of downtown Austin for years.

A chill ran down Claudia's spine as she waited for Cody. He had dropped her off before going to park the car. Pam and her husband had not yet arrived. She nodded to passersby whom she recognized, and she stared at the grackle swarming overhead. They reminded her of a swarm from a horror movie, the sound of their wings echoing eerily off the bridge that took traffic south across the water. At twilight, downtown was overrun with them as they lit on the uppermost branches of the cedar trees lining the water and the power lines overhead.

Cody tapped her on the shoulder and she jumped.

"I'm sorry," he said. "I didn't mean to surprise you."

She nodded. "Let's go in. We can catch up with them inside."

Cody's chest swelled as Claudia took his arm. He put his hand on hers, patting it as if they were an old couple.

Although the building they were celebrating was new, it had been designed to fit in with the existing architecture of downtown, so it looked, on the outside, as if it had been there for years. The inside was brightly lit, and both Cody and Claudia squinted when they entered, waiting for their eyes to adjust to the sudden harsh light. The floors were wood, shone to a high gloss, and the walls were made of native limestone, hung with art by local artists. They stopped at the entry table and filled out the required nametags. Cody stood back as person after person hugged Claudia. Most did not bother to even ask who he was or to wait for an introduction.

Pam finally arrived, and she and Claudia hugged as though they had not just seen each other twenty minutes before.

"Where's James?" Claudia asked.

"You know how he is," Pam said as she shook hands with yet another person. "Already at the bar."

Cody looked around the room, suddenly wondering whether agreeing to come had been the best thing for him to do. "That sounds like a good idea." He could sense that the two women had something else to say to each other. He took their drink orders and walked in the direction that Pam indicated. He was going to need a drink.

Pam and Claudia smiled as they watched him go, Pam tilting her head to the side as she enjoyed the rear view.

"So, what did you and the young man talk about on the way over here? He is kind of cute, you know. At least he is polite. James complained all the way over here about having to go, as if I made him come. I was the one that wanted him to stay home. He took one look at my outfit and decided he needed to come to make my life miserable."

"You two are too much. He still has a jealous streak after all these years? You complain about him so much, I don't understand why you stay with him."

Pam looked at her nails. "Please. That is simple. We have children. Sometimes it is just easier to love the one you're with. And where would a divorce leave me other than alone and my children with God knows what types of issues. All couples have complaints. I'm sure he has some about me, too."

They laughed.

"But you always talk about how inconsiderate he is and stuff. I don't know why you put up with it."

"No, of course you don't. You are not married. And you throw away men like used Kleenex. You would have dumped Jackson had he not dumped you, remember?" Pam raised her eyebrows. "That is why I can't understand your mother. I can't believe she left your dad after more than thirty-two years of marriage. What is she going to do now, go out and look for a new man?"

"I don't know," Claudia said. "I don't get it either. And I had no idea that it was that bad for her." They paused. "Cody can come back now." Claudia licked her lips and looked in the direction of the bar for Cody. "I sure could use that drink he was supposed to be bringing us."

"Don't tell me you are going to stick by him all night? You need to work this thing, girl. There are quite a few eligibles who are much more your speed here. Hop to it." They laughed. "You might as well. Looks like your boy is quite busy." Pam pointed over to the far corner of the room, where Cody was still standing in the bar line. He appeared to be engaged in conversation with two women, one on either side. "Those two won't be letting him escape any time soon. They are on the prowl. Look at how they are dressed. You might as well go on and mingle." Pam walked away, waving at someone she knew.

Claudia glanced over to where Cody was standing. Pam was right, the two ladies he was talking with were showing as much cleavage as possible. One reached out, touching Cody's arm seductively, and laughed. Claudia was almost a little bit jealous at the thought of someone moving in on him, but she quickly let it go. She and Cody made eye contact, and he shrugged, looking apologetic. By the looks of the line at the bar, he would be occupied for awhile.

One of the pieces of art on the far wall caught her eye and she walked over to it. Claudia leaned close, hoping to read the plaque stating the name of the artist. As she expected, everything was for sale. This type of display was popular with many of the businesses and restaurants around town, although Claudia had no idea how effective it was. She did not know anyone that had ever purchased anything shown this way. Still, she dug in her purse for the small notebook she carried. This piece would be a great fit over the sofa table in her entryway.

Someone giggled behind her, and she turned around to look up. Her eyes grew wide with surprise, and she dropped her handbag on the floor. Jackson was almost directly behind her.

"I can get that," he said.

Claudia was already reaching for the bag, but Jackson got to it first. They bumped heads.

"I'm sorry," he said.

She glared. "No problem."

He stared at her. "Claudia. I'm surprised to see you here. You never come to these things."

"It wasn't my idea." She snatched her purse from his grasp. "Pam asked me to come with them. With her." Of all the people to run into. The anger that she felt surprised her.

"Everything okay?" he asked.

"Peachy." How the hell was everything supposed to be, she wondered. Did he expect her to run to him with open arms? While it appeared that Jackson had moved on, the wound was still fresh for her. She was not about to admit that to him, though.

Just then, the woman he was with cleared her throat. "Stoney," she said, tapping him.

"Oh, I'm sorry. This is Claudia. Remember, I told you about her. My ex?"

"Stoney? I thought you didn't like anyone to call you that." It was Claudia's turn to raise her eyebrows. Most people would not even know Jackson's first name. "Pleased to meet you," Claudia said to Jackson's date. The woman did not smile or extend her hand for a handshake. She just stared, letting her eyes roam disdainfully over Claudia from head to toe, taking her in.

Claudia felt as if she should square off for a fight. She stared back equally hard. Finally she spoke, slicing through the awkward silence between them. "Well, it was nice to see you, Jackson." She looked at the woman for another minute, taking in her Barbie-doll perfect features and her skin so pale it was almost translucent. She hated her immediately without knowing a thing about her.

Her interest in the artwork was gone. She had even less

interest in talking to Jackson and his date. The woman brushed some imaginary lint from Jackson's well-fitted suit, then hooked her arm in his, as if she was afraid he would get away, or afraid that Claudia might bite. Claudia's hand trembled as she made a pretense of writing down the artist's name before moving on to the next picture.

Picture after picture flew by Claudia's eyes. She took none of them in. Occasionally, she glanced over at the bar area, where Cody was still patiently waiting in line. She mulled over the meeting with Jackson, hoping she had not looked too surprised when she'd seen him with his new friend. She imagined him and his date cuddled up some-where romantic, and she felt sickened. Her heart was still beating fast, damn him. Why couldn't he have been the one to see her with her date for the night instead?

"Are you buying art?" Jackson spoke to Claudia smoothly, smiling.

How could he act as if nothing had happened between them? "Where's your friend?" Claudia asked.

"She is getting a drink. You look fabulous. I don't think I can remember the last time you cut your hair," he said.

He reached his hand toward her head, and she stepped back. He stiffened.

"Thanks. Well, you sure didn't waste any time. What has it been, three days since you dumped me?"

"Claudia, you got it all wrong. She is just a friend, a colleague."

Claudia nodded. "Right. And that is why she looked me up and down like she was getting ready for a catfight. I felt like she was going to take off her earrings and dig out the Vaseline. I was expecting her to start smearing it all over her pretty face any minute."

He laughed. "Did she look at you like that really? I don't think so. What reason would she have?"

"You tell me. Is she the real reason you left? Were you seeing someone else? You could have told me. I can take it. I'm a big girl, you know." Claudia breathed in, deep and long. She did not want to cry. She fought back the tears that were stinging her nose.

His voice warmed. "You know that is not it. You left me about two years before we really broke up. Your work was your other man. You never took any time to think about or be with me unless I forced it. And you didn't want to get married, not really. Every time I brought it up, you acted like I had the plague or something. Tell me that isn't true?" He paused. "And it isn't like you are here alone. I saw you come in with that boy scout over there."

Claudia held up her hand. "Let's not go there, okay? If you cared you wouldn't have left. At least I didn't give up. You did that."

Claudia turned and left him standing there. She headed in Cody's direction just as the tears began to run down her face. Her makeup was ruined. She burst into the restroom, struggling to make it to a stall. She barely made it before she threw up.

Chapter 33

"What just happened?" Cody had one drink in each hand. "I was just on my way back to her and next thing I know she was flying by me in hysterics. What the hell did that guy say to her?"

Pam shrugged. "No telling. I didn't know he was going to be here or we wouldn't have come. I also had no idea that Claudia was this upset about the whole thing."

"One of us needs to go in there and check on her. I don't think—"

Pam walked into the bathroom without answering. Her mouth had dropped open as she'd watched the whole scenario unfold from across the room; she had never seen Claudia so upset. It was unlike Claudia to let someone else get the best of her like that.

The small bathroom was neat and still smelled new. Pam tried to be discreet as she peered under the first stall or two, looking for Claudia's shoes.

"Claudia," she called. "You okay, honey?"

"Since when do you call me honey? And you can save that pitiful voice for someone who needs it." Claudia threw open the door. It slammed back against the hinges so hard that Pam jumped. "I'm fine. I just surprised myself, that's all."

"Really? Is that why you came running into the bathroom like you did?"

Claudia shook her head. "I guess I wasn't prepared for feeling the way I did when I saw him. It hurt more than I thought. Him breaking up with me." She looked away. "But I'm okay. I just want to go home and have a long bath. We just all need to move on. That's what I wanted."

Pam shrugged. "If you say so," she said. "So there is nothing I can do?"

"How could you do anything but what you have already done? You have tried to make me feel better and let me whine and complain in your ear. What more can I ask for?" Claudia smiled weakly, wiping at her nose with tissue. "You know, he had the nerve to complain about me working so hard. As if a good work ethic is a bad thing."

"It isn't. But you have to admit that you have spent so much time working over the past few years that your love life and friendships have been put on the back burner—"

"Not true."

"Uh-huh. Keep fooling yourself. How many nights or weekends have you told me we would go do something, and then stood me up to work instead?"

Claudia didn't answer.

"That's what I thought." Pam rubbed one hand along Claudia's back and smiled. "You sure you want to go home? There are a lot of fine men out there, not to mention that Cody." A mischievous grin danced across her face. "I must say he ain't that bad looking. Are you going to tell me how old he is? I would guess about twenty-five—"

"I really don't need to try to meet anyone tonight. I would just dump on them. I need to go home. And I told you, Cody's age is immaterial. It is just not that kind of party between us." Claudia wiped at her eyes.

"Say what you want. Just fix yourself up a little before you go out there, okay? No need to broadcast that you have been crying to the world." She patted her friend on the shoulder, then hugged her. "I'm surprised you even admitted your feelings as much as you did, but I am glad you can be honest with yourself now. You try to be so hard all the time, but you know what my momma would have said, right?"

Claudia rolled her eyes. Her mother was the nagging one, but Pam's mother was certainly the strange one in the group; she had been into anything New Age before New Age was in fashion, the perpetual flower child. Claudia knew what Pam was going to say. She had heard it before.

"She would have said that, sometimes, even the hardest rock has water inside. Everyone has a little soft spot somewhere, Claudia. It's time you took care of yours."

Outside the building, a light wind was finally blowing. Claudia dialed the number to the cab company on her phone, then wrapped her arms around her body, almost as if she were hugging herself. All she wanted was to go home. She tapped her foot impatiently, willing the cab to arrive soon. She looked up as Cody virtually burst from the building.

"I guess this means you are leaving," he said. "Let me get the car. I can take you there."

Claudia bit her lip. "No, I just really need to be alone. I'm sorry."

"I saw how upset you were in there. Pam told me that

was your ex. Maybe what you need is company, someone to talk it through with you."

"I'm fine," Claudia murmured clenching her teeth slightly as she spoke. "You go back in and have a good time. I'm sure you will find some nice young ladies in there who are very eager to make some good conversation." She turned back toward the street.

Cody's face darkened. If he didn't know any better, he would think that Claudia was trying to get rid of him. "But I came here to make conversation with *you*. Sometimes, when things get rough, it is better not to be alone, no matter how much we want to be." He reached out, rubbing the back of his hand along her shoulder. "What do you think?"

Claudia flinched. Who did he think he was? "I told you what I thought—you need to go back inside and leave me alone. I am a big girl, I can get home by myself."

"No need to be so nasty," Cody said. "It's just that when I have a date—"

"Let's get something straight. You were not a date. You were an escort, nothing more." Claudia's eyes narrowed.

A brightly colored car emblazoned with a taxicab sign pulled up.

Cody took a deep breath. "Okay, fine. But can this escort take you home properly?"

He waited as Claudia put her hand on the door handle. She hesitated but did not open the door. Instead she looked down at the ground, and then over at Cody.

Why was she being so mean to him? It wasn't his fault either. She bent down and looked into the cab window. "Sorry," she said. "Never mind." She let him pull away.

Cody pursed his lips. Claudia's words had smarted, but he had not come this far after months of planning to be turned away so easily. He counted to ten, telling himself to breathe slowly. Breathe in. Breathe out. He tried to understand Claudia's hurt. All he wanted to do was to help, right? Hopefully, she would let him.

They did not speak as he put his arm on her elbow and started to walk toward his car, parked almost two blocks away. She would finally see that he would be good for her.

Chapter 34

Austin was nothing like she expected and a far cry from crowded New York. When Marina pulled up in her rental car, the street was virtually deserted. The only word that came to mind to describe what she saw was *quaint*, very different from midtown Manhattan. The three people she did see all said hello. She could get used to this place.

Marina felt some of her tension begin to melt away as soon as she checked into her downtown hotel; she felt like half of some major battle was over. Having arrived early in the morning, long before the workday began, she went up to her room, took a hot shower, and sank into the warm bed, where she slept a dreamless sleep. It was late in the day when she awoke. She drew back the curtains. From her window she looked over into the lake a few blocks away. Dusk was already falling. Marina jumped into her clothes and crossed her fingers; hopefully, the business office would still be open. She had some sleuthing to do.

Marina peered through the glass door, into what the hotel had billed as "state-of-the-art" business facilities. In reality, all she saw was one small room with an empty desk in front. She opened the door—there were about three computers in the room, as well as a few phones and fax machines. A well-dressed young man emerged from some-where in the back of the room and took a seat at the desk. He smiled at Marina.

"May I help you?" he asked.

"Maybe." She smiled, clutching the slip of paper from the file in her fingers. "I need to find an address. You wouldn't happen to have reverse phone directory, would you?"

He frowned, then shook his head. "No, I don't think so. Our offerings are pretty basic. But we do have a phone book."

"That won't help me. I already have a phone number. I need to find out who it belongs to."

"Okay, I get you. We get a lot of salespeople in here look-ing for information like that. Are you in sales?"

Marina nodded. He really had no need to know her busi-ness, so she didn't bother to elaborate. She knew he was just trying to be friendly, but she felt the beginnings of annoy-ance creeping up on her.

"What I usually suggest is that you go online, and type the phone number in the Google search engine. That should bring up the information you need." He pointed in the di-rection of the small computer area. "Let me know if you need anything else. We also offer fax and mailing services. We can bill everything to your room if you like, okay?" He handed her a lined pad, along with a pen and pencil. "These are compliments of business services."

In less than two minutes, Marina was sitting in front of the computer. Her palms were sweating, and she rubbed them together. It was hard to believe that she had waited as long as she had to do this. What would Cody say to her? she wondered. She typed the phone number in the browser, just as the man at the desk suggested. One listing came up. She clicked on it for further detail, and there it was, plain as day, all the information she could have possibly hoped to get.

The sight of Cody's address caused her to suck in her breath. Tears sprung to her eyes, and she wiped them away. She had not expected to react so strongly, but she really hadn't expected to be able to find anything either. She took a few deep breaths. She opened another browser, searching the county real estate records. So much information was in the public domain, and now most of it was online. If Marina had known tracking down what she wanted was this easy, she would have done it sooner.

Marina stared at the name that came up in response to her search, and she rubbed her temples. She closed her eyes, then opened them again. She must be seeing wrong. Cody lived in a multiunit building—she would have guessed that much—but the building was listed as being owned by none other than Jason Marlboro. She was reasonably sure that she knew that name well.

Her hands trembled as she grabbed her purse, dumping the contents onto the tabletop. She located her worn address book and thumbed through to the Ms. Jason Marlboro was there, plain as day. He was Wesley's cousin. Her stomach sank. Who was not involved in Wesley's deceit? Wesley must have known where Cody was all along.

It took awhile for Marina to convince herself of what she had to do next. She went back to her room and had a good cry as emotions poured over her like a torrential rain. Finally, she put herself back together and called valet parking to bring her car around. She had come this far, she might as well go all the way. If she did not talk to Cody now, it would nag her the rest of her life.

By the time she parked her car near the Congress Square apartment building, Marina's emotions had run the full spectrum from happy, to sad, to angry. She looked at the tiny Post-it note in her hand and rechecked the address once again. This was definitely the right place. Marina could not tell much about the neighborhood by the dim streetlights, but the unfamiliarity of the place made her uncomfortable. She put her head down on the steering wheel and counted to ten to try and ease her stomach and her mind. Unnerved and uncomfortable in an unknown city and neighborhood, she grabbed her purse and held her keys between her fingers in case she had to defend herself. Never having to use the techniques she'd learned in self-defense classes before, she prayed that they really worked. Her grip on the keys was so tight that her fingers smarted where the keys dug into the sides of her fingers, but she didn't loosen her grip. She exited her car and locked it, double-checking the doors to make sure.

The signs on the building were clear, and Marina easily found her way to the metal steps that led to Cody's apartment. As she walked, each of her steps echoed on the asphalt as if there were no other living person around for miles to absorb the noise. The hairs on the back of her neck stood on end as she stared at the number on the door. She could barely see it; the single lightbulb outside the door was missing. Some more breathing exercises. Either Cody was home or he wasn't. Marina stood in the semidarkness for several minutes, straining her ears in an attempt to hear any noise from inside. She took one last breath in, and then knocked on the door. A part of her hoped that he wasn't in, and relief washed over her as the door was not answered.

Marina raised her hand to knock again, and suddenly,

the door swung open. She drew in her breath, feeling faint, at first unable to comprehend what she was seeing. She had prepared herself for several different scenarios, everything, she thought, including a woman answering the door. In her mind, that would have been the worst and most awkward thing that could have happened. She would have never expected this. Marina's hand trembled as she covered her mouth, steadying herself against the wrought-iron railing next to her. She looked at Wesley inside Cody's apartment, and confusion flooded her mind. She didn't have time to make sense of anything or ask any questions. Wesley grabbed her by the wrist, yanked her inside the door, and slammed it shut behind them.

Chapter 35

It took Claudia a minute to calm down once she got into the car with Cody. She sat with her arms folded in front of her, surprised at the severity of her reaction to seeing Jackson. She could not remember a time since she was six that being upset had made her physically sick like that.

Cody glanced in her direction, and their eyes met. She looked down at her shoes, embarrassed. It wasn't his fault.

"You okay?" His voice was calm.

She nodded.

He cleared his throat. "You think you might want to come over to have a drink or something? You were pretty upset. Help you calm down?"

Claudia felt her back tense. She shook her head, then thought better of it. "S-ure. I think I need that." It would be better for her to go, calm down for awhile before she went home to face her mother.

"I don't live far."

"Right downtown, huh?"

He nodded. "Just about."

The car was silent as Cody drove around the block and over the bridge, heading toward his apartment complex.

He pulled into the parking lot and stopped near a space near a Dumpster.

"I don't get the greatest space in the world, but the apartment more than makes up for it." He smiled, his face nervous as he turned off the car. He ran around to the other side and opened her door before Claudia even had the chance to take off her seat belt.

She felt the stress starting to leave already. She smiled weakly, not having the energy to fully appreciate his gesture. She followed him from the parking lot and up the small metal staircase to his door.

They paused at the top, and Cody frowned. He heard voices inside his apartment. He did not remember leaving a radio or television on, but he did not want to alarm Claudia.

What now? he wondered. First, his night with Claudia had not gone as he'd expected, and now this. *Damn,* he thought, *not again.* He wondered if Wesley had sent more goons to rough him up again, and if so, for what reason? He had moved on as he'd promised and not done any more snooping around. He was through as through could be with Marina. He stood at the top of the steps, outside his door, listening as hard as he could to try and make out something, anything.

"Everything okay?" Claudia asked.

"Hmm. Hmm," he lied. He knew there was more than one person in there. He could make out one person, a man's voice.

"I don't know what possessed you to come here," it said.

Cody could hear no answer. Something knocking. Something slamming.

"Uh. I just assumed you lived alone," Claudia said. "If this is a problem, I can get a cab and go home, you know."

"No, really. It's fine." Cody's pulse quickened. Should he go to the police? What if it was someone Wesley sent? He might have to rehash his past, and Cody knew for sure he had no desire to go there. He heard something that sounded like whimpering. His brow furrowed. Was someone hurt, he wondered?

Slowly, Cody raised his hand to try the knob, not expecting the door to move. It swung open easily. Wesley stopped midsentence, and Cody surveyed the room. A lamp was knocked over, and almost all of the lights were out. Claudia looked over his shoulder.

Cody realized that Wesley and Marina were somehow inside his apartment. He made eye contact with Wesley, whose craggy features were taking on a sinister look. He smiled, a slow, deliberate, open mouth smile, his lips spreading into a sneer.

"Well, your boyfriend's here," he said. "And looks like he has company. Good to see that someone has moved on."

Cody shifted his gaze to his easy chair. Marina sat there, looking crumpled, and her shirt was torn on the right shoulder. Her cheek under her right eye had already begun to bruise. She attempted to stand up, and Wesley pushed her back down into the chair.

"Is this who you wanted to see? Well, here he is. Ask him anything you want. You came all this way."

"What the hell are you two doing here? In my apartment?" Cody could not believe his eyes. He had just made up his mind that he was done with both Wesley and Marina, and here they were in his apartment, and from Marina's obviously disheveled appearance, he could tell that they were not getting along too well. He pursed his lips. He wanted them to take whatever drama was going on between them elsewhere, but he was not prepared for what he felt on seeing Marina again.

"Um, I should leave," Claudia said.

Cody put his hand on her arm.

"She came looking for you. Aren't you glad to see her?" Wesley sneared. He looked at Claudia. "But it looks like maybe we are interrupting something."

Cody's head reeled. A few months ago, he would have been glad to see Marina, but right now, the only thing he could feel was anger mixed with embarrassment. His face darkened. The feeling surprised him; he had been telling himself that he was over her, but it wasn't until right now that he realized that not only was he over her but he hated her. Not only had she kicked him to the curb the way she had, but she had also severed any ties that he could possibly have to his children. And now, she most certainly had messed up any chance he would ever have with Claudia. He *had* moved on. Time had put some much-needed distance between the two of them. He wasn't glad to see her—instead, he was mad for being discarded like a wet dishrag.

"I—I needed to talk to you. I had to know some things," Marina said.

"Know what? That you used me up and spit me out? That your husband is a gangster in training? I have nothing to say to you. I have let the two of you make my life miserable. I keep wondering what I did to deserve the way you treated me, and I can't figure it out. And now, he has me looking over my shoulder and getting beat up by thugs on a regular basis, just because I asked a few legitimate questions. Go back home and leave me the hell alone," Cody shouted, clenching his teeth. He closed his eyes, then opened them again in an effort to calm himself down.

Claudia cringed, backing up toward the door. "You know what. I think I should go. I don't think I need to be here." She turned and snatched the door open.

"Wait," Cody said.

She held up her hand to stop his talking, then left quickly, stumbling over the doorjamb.

They were all silent as they listened to her clump down the metal staircase.

Wesley smirked.

Cody clenched and then opened his fists.

Marina got back up from the chair, and this time, Wesley let her stand. Both men stood stock still, mouths agape.

"Get the hell out of my house and leave me alone, okay? I want no part of either one of you. I was doing a good job of moving on, or so I thought, and I come home to this shit." He paced the room, waving his arms about. "You need to take your domestic disputes somewhere else. You understand?"

Wesley grinned. Marina began to cry. Cody grabbed her by the arm and pushed her to the door.

"I just need to know what—"

"Don't," he said. "It's too late for that."

They paused on the landing. Wesley turned back to Cody.

"I had you wrong," he said. "You won't hear from me again."

Cody slammed the door behind them. His eyes stung and his head throbbed. Why was his life so fucked up? He went to the kitchen to pour himself a drink.

Chapter 36

Claudia dialed Austin Cab before she even hit the bottom of the steps. She couldn't wait to get away from Cody and whatever it was he was messed up in. Those people in his apartment seemed to be a bunch of crazies, and she definitely needed no part of someone else's drama. She chuckled as she looked down the street for the cab. It was comical, really. Just a few days ago, hadn't she told Pam that her love life with Jackson had been boring? Talk about out of the frying pan.

The cab pulled up and Claudia jumped in, still thinking about Cody. She knew that it had been a bad idea to go home with him. It was a good thing that his friends had showed up. Being as angry as she was at Jackson, she might have done something she would have regretted later.

Was that woman an ex-girlfriend? Her face was vivid in Claudia's mind. Her makeup had been streaked all down her face, as if she had been crying too, and she'd had a small bruise under one of her eyes. Had that man beat her up or something? It was all too shady. She shook her head as she thought about it. The funny thing was, the woman looked slightly familiar. She probably just had one of those faces.

By the time the cab turned onto her street, Claudia felt

silly for leaving the opening so abruptly. Her life used to be so orderly, but recently everything seemed to be spinning out of control. Claudia did not like the feeling it gave her. She missed being on top of things.

Henrietta was waiting for her, sitting in the kitchen in the dark with an open bottle of wine. She didn't speak, instead she took one look at Claudia's tearstained face and reached for another glass. She filled it to the top and then slid it across the table toward her daughter. Claudia looked from the glass to her mother and then pulled out the chair to sit down.

"Ma, what are you doing?" she said. Claudia could not remember the last time she'd seen her mother drinking anything but unsweetened tea or Diet Coke.

"I'm thinking," she said. "And I'm having a drink."

Claudia was confused. She was not used to seeing her mother this way. She was used to her complaining and picking at Claudia for whatever the reason of the day was. But Henrietta hadn't seemed concerned about Claudia at all lately, and it was disconcerting. Claudia pushed her problems to the back of her mind. "You want to talk about it at all? Are you thinking about you and Dad?"

"Sort of, I guess, in a philosophical kind of way."

Claudia knew her mother to be a lot of things, but philosophical was not one of them. Cynical maybe, but the rest of this was new. Claudia was beginning to feel as if there was a whole part of her mother that she knew nothing about, or at least that she'd never taken the time to get to know. She took a sip of the wine her mother had given her and grimaced slightly at the tart taste. It wasn't even a good wine. She put her glass on the table with a thud and wiped at the little bit that sloshed onto the table. She waited for her mother to talk.

"What happened to your date?" Henrietta asked.

"Please. Let's not talk about that, okay?"

Henrietta raised her eyebrows. "Was it that bad?"

"And then some. Drama-full." Claudia gulped her wine. They were silent for a minute.

"Didn't you come home in a cab? He must not have been the gentleman I thought."

"Can we not talk about it?"

"If that's what you want. What else is on your mind? You have been so short with me since I got here, and I know you are not *that* upset about me and your father. How is work going?"

"Well, it's going. Last week, it was fine. I was a superstar. This week, I'm not so sure."

Henrietta's eyes widened. "Really? I thought you liked your job so much. You are always there."

"I do like it, Ma. I just found out some disturbing news, though. Plans for my department that I don't exactly agree with."

She paused.

Henrietta waited for her to elaborate.

"I think they are going to move some of the positions that report to me out of the country."

"Does that mean you will be out of a job?"

Claudia shook her head. "No, not exactly. But some of the people who report to me will. They think it's cheaper for the company that way."

"So, what's the problem? Your job is secure."

"But it's not about me. I will be fine. But some of those other people might not be."

Henrietta opened her mouth wide, feigning surprise. "What is this I'm hearing? Miss Claudia has concern for someone else?"

Claudia pursed her lips. "You can stop now, Ma. It's not always about me."

"Do tell. You would never know it. So, do you have a better plan?"

"No, not really. I'm still trying to gather all the facts."

"Well, it's one thing to be concerned for people, but it's another thing to act on it."

Claudia nodded. She knew she had a lot to think about. She wanted to explore all of the possibilities before she talked with her boss further.

"So, are you going to fill me in on this event you went to? You left here all excited and gussied up, but I don't hear any talking. Tell me why you took a cab home. What happened to your friend. Did you fight?"

"Not exactly. I saw Jackson there. With another woman, and I wanted to leave. He offered to bring me home, but instead we went to his place."

"And . . ." Henrietta leaned forward in her seat, grinning.

"Ma, stop. Now you know if anything happened like you think I wouldn't be sharing it with you like that." Claudia paused. "When we got to his house, there were people there waiting for him. It looked like it could get kinda rough. So, I left. I went downstairs and got a cab."

"Kinda rough? What happened to all this concern for others I just heard a minute ago. What if he needed you to help diffuse the situation?"

"What? I didn't know those folks or know what was going on. I just knew I needed to get home." She wrinkled her nose. "Maybe I was just a little on the rude side."

"Uh-huh." Henrietta sipped her wine and then rubbed the kitchen table with a napkin in a circular motion, as if wiping up a big spill.

Claudia knew this was a prelude to one of her mother's soliloquies. It was one of those actions that telegraphed the fact that she was about to lay down the law according to Henrietta, and Claudia braced herself for the onslaught.

"Well, it sounds to me that you might have treated that boy wrong, you know. You used him just a little bit, didn't you? The least you could have done was to wait a minute and make sure he was alright." She didn't wait for an answer. "I could tell when I saw him standing up in here that you weren't interested in him one bit. I know you called him because you didn't want to be dateless, and that is not fair, because he likes you. You need to call that boy and apologize."

Claudia opened her mouth to speak, but her mother held up her hand to stop her.

"Not done. I know you are grown and I can't tell you what to do. It ain't like you listen to me half the time anyway. Sometimes I believe you think you are too grown to listen to a mother's advice anymore, or that you think I am turning into a crazy, nit-picking old woman, but that's okay. You just need to hear me out. I may not be the career woman you are, but I have done more living than a little bit. I am just trying to talk to you like two adult women, sitting here, telling each other the truth. And it was not fair of you to bring that young man into the middle of your mess with Jackson. You weren't done with him and you know it, even if he said he was done with you. Am I right?"

Claudia hesitated and then nodded. She blinked as she felt tears begin to well up in her eyes. Her mother was right, she had been unfair to Cody.

"And something else. You were with Jackson for so long, if you two are going to be apart, you need to learn to like yourself, be by yourself before you go and start jumping into something else. Alone isn't so bad, you know. You just have to learn to enjoy your own company, that's all. Can't nobody make you happy but yourself. You need to make yourself complete."

Claudia was surprised by this last comment. Her mother had always been "her father's wife." The last thing Claudia had expected her mother to say was that she could be okay by herself. "But you have been pushing me to get married—"

"That's true," Henrietta said. "But that is because I thought my baby had it all together, and I do want to see grandchildren before I die." She grinned. "But it is obvious you have some more work to do on yourself. You have gotten so caught up in this career thing that you have lost touch with all the things you used to say you like. What are you going to do when all those jobs that report to you go south and then they decide you are no longer needed? Start over somewhere else?" She paused. "Do you remember telling me that you wanted a house full of kids? Not that you can't change your mind, but you never used to talk about being an executive or anything like that. You used to talk about being happy, and none of the things that you used to say would make you happy had a thing to do with money."

"I have just been so busy, Ma, that's all."

"That is what I am talking about. Look where that has gotten you. You used to be close to your family, your cousins. I bet you can't tell me the last time you talked to any of them. Work can't be your life. I understand that you enjoy it, but you have to be balanced, if that is at all possible. If you don't, who will you give this lecture to twenty years from now?" She smiled.

The tears now rolled freely down Claudia's cheeks. All the frustration she had been feeling the past few weeks was now pouring out of her. "I don't know what to do," she sobbed.

"And I can't tell you what to do. I know you have been annoyed with me lately. But I just wanted the best for you. But no one can figure what's best better than you. And while you are looking, don't overlook those things closest to you, know what I mean? There will always be something or someone out there that is bigger or better for you."

"Yeah, I guess they do say that the grass is always greener on the other side, huh?"

"I wasn't going to say that, but if you want to use an old cliché, yes, that is true. There will always be someone who seems more well off that you can strive to be like, or always someone who seems like they may make a better mate, but don't forget to ask yourself if those things will make you happy. Because like Erma Bombeck said, that greener grass may be over the septic tank." Henrietta drained her wineglass and stood up, smoothing her skirt. "But all that is just an old, annoying woman that has had too much wine talking. You are a smart girl. I raised you myself, so I know." She smiled, then reached over and stroked Claudia's cheek.

Claudia smiled through her tears, surprised at her mother's touch. She wiped her face as relief washed over her.

"I've gotta go and sleep some of this off."

"Thanks, Ma," Claudia said. She felt as if she were twelve years old again and had just been scolded, but she didn't mind.

Henrietta waved her hand as she walked away, as if to dismiss Claudia's thanks.

"So, Ma, you never told me why you left Dad. Did that decision make you happy?"

Henrietta paused, then shrugged. "I guess it did. I spent a lot of years with your father, and not all of them were good. But they weren't all bad either. The verdict is still out. That damn green grass." She winked, then turned and continued down the hallway, one hand traveling along the wall.

Her daughter watched her for a minute, and for the first time Claudia could see that her mother had indeed aged, or at least she appeared as if she had. She was glad that her mother had been frank with her. Now some things were just a tiny bit clearer for her.

So much crying in one evening had totally wrecked Claudia's makeup. As she washed her face, she contemplated the things her mother had said. Claudia hated when Henrietta was right, for no other reason than Henrietta was her mother. The first thing she did when she was done removing her makeup was look up Cody's number. She reached for the phone and hoped he wasn't too mad at her for being rude. She still had no idea what to do about Jackson. She wasn't even sure how she really felt yet. From the looks of things, she no longer had any real choice. He had apparently moved on and had started dating other people already. But at the very least, she owed Cody an apology.

Chapter 37

Tears rolled down Marina's face as Wesley practically dragged her to her car. She could taste the salt as they seeped into her mouth. Her arm ached where his hand chafed her bare skin. She would have another set of bruises tomorrow, but she didn't care. Her feelings were more bruised than her arm could ever be. She was stunned; Cody had not even wanted to hear what she had to say. He had not even given her a chance to speak, apparently truly not caring about her anymore, just like Wesley had said. Not that she could blame him. Who knew what lies he had been told. If the shoe were on the other foot, she would be bitter too. Her father was right. It was all water under the bridge and it could not be relived. She had made her bed by letting Wesley and her father push her around; now she would have to sleep in it.

"Stop whining and get in the car and drive. We are going back to the hotel to get your shit," Wesley snarled. "We are out of here first thing in the morning." He practically shoved her into the driver's side of the rental car and slammed the door. Marina put her head down on the steering wheel, sobbing harder. Her nose was stuffed up and her eyes stung, not to mention the various aches and pains she felt. She was just as bad as Wesley. She should have been stronger instead of afraid. She deserved all of this.

He snatched his door open and folded himself into the car. "I can't believe you came all this way. But I am glad you did." Wesley closed the door. "Quit crying and wipe your face." He handed her a tissue, and for a split second, Marina thought she might have sensed a little tenderness on his part, but it was gone as soon as it had appeared. The old Wesley was back in place. "Drive this car. Now." His voice thundered through the car. Marina shuddered, her tears drying up.

Her emotions were vacillating again. She moved away from feeling sorry for herself and was back to being angry. This time she was angry at herself. How could she have been so stupid? Now her father and husband would probably never let her be alone again, at least not for several months. She was going home to a prison.

She listened to Wesley's scolding. His incessant yammer made the twenty-minute trip seem like it was taking hours. She stared into space, almost driving on automatic. The streets looked different in the now total darkness. Marina did not recognize where she was. Somehow, she had gotten away from the main road, and they were now on a road that was narrow, and dark, with one lane in each direction. She slowed down, not able to see the shoulder, trying to follow the bends in the road as closely as possible.

"If you had told me how much you really wanted to know about what happened, I would have told you," he said, his eyes glaring.

The only other time Marina remembered her husband being this angry was when she'd had to tell him that she was pregnant. It was her own fault; she should have been stronger and not slept with Cody that last time, anyway, or better yet, she should have not given in to her father's pressure. She tried to concentrate on the road, and Wesley did not seem to notice the changes in the landscape.

"Was it really necessary for you to go and put this kind of strain on our relationship? Did you have to go to your father?"

Marina snapped her head around and glared at Wesley. "I see. All you really care about is what my father thinks about this whole thing. Do you have any original ideas, Wesley? Any feelings of your own?" she asked. "I bet he told you to come after me too, right? You would have just let me fade into oblivion if he hadn't sent you down here to get me. You could give a shit about our relationship!"

Wesley raised his eyebrows, pointing toward the steering wheel. "You better pay attention to your driving." He turned to stare out the window. "I don't know why you couldn't just do as you know you should. You should let us take care of things for you. The men. You would have had everything you could have ever wanted—"

"Right. Did I mention that you play the part of minion very well? Why can't you grow a spine and act like you really care about us?" Marina jerked the steering wheel. They swerved across the yellow line dividing the road.

"Be careful," Wesley bellowed. Marina jumped as he reached across the car and placed his hand on the wheel, straightening the car. "Do I have to do everything?"

A new wave of anger came across Marina. She shoved his hand back across the car. Why did he think she was so helpless and needed to be protected? "You let me drive. I can handle this," she said. "There is no need to be so dramatic."

Wesley yelled as a huge deer appeared in the headlights

of their car. Marina stared, frozen, as the car barreled forward. Wesley reached across again and turned the wheel. The car careened off the side of the road, but there was no shoulder to stop him as he'd planned.

The deer turned his head to watch the car go over the ravine, then galloped away, his small family behind him.

Time moved in slow motion. Marina and Wesley both screamed as they fell, and then all was black.

Chapter 38

The parking lot of Magnolia Café was shrouded in shadows, but full. Claudia circled the block once to look for a space. She finally found one, in the corner near a large utility pole. She pulled her car into the tight spot, hoping they wouldn't tow at night. She locked the car and then cautiously made her way to the door of the popular restaurant, one of the few twenty-four-hour eateries in town. Hopefully, there would not be much of a wait.

Cody was already waiting inside the door. He smiled weakly as she walked in. She raised her eyebrows and rubbed the goose bumps that had appeared on her arms, relief spreading through her. A part of her was surprised that he'd even agreed to come back out and meet her after the way she had treated him. They did not speak. He put his hand in the small of her back and guided her to a table in the corner of the small restaurant.

He did not smile as they slid into the small booth. Claudia sensed an uneasiness about him that she did not remember from before.

"I didn't think you would come." She played with her silverware. Her words were awkward and uneasy.

Cody did not reply. Instead he cleared his throat.

"I thought I owed you an apology, and I didn't want you to think I was that uncaring."

"I didn't think that. I just thought you were having a bad night. Pam told me about your ex, so you shouldn't have had to deal with mine."

"I know she did, but I didn't have to be so rude. None of that was your fault. And you were obviously having issues of your own."

A waitress interrupted them, placing two mugs down on the table. She waited a minute, then when they did not order anything else, she left.

"I took the liberty of ordering you a latte before you came. I think I remembered it right," he said. "I got here a few minutes ago and walked to the door when I saw you coming."

Claudia nodded, and then took a sip of her drink. It was perfect, and she smiled at Cody's unexpected thoughtfulness.

The two of them made small talk about the art in the room and the restaurant while they finished their drinks. Claudia avoided looking at him directly. Did he have to be so nice about the whole thing? They alternated between strained silence and meaningless conversation. He still looked good to her, but there was no magic between them, confirming the fact that she was doing the right thing by keeping their relationship solely on a platonic level. Slowly, she began to feel better.

"Look, I appreciate that you wanted to apologize, believe me. Your apology has definitely been one of the highlights of my day," he said. "If you need anything, I will be there for you. And I need to be frank, I want you to let me be there for you. I like you and I would like to get to know you better."

Claudia sighed, biting her lip. He still wasn't getting it. "I need to be frank too. This apology is just that—an apology. We really can't have anything more right now, even if we didn't work together. I need to take some time and find out what it is I want before I concentrate on being with anyone else or getting to know anyone better. There have to be a million women out there who are much more ready for what you have to offer than I am. It wouldn't be fair."

Cody nodded, his face darkening. "Well, I guess we better go then, huh?" He stood, placing several dollars on the table. "Let me walk you to your car."

Claudia followed, unable to read his expression. They walked out of the restaurant and back to the parking lot in silence.

"This isn't exactly the safest parking spot in the place, huh?"

"Nope, it's not, but it was the only one." Claudia smiled weakly, glad to be changing the subject. She used her car remote to unlock the door.

Cody opened the door for her. "Get in, I will wait until you get started."

"You don't have to—"

"But it's okay. Really. I want to." He closed the door behind her and stepped back.

Claudia fumbled with her keys, then finally they found their home in the ignition of her car. Her hands shook, but she did not know why. The car didn't turn over, and she tried again. The lights and radio came on inside the car, but that was it. She rolled down the window and called out to Cody.

"You think you could give me a jump? I think my battery is dead."

"You got cables?"

She shook her head.

"I don't think it would matter anyway, you are parked so far in there, it would be hard to reach the front of your car with that pole in the way. Maybe you can call Triple A or something."

"Well, I could, if I had it. But I don't. I am just not having a good day." She sat back in her seat hard, thudding against the upholstery. *If it isn't one thing,* she thought, *it's another.*

"I'll tell you what," Cody said. "Why don't you let me drive you home. You can deal with your car tomorrow. It has been a long day."

"You sure you won't mind? You remember where I live, right? Isn't that far for you?"

He nodded. "I think I do owe you a ride anyway, that is, if you will allow me to give you one." He smiled. "And it is no trouble at all."

Claudia paused. She really had no choice. It was almost eleven, and she certainly couldn't ask her mother to come out at this late hour to come and get her. And knowing Pam, it would take her until daylight to get herself together enough. Claudia nodded, then locked her car once again.

Cody was not parked far away. Claudia slid into the front passenger seat of Cody's car. This wasn't working out so badly after all, she thought. He could have been angry and left her right there in the parking lot.

Suddenly curious, she automatically looked around the car for clues about Cody, but found nothing. The car was immaculate and smelled as if it had just been washed. He reached under his steering wheel to a small space there and found a box of mints, which he offered to Claudia. She refused, but smiled. He was still being a gentleman. He shrugged his large, muscular shoulders, then started his car and pulled onto the deserted street. They headed south, toward the loop that would lead him to Claudia's neighborhood. Neither one of them spoke, and Claudia wished he would turn on the radio or something, so that she would not hear her heart beating inside her chest. The sound was pounding in her ear and she fidgeted in her seat, but she could not understand her uncomfortableness. They rode in silence.

"Um, that was my turnoff," Claudia said.

"Oh? I didn't notice. I know another way." He glanced into his rearview mirror.

Interstate 35 was directly ahead, and Claudia felt the hairs on the back of her neck begin to rise as she watched Cody pull onto it. She had lived in the Austin area a long time, all of her life. There was no other way to get to her west Austin neighborhood than the road that Cody had just driven by, at least not that she could recall. Still, the city was growing so quickly, maybe there was something he knew that she didn't.

"Did they build some new road down this way or something? When I was a kid, this was all farmland." Her mouth twitched.

"Was it? That's hard to imagine now." Cody cleared his throat.

"This city is growing so fast it is hard to keep up." Claudia was dying to ask him about the route he was taking, but she didn't want him to think she didn't trust him. They had gotten off on such a bad foot already, and because they worked together it was inevitable that they would continue to run into each other, even if they never went out socially again.

He didn't answer her. Instead, he pressed his foot on the gas, bringing the car up over the sixty-five-mile-an-hour posted limit.

"I'm not in a hurry," Claudia said. She pressed her hands into her thighs tightly, as if the pressure would hold her in her seat. "You can take it easy."

"You can take it easy too." Cody reached over and put his hand on her knee.

Claudia froze. A shadow spread over Cody's face, and where his features had before appeared symmetrical and attractive, Claudia now saw desperation. Her stomach jumped.

"You are too beautiful to be treated the way I saw him treat you. He shouldn't have had that woman all over him. He knew you were there, he should have had more concern for your feelings."

She moved his hand and placed it on the seat beside her.

"Oh, but it's okay. I shouldn't have been upset. We aren't together anymore, you know." A lump rose in her throat as she spoke. Claudia suddenly felt the need to explain to Cody. He seemed to press down harder on the gas. She glanced at the speedometer as the car approached eighty.

"Where are we going?" Her voice was strained and her head began to throb.

"I'm taking you away. You don't need any of this. He treats you badly, and you work too hard. And your friend Pam, she isn't a good influence. You just need to be who you are and not listen to her. You were perfect before. You didn't need to change to impress him or anybody else. You need me. I want to take care of you, I told you that. We were going just fine, getting to know each other and everything. Don't let those idiots you saw in my apartment turn you off." Cody's nose flared. He was tired of Marina and her nonsense. She had messed up his life before, and he wasn't about to let her and her family mess things up with Claudia too. How could he move on with her coming back to haunt him like that?

The car swerved.

"Away? Away from what? I don't want to go anywhere. Please keep your eyes on the road."

"Yes you do. You just don't know it yet. I am going to take care of things for you. You won't have to ever worry about being treated the way you were again. I am going to be everything you ever wanted in a man. Just wait and see."

Claudia's stomach did a somersault. Was she being kidnapped? "Cody, where are you taking me?" she asked again. "You could get in serious trouble for this—taking someone against their will. I just want to go home." Her face stung.

"No need to cry. Please, don't do that," he begged. "I am not going to hurt you, you'll see, I just want to take care of you."

Claudia knew she would have to think of something, if she didn't want to end up on the evening news. She also did not want Cody to panic. He was much bigger than she was and could overpower her any time he wanted. She struggled to appear calm, although her heart was beating so quickly that she could hear it roaring in her head. Cody was scaring her.

"Maybe you should slow down so we can get there in one piece." She stared at his foot. The speedometer appeared to inch downward. Tears were now streaming down her face. She had to think quickly. She reached for her handbag.

"What are you doing?" Cody took one hand off the wheel and gripped Claudia's wrist.

"You are hurting me. I am just getting a tissue. I need to wipe my face." The car engine roared as they stared at each other too long.

Finally, Cody released his grip on Claudia and she opened, then closed, her fingers. The blood flowed back into her hand.

"Can I get my tissue?" she asked.

He nodded.

Without opening her bag fully, Claudia reached down into it, fumbling. She was glad that she did not carry a more fashionable purse. The size of her bag was yet another thing that Pam always teased her about, but she had never been able to bring herself to downsize. Claudia needed what she needed when she needed it and didn't want to be caught unprepared because something hadn't fit in her bag that day.

Her fingers found what they were looking for, and Claudia was grateful for her refusal to be a slave to fashion. She used her thumb to pry open her phone and press the keys firmly. She left it open, hoping that whomever she'd called would not hang up. Thank God for auto-dial.

She pulled out a tissue, an old one, and wiped her face, placing her bag gingerly on her lap. She took a deep breath.

"Where are you taking me?"

Cody searched her face, then smiled. "Not far, just away from those people. Where we can talk," he said.

"They will worry. They are going to look for me."

"That's okay. You are going to call them and tell them you are all right. Give me a few hours and you won't want to go back."

Claudia licked her lips, unsure of how to take that. She

cleared her throat. "San Marcos is the next exit," she said. "The best outlets in the whole world are there."

"You don't have to talk so loud. All you women like to shop, I know. I get the picture. Lucky for you we aren't going that far from there, near Aquarena Springs."

"Aquarena Springs? You mean, near exit 206?" she almost shouted.

"Why are you talking like that? You okay? I am not going to hurt you. Think of this as a date, okay?"

Claudia pulled her bag closer to her. "I am not talking funny. I just know the place, that's all. Pam got married there, near the aquarium. It was very beautiful."

"We can do that too. If you want. We can do anything you want. Just say the word."

Unable to control herself any longer, Claudia burst into tears. "I want to go back home, to Austin." She was sobbing. The salt from the tears streaming down her face made her face itch. Her nose was running, and she dabbed at it with the almost disintegrated tissue. She shifted her legs and her purse fell to the ground. The phone slid out.

Cody's mouth dropped open. "Did you call anybody?" His chest heaved. "Answer me." He pulled the car to the side of the road. "Did you?"

Claudia cringed in her seat. She tried to open the door but knew it was locked. It didn't budge. She sobbed harder, pressing into her seat so hard that she could feel the springs in it. She shook her head.

Cody struck the steering wheel, and it shuddered from the force of his blow. Claudia jumped, wailing louder. She had never felt so helpless in her life.

"Dammit, Claudia," he said. "I just wanted to help you. Why won't you let me? I love you, don't you see that?

Didn't your mother ever tell you that you have to love the ones who love you, huh? I am a good man, but I keep getting thrown away. Stop crying, I didn't want that. I didn't want to make you upset. It's not good. You will make yourself sick."

"You're scaring me. Why are you doing this?"

"It's okay. Maybe I was a little dramatic. I didn't mean it. It's just that my life has been such a mess recently. Nothing seems to turn out how I want. I wanted us to get to know each other. I have been planning to meet you for weeks, ask you out. I didn't mean—"

Claudia opened her mouth to speak, and tears rolled around her lips. The salt, mixed with the remnants of her makeup, tasted acidic. She wiped at her mouth with the back of her hand.

Suddenly, a loud thud shook the car and both of their heads snapped up. Claudia exhaled and closed her eyes. She laid her head back on the headrest. Her call had worked. Standing on either side of the car were two Texas State Troopers. Someone had gotten her call and called the cops. She had never been so glad to see law enforcement officers in her life.

Cody glanced into his rearview mirror as one of the officers shone a light inside the car, then knocked on the window. A patrol car was directly behind him, its lights flashing. Cody squinted as the flash made his eyes hurt. He thought for a minute, then slowly rolled down the window.

Chapter 39

A nurse rushed toward the open emergency room doors. A paramedic handed her Marina's wallet.

"Any info in here?" she asked. "They have anyone to call?" She was the head nurse for the shift; the radio operator had already let her know the situation before she arrived.

He nodded. "The female is semi-coherent. She keeps saying something about her father. They are out-of-towners."

She flipped through the wallet, examining its contents. There was a stack of business cards where cash might go. She thumbed through them and picked up the phone. One of these had to lead her to some kinfolk.

Mario Chivers waved good-bye to his secretary just as the phone rang.

"I'll get it," she said.

He stopped her, glancing at his watch. "No, you go ahead. I'll take care of it myself." Whoever it was, it was probably personal. It was late, well after seven. He grabbed the phone as she continued toward the front lobby.

"Mario Chivers." His voice was weary.

"Yes, I was looking for Marina Piscato's father."

"Speaking." His pace quickened.

The person on the other end of the line cleared their throat.

"There has been an accident. Marina and her husband have just been brought into the emergency room—"

"Oh, not Marina," he shouted.

Her voice faded away from his ears, and a dull pain hit his chest. Mario dropped the phone and felt himself slipping away. He watched the handset fall, then clang and bounce off the side of the desk. He hit the floor with a thud.

Chapter 40

The hiss of life-support machines resounded throughout the otherwise quiet hospital floor. Marina stood in the doorway to her father's room, fighting back the tears. He would be moving to a new floor tomorrow, hopefully one with more sounds of life. Mario was making it through. So much had happened over the past few months. It was a good thing that he was such a tough man.

Her thoughts were interrupted by a soft touch on her shoulder. She jumped, surprised. She had not heard Wesley approach. He looked at her, questions written all over his face.

"How're you holding up?" he said.

"I'm fine. But my father—"

"Will be fine, according to the doctor. I had a long chat with him. He says that Mario will be able to come home soon. But he is going to need a full-time nurse for awhile."

Marina exhaled, relieved. Her father's condition had been touch and go. After the stroke, it had taken him a full three months to even sit up. "I still can't help but think that this is somehow my fault. If I hadn't run off to Austin, none. of this might have happened." She paused. "What are you doing here, anyway?"

Wesley looked down, resting on his cane. "I come to check on him regularly."

"That's not necessary. I can take care of him. If you are thinking that maybe you will get in on his good graces somehow, you can forget it."

Wesley winced. "Nothing like that. He treated me well."

Marina sucked her teeth. She was going to make sure that Wesley was long gone from her family.

"I know you could care less. I deserve that." He searched her face for a kernel of softness but couldn't find one. "Well, you know you can't blame yourself. About your dad, I mean. You weren't the only stressor in his life, you know that. Just be thankful that it all worked out. He is going to be fine. And think of the good that came of it. You discovered your strength. He would be so proud of all you have done." He attempted a smile.

"That's true. I did." It was still hard for her not to feel guilty. Her father did have his stroke just as he was finding out about the accident. He'd passed out before he even got to hear that Marina's injuries were minor. It was Wesley who had almost lost a leg.

They turned and walked away from the door, toward the elevator. Wesley limped slightly, leaning on his cane for support. Visiting hours were over, and her father had finally fallen asleep. "It's strange how tragedy brings people closer together."

He nodded. "Tell me about it. It did wonders for us. I can almost live with you not wanting to be married to me anymore. We are getting to know each other now. That's funny, isn't it?"

Marina looked at Wesley. Their divorce would be final in a couple of days. He was still as clueless as ever. She was

talking about her and her father reaching a new under-
standing, and he thought she was talking about the two of
them. She was on speaking terms with Wesley, although she
was not sure she should be. He had done enough to her to
warrant her never talking to him again.

The elevator doors opened and they stepped onto it. Just
before the doors closed, one of the nurses at the desk waved
at them. Marina waved back. She had come to know all of
them on a first-name basis in the past few weeks.

"I think the main thing I worked out is that I am not mad
at my father. I understand why he did what he did, but I
can't say I agree with him. And I still can't believe that the
woman I thought was my mother is not even a blood rela-
tive. I used to think we were so much alike. No wonder she
was unstable all those years. It must have been quite a
strain raising another woman's child, always wondering
where her birth mother was. But meeting my birth mother
answers a lot of questions. And it was a good thing for me
that my father was finally able to track her down. We called
her, and she found out about the accident and came right
away, just like that." Marina snapped her fingers. "She even
looks like me." After the accident, the whole truth had
come out. Marina had discovered that she was actually her
father's love child, just as he had insinuated that day in his
office.

"That she does," Wesley said. "But I still don't get why
she just let your father take you like that. I had no idea how
not knowing could make a person so tormented." He
paused, realizing what he was saying. He had put Marina
through the very same thing. "I'm sorry I put you through
all that."

Marina studied the tiles on the elevator floor. "Well, she

knew all along. My father sent her occasional pictures and updates. We didn't know, of course. She didn't want to interrupt my life. How can children be expected to understand some of the intricacies of the mistakes and decisions that adults make? It was very unselfish of her. She thought I would have a better life that way." She lowered her voice. "Maybe my twins will too."

"It's your decision. But there is no use dwelling on all that now. You have made some very good decisions. We all need to move forward now. And you have to keep the business running."

"I know. I have that big meeting tomorrow too."

"You know, your father had me thinking that you didn't have much of a head for business, but you did well. You stepped right in and took over. And that move you are making with that small outsourcing company. I think it's a good one."

"Oh?" she said, nodding. "Someone had to do the right thing. It's the least I can do."

"I don't understand."

"You wouldn't. I figured out a way to at least right some of the wrong that you and my father did. Let me break it down. You guys made Cody almost go nuts. He made someone else's life hell. That person is Claudia Barrett."

Marina could see recognition in his eyes.

"The president of that outsourcing company?"

"You got it."

Chapter 41

The revolving door hissed. Claudia moved with it and looked down at the floor. She walked with deliberation and listened to the clicking sound her totally unsensible shoes made as she floated across the old hotel lobby. They were already hurting her feet, but they damn sure looked good.

The lobby was ornate, decorated with limestone and marble from nearby quarries, and it smelled of cigar smoke wafting from the bar in its corner. She looked up, making eye contact with the concierge. He nodded and smiled. Knowing he was watching her, she silently accepted the compliment and sashayed appropriately, stepping onto the waiting elevator.

The elevator doors opened at the top floor, and Claudia quickly made her way to a door at the end of the hallway. She knocked, and the unlocked door floated open.

Jackson was waiting for her. He stepped aside, and Claudia caught her breath. Although it was midday, the room was pleasingly semi-dark. A smile flitted across her lips. A single strand of white Christmas lights was strewn across the top of the draperies, and rose petals laid a pathway that led to the bed. The music of Maxwell played softly in the background.

"This is nice," she said. She looked at him, noting that he appeared more distinguished than he had before. He took her hand and led her to a small, antique-looking sofa opposite the bed. She sat, immediately kicking off her shoes. She wiggled her toes, savoring the freedom. She loved them when she bought them, but she knew they wouldn't last long. They were foot jewelry, as Pam called them, and Claudia knew they had their intended effect by the way Jackson's eyes lingered on her legs.

There were two champagne flutes on the coffee table in front of the sofa, and a small bucket with ice. Jackson reached over and picked up the bottle of champagne and uncorked it. He was silent as he filled the glasses.

"Before we toast, I have something for you." He spoke softly, but his deep voice sounded loud in the small room. He handed her a legal-sized silver box.

"What is this?" she asked. "You didn't have to get me anything. I am the one who should be buying you a thank-you gift. Who knows what would have happened if you had hung up that day?"

"Why would I have hung up? I knew it was you, thanks to caller ID. I am just glad that my last name begins with a B. I could have been the last person in your phone book instead of the first. It's no big deal. Take a look."

Claudia removed the cover on the heavy metal box. Inside she found a black leather-bound book. In the lower right-hand corner of the cover were Jackson's initials, engraved in gold filigree—SJB for Stonewall Jackson Baxter. She ran her fingers over the letters, savoring the luxuriousness of the well-used leather, and she opened it slowly. It was a notebook. She looked at Jackson, her eyebrows raised.

"It's my journal. My thoughts are in there. The good and

the bad. How I felt when you seemed to be so into work and not me. How I felt when I left. How I missed you. How badly I wanted you to be my wife. My pride wouldn't let me talk about it too much, so I wrote it down."

"I can't take this. This is private."

"But I want you to have it. So if you are ever doubting the way I feel about you again, you can read it. Ask me what's wrong next time instead of withdrawing from me, okay? We will never get anywhere if we try to bury ourselves in other parts of our lives. Nothing gets solved that way."

Claudia sniffed and looked down at her freshly painted toes. Her eyes stung. He was right. So was her mother and so was Pam. She had buried herself so deeply in her work that she had neglected other parts of her life.

Jackson put his finger under her chin and raised her head. He pulled her to him and kissed her gently, wiping away her tears. "That's all over now," he said. "And we are not going back there again." He handed her a champagne flute and they sipped.

"Oh, and these are for you too."

"You can stop with the gifts."

"Not yet. You had better get used to it. I didn't realize you felt I wasn't being romantic. I have some making up to do. And this is really no big deal. It's just some chocolate. Your favorite chocolate."

"You would give me my most favorite thing in the world. I am going to save this for a rainy day, when I really need it." She smiled and took a step forward. "But what I really need right now is you."

"Not yet. Are you sure you don't want to press charges against Cody? It's not too late. Look at the bruises on your wrists. It's been awhile, and they are only now starting to fade."

She shook her head. "I was so angry at first, but not at him. I was mad at myself for trusting him and being so comfortable. But then I talked with his ex-girlfriend and I heard his story. I felt sorry for him."

"I guess I would be a man on the edge too if I had been through what he had. I hope he gets some help." Jackson chuckled. "That Marina must have been something else, to make a man go that crazy after they broke up."

"Don't tease. It's serious. They are still trying to track down her kids. I want you to help. You are a lawyer. What happened to him isn't right. He should at least know where they are, don't you think?"

"He should, I agree, but I was talking about psychological help, not legal help. And why would I want to help him? He was trying to steal my woman." He kissed Claudia gently on the bridge of her nose. "And besides, that isn't exactly my field."

She cleared her throat. "Uhm, no. That wasn't how it went. You have a strange memory. You dumped me, remember. And you know that Black people don't go to psychologists. They go to church."

"Well, he needs to get him some religion, then." Jackson took the champagne glasses and set them on the table. "Besides, with my new client, CB Outsourcing—"

Claudia held up her hand. "Don't go there. My company is itty-bitty and barely off the ground. It's not going to go away, anyway. My main client *is* Chivers Technologies, remember. Both of us will probably have to look that woman in the face a whole lot over the next few months. How are you going to feel if you know that you didn't do everything you could?"

"I know, I know." Jackson took Claudia's hand in his and led her to the other side of the room, stopping by the side of the bed. He unbuttoned her dress, slowly, as if each button were different than the one before it.

Butterflies flitted about Claudia's stomach as if this were the first time they had ever been together. She opened her mouth to speak, but he shushed her and gently moved her back onto the bed.

Epilogue

The air-conditioning had never seemed to work right in the church, even back when they'd first installed it. There was standing room only today, and people were starting to glow from the heat. Claudia gladly accepted an old-fashioned paper fan from the elderly usher. She fidgeted in her seat, feeling hot and sweaty in her panty hose. She tugged at the top of them. They did not fit right, and the elastic at the top kept rolling down over her swollen belly.

"Will you quit doing that?" Pam said. "You keep poking me with your elbow."

"I can't help it. These stupid hose keep rolling down and I am afraid when I stand up they will fall down around my ankles."

Pam laughed. "This is my fourth time being pregnant, and that has never happened to me. You should have just left them off. No one would have noticed anyway."

"I don't know. You know my mother has an eagle eye. She would have been hounding me about messing up her ceremony by coming in with a naked butt and all. She has been acting like this is the first time she and Daddy are getting married. It's not like it is a big deal."

"But it is. I think it is sweet that they are renewing their vows."

"Tcch. You would. You are the same woman that romanticized being pregnant. This is horrible. I can't see how you keep doing it."

"I couldn't let you go through it alone. You my girl." Pam chuckled again and patted Claudia's hand.

"Whatever. You shoot me if I try this again. Jackson is going to get a vasectomy. Snip. Snip." She moved her fingers in the air like scissors.

"You're just talking. Motherhood is wonderful. And the pathway there ain't too bad either. My sweetie knows what to do. Don't let anybody ever tell you that white man can't jump, 'cause he jumps all over—"

"Alrighty then. That is not the picture I wanted in my head while my mother renews her vows. Do you have to be so, you know, in church?" Claudia raised her eyebrows and ran her hand over her head, smoothing some of her hair, which was beginning to rise in the heat.

"You are never going to loosen up, huh?"

The organist came from a room at the side of the altar and made her way to the area where the musicians sat waiting, a signal that the ceremony was about to begin. A whisper went through the church just as Jackson came scurrying down the side aisle.

"Here comes your other half," Pam said, gesturing in his direction. "Is he ever on time for anything?" she asked.

Claudia whipped her head around. "I know you aren't talking about him, Miss Late-For-Everything. Move over a little so he can sit down. I will have you know he was right on time for our wedding. And ahead of time for our first anniversary, which is next week. He has already planned us a little getaway." She grinned, flashing her teeth. "Besides, he was working."

"On the case with Cody?" Pam asked.

"Probably."

"How does he feel about your new business venture? Is he as surprised as I was? You loved that company so much I am surprised you went out on your own."

"When I heard about all those jobs being lost, it wasn't about me anymore. He's fine with it. He really likes the idea."

"You know you have a good man. Not many men would do what he is doing."

"I know that's right. I'm just glad he located those kids for those people. They couldn't find them because they were looking in the wrong places. They weren't in Puerto Rico after all. They were right in mainland United States all the time."

"So what is going to happen? Those two are still weird, if you ask me. Are they going to get together?"

Claudia shook her head. "I don't think so, but I guess they will work out something. I think Cody is actually going to raise them. Marina will get visitation."

Jackson entered the pew and Claudia gazed into his eyes, beaming. She inhaled, and the air she breathed filled with his cologne. It was new, but it had a familiar musk undertone.

"How'd it go?" she asked.

"Good. They are going to work it out."

The church doors opened for the small processional, and they stood. Claudia smiled and slipped her hand into Jackson's. He wasn't getting away again.